Praise f...

LINDA HOWARD

"You can't read just one Linda Howard!"
—*New York Times* bestselling author
Catherine Coulter

"This master storyteller takes our breath away."
—*RT Book Reviews*

SHERRYL WOODS

"Sherryl Woods always delights her readers—
including me!"
—#1 *New York Times* bestselling author
Debbie Macomber

"Redolent with Southern small-town atmosphere…
emotionally rich."
—*Library Journal* on *A Slice of Heaven*

EMILIE RICHARDS

"This quintessential beach read is full of intrigue,
romance, comedy and a splash of mystery."
—*Publishers Weekly* on *Happiness Key*

"A romance in the best sense, appealing to the
reader's craving for exotic landscapes,
treacherous villains and family secrets."
—*Cleveland Plain Dealer* on *Beautiful Lies*

LINDA HOWARD
SHERRYL WOODS
EMILIE RICHARDS

a mother's touch

MIRA®

ISBN-13: 978-0-7783-2866-7

A MOTHER'S TOUCH

CONTENTS

THE WAY HOME

Linda Howard

Prologue

The Beginning

Saxon Malone didn't look at her as he said, "This won't work. You can be either my secretary or my mistress, but you can't be both. Choose."

Anna Sharp paused, her nimble fingers poised in suspended animation over the stack of papers she had been sorting in search of the contract he had requested. His request had come out of the blue, and she felt as if the breath had been knocked out of her. *Choose,* he'd said. It was one or the other. Saxon always said exactly what he meant and backed up what he'd said.

In a flash of clarity she saw precisely how it would be, depending on which answer she gave. If she chose to be his secretary, he would never again make any move toward her that could be construed as personal. She knew Saxon well, knew his iron will and how completely he could compartmentalize his life. His personal life never bled over into business, or vice versa. If she chose to be his lover—no, his *mistress*—he would

expect to completely support her, just as sugar daddies
had traditionally done over the centuries, and in
exchange she would be sexually available to him whenever he had the time or inclination to visit. She would be
expected to give him total fidelity while he promised
nothing in return, neither faithfulness nor a future.

Common sense and self-respect demanded that she
choose the upright position of secretary as opposed to
the horizontal position of mistress, yet still she hesitated. She had been Saxon's secretary for a year, and had
loved him for most of that time. If she chose her job, he
would never allow her to get any closer to him than she
was right now. As his mistress, at least she would have
the freedom to express her love in her own way and the
hours spent in his arms as a talisman against a future
without him, which she would eventually have to face.
Saxon wasn't a staying man, one with whom a woman
could plan a life. He didn't tolerate any ties.

She said, her voice low, "If I choose to be your mistress, then what?"

He finally looked up, and his dark green eyes were
piercing. "Then I get a new secretary," he said flatly.
"And don't expect me to ever offer marriage, because I
won't. Under any circumstances."

She took a deep breath. He couldn't have stated it any
plainer than that. The wildfire physical attraction that had
overtaken them the night before would never become
anything stronger, at least not for him. He wouldn't per-
mit it.

She wondered how he could remain so impassive
after the hours of fierce lovemaking they had shared on
the very carpet beneath her feet. If it had been one hasty

mating, perhaps they would have been able to ignore it as an aberration, but the fact was that they had made love over and over again in a prolonged frenzy, and there was no pretending otherwise. His office was permeated with sexual memories; he had taken her on the floor, on the couch, on the desk that was now covered with contracts and proposals; they had even made love in his washroom. He hadn't been a gentle lover; he'd been demanding, fierce, almost out of control, but generous in the way he had made certain she'd been as satisfied as he by each encounter. The thought of never again knowing that degree of passion made her heart squeeze painfully.

She was twenty-seven and had never loved before—never even, as a teenager, had the usual assortment of crushes or gone steady. If she passed up this chance she might never have another, and certainly never another with Saxon.

So, in full possession of her faculties, she took the step that would make her Saxon Malone's kept woman. "I choose to be your mistress," she said softly. "On one condition."

There was a hot flare in his deep-set eyes that just as quickly cooled at her last words. "No conditions."

"There has to be this one," she insisted. "I'm not naive enough to think this relationship—"

"It isn't a relationship. It's an arrangement."

"—this *arrangement* will last forever. I want to have the security of supporting myself, earning my own way, so I won't suddenly find myself without a place to live or the means of making a living."

"*I'll* support you, and believe me, you'll earn every

penny of it," he said, his eyes moving down her body in a way that made her feel suddenly naked, her flesh too hot and too tight. "I'll set up a stock portfolio for you, but I don't want you working, and that's final."

She hated it that he would put their relationship—for it *was* a relationship, despite his insistence to the contrary—on such a mercenary basis, but she knew it was the only basis he could agree to. She, on the other hand, would take him on any basis he desired.

"All right," she said, automatically searching for the words he could accept and understand, words that lacked any hint of emotion. "It's a deal."

He stared at her in silence for a long minute, his face as unreadable as usual. Only the heat in his eyes gave him away. Then he rose deliberately to his feet and walked to the door, which he closed and locked, even though it was after quitting time and they were alone. When he turned back to her, Anna could plainly see his arousal, and her entire body tightened in response. Her breath was already coming fast and shallow as he reached for her.

"Then you might as well begin now," he said, and drew her to him.

Chapter One

Two years later

Anna heard his key in the door and sat up straight on the sofa, her heart suddenly beating faster. He was back a day earlier than he'd told her, and of course he hadn't called; he never called her when he was gone on a trip, because that would be too much like acknowledging a relationship, just as he insisted, even after two years, on maintaining separate residences. He still had to go home every morning to change clothes before he went to work.

She didn't jump up to run into his arms; that, too, was something that would make him uncomfortable. By now, she knew the man she loved very well. He couldn't accept anything that resembled caring, though she didn't know why. He was very careful never to appear to be rushing to see her; he never called her by a pet name, never gave her any fleeting, casual caresses, never whispered love words to her even during the most intense lovemaking. What he said to her in bed were always words of sexual need and excitement, his voice guttural with tension, but he was a sensual, giving lover. She loved making love with him, not only because of the satisfaction he always gave her, but because under the guise of physical desire she was able to give him all the affection he couldn't accept outside of bed.

When they were making love she had a reason for touching him, kissing him, holding him close, and during those moments he was free with his own caresses. During the long, dark nights he was insatiable, not just for sex but for the closeness of her; she slept every night in his arms, and if for some reason she moved away from him during the night he would wake and reach for her, settling her against him once more. Come morning, he would withdraw back into his solitary shell, but during the nights he was completely hers. Sometimes she felt that he needed the nights as intensely as she did, and for the same reasons. They were the only times when he allowed himself to give and accept love in any form.

So she forced herself to sit still, and kept the book she'd been reading open on her lap. It wasn't until the door had opened and she heard the thump of his suitcase hitting the floor that she allowed herself to look up and smile. Her heart leaped at the first sight of him, just as it had been doing for three years, and pain squeezed her insides at the thought of never seeing him again. She had one more night with him, one more chance, and then she would have to end it.

He looked tired; there were dark shadows under his eyes, and the grooves bracketing his beautiful mouth were deeper. Even so, not for the first time, she was struck by how incredibly good-looking he was, with his olive-toned skin, dark hair and the pure, dark green of his eyes. He had never mentioned his parents, and now she wondered about them, about the combination of genes that had produced such striking coloring, but that was another thing she couldn't ask.

He took off his suit jacket and hung it neatly in the closet, and while he was doing that, Anna went over to the small bar and poured him two fingers of Scotch, neat. He took the drink from her with a sigh of appreciation, and sipped it while he began loosening the knot of his tie. Anna stepped back, not wanting to crowd him, but her eyes lingered on his wide, muscled chest, and her body began to quicken in that familiar way.

"Did the trip go all right?" she asked. Business was always a safe topic.

"Yeah. Carlucci was overextended, just like you said." He finished the drink with a quick toss of his wrist, then set the glass aside and put his hands on her waist. Anna tilted her head back, surprise in her eyes. What was he doing? He always followed a pattern when he returned from a trip: he would shower while she prepared a light meal; they would eat; he would read the newspaper, or they would talk about his trip; and finally they would go to bed. Only then would he unleash his sensuality, and they would make love for hours. He had done that for two years, so why was he breaking his own pattern by reaching for her almost as soon as he was in the door?

She couldn't read the expression in his green eyes; they were too shuttered, but were glittering oddly. His fingers bit into her waist.

"Is something wrong?" she asked, anxiety creeping into her tone.

He gave a harsh, strained laugh. "No, nothing's wrong. It was a bitch of a trip, that's all." Even as he spoke, he was moving them toward the bedroom. Once there, he turned her around and began undressing her, pulling at her clothes in his impatience. She stood docilely, her gaze locked on his face. Was it her imagination, or did a flicker of relief cross his face when at last she was nude and he pulled her against him? He wrapped his arms tightly around her, almost crushing her. His shirt buttons dug into her breasts, and she squirmed a little, docility giving way to a growing arousal. Her response to him was always strong and immediate, rising to meet his.

She tugged at his shirt. "Don't you think you'd be better off without this?" she whispered. "And this?" She slipped her hands between them and began unbuckling his belt.

He was breathing harder, his body heat burning her even through his clothes. Instead of stepping back so he could undress, he tightened his arms around her and lifted her off her feet, then carried her to the bed. He let himself fall backward, with her still in his arms, then rolled so that she was beneath him. She made a tight little sound in her throat when he used his muscular thigh to spread her legs, and his hips settled into the notch he'd just made.

"Anna." Her name was a groan coming from deep in his chest. He caught her face between his hands and ground his mouth against hers, then reached down between their bodies to open his pants. He was in a frenzy, and she didn't know why, but she sensed his desperate need of her and held herself still for him. He entered her with a heavy surge that made her arch off the bed. She wasn't ready, and his entry was painful, but she pushed her fingers into his hair and clasped his head, trying to give him what comfort she could, though she didn't know what was wrong.

Once he was inside her, however, the desperation faded from his eyes and she felt the tension in his muscles subside. He sank against her with a muted groan of pleasure, his heavy weight crushing her into the bed. After a moment he propped himself on his elbows. "I'm sorry," he whispered. "I didn't mean to hurt you."

She gave him a gentle smile and smoothed his hair. "I know," she replied, applying pressure to his head to force him down within kissing range. Her body had accustomed itself to him, and the pain of his rough entry was gone, leaving only the almost incandescent joy of making love with him. She had never said it aloud, but her body said it, and she always echoed it in her mind: *I love you.* She said the inner words again as he began moving, and she wondered if it would be for the last time.

Later, she woke from a light doze to hear the shower running. She knew she should get up and begin preparations for a meal, but she was caught in a strange inertia. She couldn't care about food when the rest of her life depended on what happened between them now. She couldn't put it off any longer.

Maybe tonight *wouldn't* be the last time. Maybe. Miracles had happened before.

She might hope for a miracle, but she was prepared for a less perfect reality. She would be moving out of this chic, comfortable apartment Saxon had provided for her. Her next living quarters wouldn't be color-coordinated, but so what? Matching carpets and curtains didn't matter. Saxon mattered, but she wouldn't be able to have him. She only hoped she would be able to keep from crying and begging; he would hate that kind of scene.

Being without him was going to be the most difficult thing she had ever faced. She loved him even more now than she had two years before, when she had agreed to be his mistress. It always squeezed her heart the way he would do something considerate, then go out of his way to make it appear as just a casual gesture that had happened to present itself, that he hadn't gone to any trouble to do something for her. And there was the concern he had shown over minor colds, the quiet way he had steadily built up an impressive stock portfolio in her name so she would be financially secure, and the way she always complimented whatever she cooked.

She had never seen anyone who needed to be loved more than Saxon, nor anyone who rejected any sign of love so fiercely.

He was almost fanatically controlled—and she adored it when his control shattered when they made love, though never before had he been as frenzied, as *needy,* as he had been tonight. Only when they were making love did she see the real Saxon, the raw passion he kept hidden the rest of the time. She cherished all of his expressions, but her most cherished image was the way he looked when they made love, his black hair damp with sweat, his eyes fierce and bright, all reserve burned away as his thrusts increased in both depth and speed.

She had no photographs of him. She would have to keep those mental images sharp and polished, so she could take them out and examine them whenever the loneliness became too intense. Later, she would painstakingly compare his beloved face with another that was equally precious, and search for the similarities that would both comfort and torment her.

She smoothed her hands over her stomach, which was still flat and revealed nothing yet of the child growing within.

She had had few symptoms to signal her pregnancy, though she was almost four months along. This last period was the first one she had skipped entirely; the first one after conception had been light, and the second one little more than heavy spotting. It was the spotting that had sent her to the doctor for a precautionary exam, which had revealed that she was in good physical condition and undoubtedly pregnant. She had had no morning sickness, only a few isolated bouts of queasiness that had held no significance except in retrospect. Her breasts were now becoming a bit tender, and she had started taking naps, but other than that she felt much as she had before. The biggest difference was in the almost overwhelming emotions she felt for this baby, Saxon's baby: delirious joy at its presence within her; fierce protectiveness; a powerful sense of physical possession; impatience to actually hold it in her arms; and an almost intolerable sense of loss, because she was terrified that she would lose the father as she gained the child.

Saxon had made it plain from the start that he would accept no strings, and a child wasn't merely a string, it was an unbreakable chain. He would find that intolerable. Just the knowledge of her pregnancy would be enough to drive him away.

She had tried to resent him, but she couldn't. She had

gone into this with her eyes open; Saxon had never tried to hide anything from her, never made any promises, had in fact gone out of his way to make certain she knew he would never offer anything more than a physical relationship. He had done nothing other than what he'd said he would do. It wasn't his fault that their birth control had failed, nor was it his fault that losing him would break her heart.

The shower had stopped running. After a minute he walked naked into the bedroom, rubbing a towel over his wet hair. A small frown pulled his brows downward when he saw she was still in bed; he draped the towel around his neck and came over to sit beside her on the bed, sliding his hand under the sheet in search of her warm, pliant body. His hand settled on her belly. "Are you all right?" he asked with concern. "Are you sure I didn't hurt you?"

She put a hand over his. "I'm fine." More than fine, lying there with his hand resting over the child he had given her.

He yawned, then shrugged to loosen the muscles of his shoulders. There was no sign now of his former tension; his expression was relaxed, his eyes lazy with satisfaction. "I'm hungry. Do you want to eat in or go out for dinner?"

"Let's eat in." She didn't want to spend their last night together in the middle of a crowded restaurant.

As he started to get up, she tightened her hand on his, keeping him in place. He gave her a look of mild surprise. She took a deep breath, knowing she had to get this over with now before she lost her nerve, yet when the words came out they weren't the ones she had planned. "I've been wondering…what would you do if I happened to get pregnant?"

Like a shutter closing, his face lost all expression and his eyes frosted over. His voice was very deep and deliberate when he said, "I told you in the beginning, I won't marry you, under any circumstances, so don't try getting pregnant to force my hand. If you're looking for marriage, I'm not the man, and maybe we should dissolve our arrangement."

The tension was back, every line of his big body taut as he sat naked on the side of the bed and waited for her answer, but she could see no sign of worry in his face. He had already made his decision, and now he was waiting to hear hers. There was such a heavy weight crushing her chest that she could hardly bear it, but his answer had been no more than what she had expected.

But she found that she couldn't say the words that would make him get up, dress and walk out. Not right now. In the morning. She wanted to have this last night with him, held close in his arms. She wanted to tell him that she loved him just one more time, in the only way he would allow.

Chapter Two

Saxon woke early the next morning and lay in the dim light of dawn, unable to go back to sleep because of the echo of tension left behind by the question Anna had asked the night before. For a few nightmarish moments he had seen his entire life caving in around him, until Anna had smiled her quiet smile and said gently, "No, I'd never try to force you to marry me. It was just a question."

She was still sleeping, her head pillowed on his left shoulder, his left arm wrapped around her, his right hand resting on her hip. From the very first he hadn't been able to sleep unless she was close to him. He had slept alone his entire adult life, but when Anna had become his mistress he had abruptly found, to his surprise, that sleeping alone was almost impossible.

It was getting worse. Business trips had never bothered him before; he had, in fact, thrived on them, but lately they had been irritating the hell out of him. This last trip had been the worst yet. The delays, glitches and aggravations hadn't been anything out of the ordinary, but what he had once taken for granted now grated almost unbearably. A late flight could send him into a rage; a mislaid blueprint was almost enough to get someone fired; a broken piece of equipment had him swearing savagely; and to top it off, he hadn't been able to sleep. The hotel noises and unfamiliar bed had been particularly annoying, though he probably wouldn't have noticed them at all if Anna had been there with him. That admission alone had been enough to make him break out in a sweat, but added to it was a gnawing need to get back home to Denver, to Anna. It wasn't until he had had her beneath him in bed, until he had felt the soft warmth of her body enfold him, that he had at last been able to relax.

He had walked through the door of the apartment and desire had hit him like a blow, low down and hard. Anna had looked up with her customary smile, her dark eyes as calm and serene as a shadowy pool, and his savage mood had faded, to be replaced by pure sexual need. Walking through that door had been like walking into a sanctuary to find a woman made specifically for him. She had poured him a drink and brushed close to him, and he had smelled the sweet scent of her skin that always clung to their sheets, the scent that had been maddeningly absent from the hotel linens. The ferocity of the desire that had taken hold of him still left him a little shaken this morning.

Anna. He had noticed that serenity, and the feminine scent of her, from the very first day when he had hired her as his secretary. He had wanted her from the beginning, but had controlled his sexual urges because he had neither wanted nor needed that sort of complication on the job. Gradually, though, the wanting had grown stronger, until it had become an unbearable need that gnawed at him day and night, and his control had begun crumbling.

Anna looked like honey, and he had been going mad wanting to taste her. She had silky, light brown hair, streaked with blond, and dark-honey eyes. Even her skin had a smooth, warm, honey tone to it. She would never be flashy, but she was so pleasant to look at that people continually turned her way. And those honey eyes had always been warm and calm and inviting, until finally he had been unable to resist the invitation. The frenzy of that first night still startled him, even in memory, because he had never lost control—until then. He had lost it with Anna, deep inside her hot, honeyed depths, and sometimes he felt that he had never gotten it back.

He had never let anyone get close to him, but after that first night he had known that he couldn't walk away from her as he had from the others. Acknowledging that simple fact had terrified him. The only way he had been able to handle it had been to completely separate her from the other parts of his life. She could be his mistress, but nothing else. He couldn't let her matter too much. He still had to constantly guard against letting her get too close; Anna could destroy him, and something deep inside him knew it. No one else had ever even threatened his defenses, and there were times when he wanted to walk out and never come back, never see her again, but he couldn't. He needed her too much, and he constantly fought to keep her from realizing it.

But their arrangement made it possible for him to sleep with her every night and lose himself over and over in her warm, pliant body. In bed he could kiss her and smooth his hands over her, wrap himself in her scent and touch. In bed he could feed his craving for honey, his savage need to touch her, to hold her close. In bed she clung to him with abandon, opening herself to him whenever he wanted, her hands sliding over him in bold, tender caresses that drove him wild. Once they were in bed together, it seemed as if she never stopped touching him, and despite himself, he reveled in it. Sometimes it was all he could do to keep from groaning in a strange, not completely physical ecstasy as she petted and stroked and cuddled.

Yet for all that they had virtually lived together for two years—the small distance that he insisted on retaining, so necessary for him, was in fact negligible in terms of time—he knew little more about her now than he had before. Anna didn't bombard anyone with the details of her past or present life, and he hadn't asked, because to do so would give her the same right to question him about his own past, which was something he seldom allowed himself to even think about. He knew how old she was, where she had been born, where she had gone to school, her social security number, her former jobs, because all that had been in her personnel record. He knew that she was conscientious, good with details and preferred a quiet life. She seldom drank alcohol, and lately seemed to have stopped drinking altogether. She read quite a bit, and her interests were wide and varied in both fiction and nonfiction. He knew that she preferred pastel colors and didn't like spicy foods.

But he didn't know if she had ever been in love, what had happened to her family—in her personnel file, "None" had been listed in the next-of-kin column—if she had been a cheerleader or ever gotten into trouble for childish pranks. He didn't know why she had moved to Denver, or what her dreams were. He knew only the surface facts that were there for anyone to see, not her memories or hopes.

Sometimes he was afraid that, because he knew so little about her, she might someday slip away from him. How could he predict what she would do when he knew nothing of her thoughts and had only himself to blame? He had never asked, never encouraged her to talk to him of those parts of her life. For the past two years he had lived in quiet terror, dreading the day when he would lose her, but unable to do anything to stop it. He didn't know how to reach out to her, how to hold her, when even the thought of letting her know how vulnerable he was to her had the power to make him physically sick.

The hunger grew in him as he thought of her, felt her lying so soft against his side, and his manhood swelled in response. If they had no other form of contact, they at least had this, the almost overwhelming sexual need for each other. He had never before wanted anything from a woman except sex; it was bitterly ironic that now he was using sex to give him at least the semblance of closeness with her. His heartbeat kicked into a faster rate as he began stroking her, easing her awake and into passion so he could ease himself into her and forget, for a while, everything but the incredible pleasure of making love to her.

It was one of those sunny days when the brightness seemed almost overwhelming, the air was clear and warm for late April, a perfect day, a mockery of a day, because she felt as if her heart were dying inside of her. She cooked breakfast, and they ate it on the terrace, as they often did during good weather. She poured him another cup of coffee and sat down across from him, then folded her hands around her chilled glass of orange juice so they wouldn't shake.

"Saxon." She couldn't look at him, so she focused on the orange juice. She felt nauseated, but it was more a symptom of heavy dread than of her pregnancy.

He had been catching up on the local news, and now he looked up at her over the top of a newspaper. She felt his attention focus on her.

"I have to leave," she said in a low voice.

His face paled, and for a long minute he sat as if turned to stone, not even blinking. A slight breeze rattled the newspaper, and finally he moved, folding the pages slowly and painstakingly, as if every movement were painful. The time had come, and he didn't know if he could bear it, if he could even speak. He looked at Anna's lowered head, at the way the sun glinted on the pale, silky streaks, and knew that he had to speak. This time, at least, he wanted to know why.

So that was the question he asked, that one word, and it came out sounding rusty. "Why?"

Anna winced at the raw edge to his voice. "Something has happened. I didn't plan it. It—it just happened."

She had fallen in love with someone else, he thought, fighting to catch his breath over the knot of agony in his chest. He had always trusted her completely, had never even entertained the thought that she might be seeing other men during his absences, but obviously he'd been wrong.

"Are you leaving me for another man?" he asked harshly.

Her head jerked up, and she stared at him, stunned by

the question. He looked back at her, his eyes fierce and greener than she had ever seen them before.

"No," she whispered. "Never that."

"Then what?" He shoved himself away from the table and stood, his big body taut with barely controlled rage.

She took a deep breath. "I'm pregnant."

Just for an instant his fierce expression didn't change; then all of a sudden his face turned to stone, blank and hard. "What did you say?"

"I'm pregnant. Almost four months. It's due around the end of September."

He turned his back on her and walked to the terrace wall to look out over the city. The line of his shoulders was rigid with anger. "By God, I never thought you'd do this," he said, his voice harshly controlled. "I've been suckered all the way, haven't I? I should have known what to expect after the question you asked last night. Marriage would be more profitable than a paternity suit, wouldn't it? But you stand to make a good profit either way."

Anna got up from the table and quietly walked back into the apartment. Saxon stood by the wall, his fists knotted as he tried to deal with both blind rage and the cold knot of betrayal, as well as the pain that waited, crouched and ready, to come to the fore at the least abatement of anger.

He was too tense to stand there long; when he couldn't bear it any longer, he followed her, determined to find out the depths of his own stupidity even though that would only deepen the pain. It was like the way a tongue would continually probe a sore tooth, in search of the pain. No matter how she tore him to shreds, he had to know, and then he would be invulnerable; no one would ever get to him again. He had once thought himself invulnerable, only to have Anna show him the chink in his emotional armor. But once he got over this, he would truly be untouchable.

Anna was calmly sitting at her desk, writing on a sheet of paper. He had expected her to be packing, at the very least, anything but sitting there scribbling away.

"What're you doing?"

She jerked a little at his harsh voice, but continued writing. Perhaps it was only that his eyes hadn't adjusted to the dimmer light, but she looked pale and drawn. He hoped savagely that she was feeling just a fraction of what he was going through right now.

"I said, what are you doing?"

She signed her name to the bottom of the page and dated it, then held it out to him. "Here," she said, using an enormous effort to keep her voice calm. "Now you won't have to worry about a paternity suit."

Saxon took the paper and turned it around to read it. He skimmed it once, then read it again with greater attention and growing disbelief.

It was short and to the point. *I swear, of my own free will, that Saxon Malone is not the father of the child I carry. He has no legal responsibility, either to me or my child.*

She stood up and moved past him. "I'll be packed and gone by tonight."

He stared down at the paper in his hand, almost dizzy with the conflicting emotions surging back and forth inside him. He couldn't believe what she had done, or how casually she had done it. With just a few words written on a sheet of paper she had prevented herself from receiving a large sum of money, because God knew he would have paid any amount, even bankrupted himself if necessary, to make certain that baby was taken care of, not like—

He started shaking, and sweat broke out on his face. Rage welled in him again. Clutching the paper in his hand, he strode into the bedroom just as she was tugging her suitcases out of the closet.

"That's a damn lie!" he shouted, and threw the crumpled paper at her.

Anna flinched but hung on to her calm demeanor. Privately she wondered how much more she could take before she broke down and began sobbing. "Of course it's a lie," she managed as she placed the suitcases on the bed.

"That baby is mine."

She gave him an odd look. "Did you have any doubt? I wasn't admitting to being unfaithful, I was trying to give you some peace of mind."

"Peace of mind!" It seemed as if all his control had been demolished. He was shouting at her again, when in the entire three years they had known each other he had never before even raised his voice to her. "How the hell am I supposed to have any peace of mind knowing that my kid…my kid—" He stopped, unable to finish the sentence.

She began emptying her dresser drawers into the open suitcases, neatly folding and placing each garment. "Knowing that your kid—what?" she prompted.

He shoved his hands into his pockets and knotted them into fists. "Are you even going to have it?" he asked raggedly.

She went stiff, then straightened to stare at him. "What do you mean by that?"

"I mean, have you already planned an abortion?"

There was no warmth or softness at all in her brown eyes now. "Why do you ask?" she questioned evenly.

"It's a reasonable question."

He really had no idea, she thought numbly. How could he even consider the idea that she might abort his child if he had any inkling at all about the way she felt? All of the love that she had expressed during those long, dark hours might as well have been kept hidden for all the notice he'd paid it. Maybe he had just accepted her passion as the skillful act of a kept woman, designed to keep a sugar daddy happy.

But she didn't say any of that. She just looked at him for a moment before stating abruptly, "No. I'm not having an abortion," then turning back to her packing.

He made an abrupt motion with his hand. "Then what? If you're going to have it, then what are you going to do with it?"

She listened to him with growing disbelief. Had she gone crazy, or had he? What did he think she was going to do? A variety of answers occurred to her, some obvious and some not so obvious. Did he expect her to list the numerous activities involved in caring for a baby, or was he asking what her plans were? Given Saxon's usual precision of speech, always saying exactly what he meant, she was even more bewildered.

"What do you mean, 'what am I going to do with it?' What mothers usually do, I suppose."

His face was grayish and covered with a sheen of sweat. "That's my baby," he said, striding forward to catch her shoulders in his hard hands. "I'll do whatever it takes to keep you from throwing it away like a piece of garbage!"

Chapter Three

Cold chills of horror trickled down her spine, rendering her momentarily incapable of speech. All she could do was endure his tight grip on her shoulders, wide eyes fastened on him and her mouth slightly parted in disbelief. She tried several times to speak, and when she finally managed it, her voice was a hoarse croak. "*Throw it away?* Dear God! That's *sick!* Why on earth would you ever say something like that?"

He was shaking. She could feel it now, in his hands; see it in the visible tremors of his big body. His distress had the effect of relieving her own as she suddenly realized that he was upset and in need of reassurance even more, perhaps, than she was, though she didn't know why. Instinct took over and ruled her actions as she placed her hands on his chest.

"I would never do anything to harm your baby," she said gently. "Never."

His trembling intensified. His green eyes were stark with some savage emotion that she couldn't read, but he took a deep breath and locked his jaw as he fought to regain control. She saw the battle, saw what it cost him to win it, but in just a moment his hands were steady and his face, if still colorless, was as blank as rock. With great care he released her shoulders and let his hands drop to his sides.

"You don't have to leave here," he said, as if that was what they had been discussing. "It's a good apartment. You could take over the lease…."

Anna whirled away from him to hide the sharp upthrust of pain, all the more hurtful because, just for a moment, she thought he had meant that things didn't have to change. But he wasn't offering to preserve the status quo; he still intended to sever the relationship. "Don't," she said, warding off the words with a hand held back toward him. "Just…don't."

"Don't what?" he challenged. "Don't try to make it comfortable for you?"

She inhaled raggedly and let her head drop as she, in turn, tried to marshal her own control, but all she could find was weariness and a need for the truth. If this was the end, why not tell him? Pride? That was a pitiful reason for hiding something that had changed her life. She took another deep breath. "Don't ask me to stay here without you," she said. "You're the reason I'm here. Without you, I have no reason to stay." She turned and faced him, lifting her head so she could see him as she said in a clear, deliberate voice, "I love you. If I hadn't, I never would have come here at all."

Shock rippled across his face, turning it even whiter. His lips moved but made no sound.

"I planned to leave because I thought that was what

you would want," she continued steadily. "You made it
more than plain from the beginning that you didn't want
any ties, so I didn't expect anything else. Even if you
wanted to continue our—our arrangement, I don't think
it's possible. I can't be a mother and continue to be your
undemanding mistress, too. Babies tend to have their
own priorities. So, under the present circumstances, I
have to leave. That doesn't mean I'll stop loving you."
Ever, she added in her thoughts.

He shook his head, either in disbelief or denial, and
moved jerkily to sit down on the bed, where he stared
unseeingly at the open suitcases.

Concern welled in her as she watched him. She had
expected him to react with anger or cold retreat, but he
truly seemed in shock, as if something terrible had happened. She walked over to sit beside him, her gaze fastened on his face in an effort to catch every fleeting
nuance of expression. Saxon was hard enough to read
when he was relaxed; his face looked like marble now.

Anna gripped her fingers tightly together. "I never expected you to act like this," she murmured. "I thought…I
guess I thought you just wouldn't care."

His head jerked up, and he gave her a look like a
sword edge, sharp and slicing. "You thought I'd just
walk away and never give another thought to either you
or the baby?" His tone was harsh with accusation.

She didn't back down. "Yes, that's exactly what I
thought. What else could I think? You've never given me
any indication that I was anything more to you than a
convenient sexual outlet."

His heart twisted painfully, and he had to look away.
She thought she was only a convenience, when he

measured his life by the time he spent with her. Not that he had ever let her know; she was right about that. He had gone out of his way to keep her from knowing. Was that why he was losing her now? He felt as if he had been shredded, but he was in too much pain to be able to tell which was hurting worse, the knowledge that he was losing her or that he had fathered a baby who was also lost to him.

"Do you have a place to go?" he asked numbly.

She sighed inaudibly, releasing the last frail grasp of hope. "No, not really, but it's okay. I've looked around a little, but I haven't wanted to commit on anything until I talked to you. I'll go to a hotel. It won't take me long to find another apartment. And you've made certain I won't be strapped financially. Thank you for that. And thank you for my baby." She managed a faint smile, but he wasn't looking at her and didn't see it.

He leaned forward and braced his elbows on his knees, massaging his forehead with one hand. Lines of weariness were cut into his face. "You don't have to go to a hotel," he muttered. "You can look for another place from here. There's no point in moving twice. And we have a lot of legal stuff to get sorted out."

"No we don't," she said. He slanted his head to the side to give her another of those incisive looks. "We don't," she insisted. "You've made certain of my financial security. I'm more than able to provide for my baby. If you think I'm going to be bleeding you dry, you can just think again!"

He straightened. "What if I want to support it? It's my kid, too. Or didn't you plan on ever letting me see it?"

She was frankly bewildered. "Do you mean you *want*

to?" She had never expected that. What she had expected was a cold and final end to their relationship.

That look of shock crossed his features once again, as if he had just realized what he'd said. He gulped and got to his feet, striding restlessly around the room. He had so much the look of a trapped animal that she took pity on him and said softly, "Never mind."

Instead of reassuring him, her words seemed to disturb him even more. He ran his hands through his hair, then turned abruptly toward the door. "I can't—I have to think things through. Stay here as long as you need."

He was gone before she could call him back, before she truly realized he was leaving. The front door slammed even before she could get up from the bed. She stared at the empty space where he had stood, and recalled the haunted look in his eyes. She recognized that he was more deeply disturbed than she had ever considered possible, but had no clue as to why. Saxon had kept his past so completely private that she knew absolutely nothing about his childhood, not even who his parents were. If he had any family at all, she didn't know about them. But then, it didn't necessarily follow that she would; after all, he still had his own apartment, and his mail still went there. Nor did she think it likely that he would have given out his mistress's telephone number so his family could contact him if he didn't answer his own phone.

She looked around at the apartment she had called home for two years. She didn't know if she would be able to stay here while she looked for someplace else, despite his generous offer. She had been telling him nothing less than the truth when she had said that she didn't want to stay here without him. The apartment was permeated with his presence, not physical reminders so much as the sharp memories that would be a long time fading. Her child had been conceived in the very bed she sat on. She thought about that for a moment; then her lips curved in a wryly gentle smile. Perhaps not; Saxon had never felt the need to limit their lovemaking to the bed, though they had usually sought it for comfort's sake. It was, she supposed, just as likely to have happened in the shower, or on the sofa, or even on the kitchen counter, one cold afternoon when he had arrived while she was cooking dinner and hadn't been inclined to wait until bedtime.

Those days of wondrous passion were over now, as she had known they would be. Even if Saxon hadn't reacted as she had anticipated, the end result was the same.

Saxon walked. He walked automatically, without aim or care. He was still reeling from the twin blows Anna had dealt him, incapable of ordering his thoughts or controlling his emotions. He had controlled every aspect of his life for so long, closing a door in his mind on the things that had happened years before, and he had thought the monster tamed, the nightmare robbed of horror. Yet all it had taken to destroy his deceptively fragile peace was the knowledge that Anna was pregnant. And she was leaving him. God, she was leaving him.

He felt like raising his fists to the sky and cursing whatever fate had done this to him, but the pain was too deep for that. He would have crouched on the sidewalk and howled like a demented animal if it would have relieved even a portion of the swelling agony in his chest and mind,

but he knew it would not. The only surcease he would find
would be where he had always found it: with Anna.

He couldn't even begin to think of the future. He had
no future, no anchor. The image of endless days stretch-
ing before him refused to form; he simply couldn't face
even one more day, let alone an eternal procession of
them. A day without Anna? Why bother?

He'd never been able to tell her how much she meant
to him. He could barely tolerate even admitting it to himself. Love, in his experience, was only an invitation to
betrayal and rejection. If he allowed himself to love, then
he was making himself vulnerable to a destruction of the
mind and soul. And no one had loved him, not ever. It
was a lesson he had learned from the earliest reaches of
memory, and he had learned it well. His very survival had
depended on the hard shell of indifference he had cultivated, so he had formed layer after layer of armor.

When had it changed from protection to prison? Did
the turtle ever long for freedom from its boxy shell, so
it could run unhindered? Probably not, but he wasn't so
lucky. Anna had said that she loved him, and even if it
wasn't true, in saying it she had given him the opportunity to stay just a little while longer, if only he had dared
to take it. He hadn't, because it would have meant shed-
ding at least a few layers of his armor, and the prospect
filled him with a terror founded in earliest childhood
and strengthened through long years of abuse.

When he arrived in front of his apartment door he
stood staring at it in bewilderment, not quite certain of
his location. When he finally realized that he was, in
fact, at his own apartment, that he had walked several
miles to reach it, he fumbled in his pocket for the keys.

The apartment was silent and musty when he entered, without any sweet welcoming presence. Anna had never been here, and it showed. He could barely stand to spend any time here. It was dark and empty, like a grave, and he was incapable of bringing any light into it. The only light he'd ever known had been Anna's, and he had shared it for too short a time, then driven her away with his own unbridled lust. He'd never been able to keep his hands off her. He had made love to her far more often than he ever would have thought possible, his male flesh rising again and again for the incredible sweetness of sinking into her and joining his body to hers. He had made her pregnant, and because of it he had lost her.

What would he do without her? He couldn't function, couldn't find it in himself to give a damn about contracts, or whether the job got done or not. Even when he had spent days on a job, he had always done it knowing that she was waiting for him. By working so hard, even if it took him away from her, he was able to take care of her and make certain she never had to do without anything. Every time he had expanded the stock portfolio he had set up for her, he had felt an intense satisfaction. Maybe he had thought that his diligent efforts in that would keep her with him, that they would show her that she was better off with him than with anyone else, or out on her own.

He couldn't let himself think, even for a moment, that she might have stayed with him only because he *was* establishing her financial security. If he thought that about Anna, then he truly had nothing left to live for. No, he had always known that she had disliked that part of their arrangement.

There had been no reason at all for her to stay…
unless she *did* love him.

For the first time, he let himself think about what she
had said. At the time, it had been too much for him to
take in, but now the words circled tentatively in his consciousness, like frail birds afraid to light.

She loved him.

He sat in the silent apartment for the rest of the day
and into the night, too far withdrawn into himself to feel
the need for light or noise, and sometime during the
dark hours he crossed an internal barrier. He felt as if he
were pinning his desperate hopes on the slimmest of
chances, as if he were shooting for the longest odds, but
he faced the cold gray fact that he could do nothing else.

If Anna loved him, he couldn't let her go like this.

Chapter Four

Anna had a bad night. She couldn't sleep; though she hadn't expected to sleep well, neither had she expected to lie awake for hours, staring at the dark ceiling and physically aching at the empty space beside her. Saxon had spent many nights away from her before, on his numerous business trips, and she had always managed to sleep. This, however, was different, an emptiness of the soul as well as of space. She had known it would be difficult, but she hadn't known it would leave this wrenching, gnawing pain inside. Despite her best efforts, she had cried until her head had started throbbing, and even then she hadn't been able to stop.

It was sheer exhaustion that finally ended the tears, but not the pain. It was with her, unabating, through the long dark hours.

If this was what the future would be like, she didn't know if she could bear it, even with the baby. She had thought that his child, immeasurably precious, would be some consolation for his absence, and though that might be so in the future, it was a hollow comfort now. She couldn't hold her baby in her arms right now, and it would be five long months before she could.

She got up toward dawn without having slept at all, and made a pot of decaffeinated coffee. Today of all days she needed the kick of caffeine, but her pregnancy forbade it. She made the coffee anyway, hoping that the ritual would fool her brain into alertness, then sat at the kitchen table with a thick robe pulled around her for comfort while she sipped the hot liquid.

Rain trickled soundlessly down the glass terrace doors and jumped in minute splashes on the drenched stone. As fine as the day before had been, the fickle April weather had turned chilly and wet as a late cold front swept in. If Saxon had been there, they would have spent the morning in bed, snuggled in the warmth of the bed covers, lazily exploring the limits of pleasure.

She swallowed painfully, then bent her head to the table as grief welled up overwhelmingly again. Though her eyes felt grainy and raw from weeping, it seemed there were still tears, still an untapped capacity for pain.

She didn't hear the door open, but the sound of footsteps on the flagstone flooring made her jerk upright, hastily wiping her face with the heels of her hands. Saxon stood before her, his dark face bleak and drawn with weariness. He still had on the same clothes he'd worn the day before, she saw, though he had thrown on a leather bomber jacket as protection against the rain. He had evidently been walking in it, because his black hair was plastered down, and rivulets of moisture ran down his face.

"Don't cry," he said in a raw, unnatural tone.

She felt embarrassed that he had caught her weeping. She had always taken pains to hide any bouts of emotion from him, knowing that they would make him uncomfortable. Nor did she look her best, with her eyes swollen and wet, her hair still tousled from a restless night, and swaddled from neck to foot in a thick robe. A mistress should always be well-groomed, she thought wryly, and almost burst into tears again.

Without shifting his gaze from her, he took off his jacket and hung it over the back of a chair. "I didn't know if you had stayed," he said, the strain still evident in his voice. "I hoped you had, but—" Then, abruptly, he moved with that shocking speed of his, scooping her up in his arms and carrying her quickly into the bedroom.

After a small startled cry, Anna clung to his shoulders. He had moved like that the first time, as if all his passion had been swelling behind the dam of his control and the dam had finally given way. He had swept her off her feet and down to the floor in the office almost in the same motion, then had come down on top of her before her surprise could give way to gladness. She had reached for him with desire that rose quickly to match his, and it had been hours before he had released her.

She could feel the same sort of fierceness in his grip now as he placed her on the bed and bent over her, loosening the robe and spreading it wide. Beneath it she wore a thin silk nightgown, but evidently even that was too much. Silently she stared up at his intent face as he lifted her free of the robe, then tugged the nightgown over her head. Her breath quickened as she lay naked before him, and she felt her breasts tighten under his gaze, as hot as any touch. A warm, heavy pooling of sensation began low in her body.

He opened her thighs and knelt between them, visually feasting on her body as he fumbled with his belt and zipper, lowering his pants enough to free himself. Then his green gaze flashed upward to meet the drowning velvet brown of hers. "If you don't want this, say so now."

She could no more have denied him, and herself, than she could willingly have stopped breathing. She lifted her slender arms in invitation, and he leaned forward in acceptance, sheathing himself in both her body and her embrace with one movement. He groaned aloud, not just at the incredible pleasure, but at the cessation of pain. For now, with her slender body held securely beneath him, and himself held just as securely within her, there was no distance between them.

Anna twisted under the buffeting of a savagely intense sensual pleasure. The shock of his cold, damp clothing on her warm bare body made her feel more naked than she ever had before. The single point of contact of bare flesh, between her legs, made her feel more sexual, made her painfully aware of his masculinity as he moved over and inside her. It was too overwhelming to sustain, and she arched into climax too soon, far too soon, because she wanted it to last forever.

He stilled, holding himself deep inside her for her pleasure, holding her face and planting lingering kisses over it. "Don't cry," he murmured, and until then she hadn't known that there were tears seeping out of her eyes. "Don't cry. It doesn't have to end now."

She had cried it aloud, she realized, had voiced her despair at the swift peaking.

He brought all the skill and knowledge of two years of intimacy into their lovemaking, finding the rhythm that was fast enough to bring her to desire again, but slow enough to keep them from reaching satisfaction. There was a different satisfaction in the lingering strokes, in the continued linking of their bodies. Neither of them wanted it to end, because as long as they were together like this they wouldn't have to face the specter of separation. Withdrawal, right now, would mean more than the end of their lovemaking; it would be a parting that neither could bear.

His clothing became not a sensual pleasure, but an intolerable barrier. She tore at the buttons on his shirt, wanting the wet cloth out of the way, needing the pressure of his skin on hers. He rose enough to shrug his wide shoulders out of the garment and toss it aside; then he lowered his chest, and she whimpered in delight at the rasp of his hair on her sensitive nipples.

He cupped her breasts in both hands and pushed them together, bending his head to brush light kisses over the tightly drawn nipples. They were a bit darker, he noticed, and the pale globes were a little swollen, signs of his baby growing within her flat belly. He shuddered with unexpected excitement at the thought, at the knowledge that the same act he was performing now had resulted in that small life.

He had to grit his teeth in an effort to keep from climaxing right then. His baby! It seemed that knowledge wasn't quite the same thing as realization, and he had just been hit by the full realization that the baby was his, part of him, sharing his genes. Blood of his blood, bone of his bone, mingled inseparably with Anna, a living part of both of them. He felt a wave of physical possession like he'd never known before, never even dreamed existed. His baby!

And his woman. Honey-sweet Anna, smooth warm skin and calm, gentle dark eyes.

The crest had been put off too long to be denied any longer. It swept over them, first engulfing her, then him, her inner trembling too much for him to bear. They heaved together in a paroxysm of pleasure, crying out, dying the death of self and surfacing into the quiet aftermath.

They lay entwined, neither of them willing to be the first to move and break the bond of flesh. Anna slid her fingers into his damp hair, loving the feel of his skull beneath her fingers. "Why did you come back?" she whispered. "It was hard enough watching you leave the first time. Did you have to put me through it again?"

She felt him tense against her. Before, she would never have let him know her feelings; she would have smiled and retreated into her role of the perfect mistress, never making demands. But she had left that shield behind, baring herself with her declaration of love, and there was no going back. She wasn't going to deny that love again.

He rolled to his side, taking her with him, wrapping his arm around her hip to keep in place. She shifted automatically, lifting her leg higher around his waist for greater comfort. He moved closer to deepen his tenuous penetration, and they both breathed infinitesimal sighs of relief.

"Do you have to go?" he finally asked. "Why can't you just stay?"

She rubbed her face against his shoulder, her dark eyes sad. "Not without you. I couldn't bear it."

She felt the effort it took him to say, "What if…what if I stay, too? What if we just go on as before?"

She lifted her head to look at him, studying his

beloved features in the rain-dimmed light. She wasn't unaware of what it had taken for him to make such an offer; he had always been so diligent in shunning even the appearance of caring, yet now he was actually reaching out to her, asking for the ties of emotion. He needed to be loved more than any man she had ever seen, but she didn't know if he could tolerate it. Love brought responsibilities, obligations. It was never free, but required a high payment in the form of compromise.

"Can you?" she asked, the sadness as evident in her tone as in her eyes. "I don't doubt that you would try, but could you stay? There's no going back. Things have changed, and they'll never be the same again."

"I know," he said, and the stark look in his eyes hurt her, because she could see that he didn't really believe he could succeed.

She had never before pried into his past, just as she had never before told him that she loved him, but their insular little world had unraveled with frightening speed and turned things upside down. Sometimes, to make a gain, you had to take a risk.

"Why did you ask me if I would throw our baby away?"

The question hung in the air between them like a sword. She felt him flinch, saw his pupils contract with shock. He would have pulled away from her then, but she tightened her leg around him and gripped his shoulder with her hand; he stopped, though he could easily have moved had he wanted to pit his strength against hers. He stayed only because he couldn't bring himself to give up her touch. She bound him with her tenderness when strength couldn't have held him.

He closed his eyes in an instinctive effort to shut out

the memory, but it didn't go away, couldn't go away with Anna's question unanswered. He had never talked about it before, never wanted to talk about it. It was a wound too deep and too raw to be eased by "talking it out." He had lived with the knowledge his entire life, and he had done what he'd had to do to survive. He had closed that part of his life away. It was like tearing his guts out now to answer, but Anna deserved at least the truth.

"My mother threw me away," he finally said in a guttural tone; then his throat shut down and he couldn't say anything else. He shook his head helplessly, but his eyes were still closed, and he didn't see the look of utter horror, swiftly followed by soul-shattering compassion, on Anna's face. She watched him through a blur of tears, but she didn't dare break down and begin crying, or do anything else that would interrupt him. Instead she gently stroked his chest, offering tactile comfort rather than verbal; she sensed that words weren't adequate to the task, and in any case, if she tried to speak, she would lose her battle with her tears.

But as the silence stretched into minutes, she realized that he wasn't going to continue, perhaps couldn't continue without prompting. She swallowed and tried to regain her composure; it was an effort, but finally she was able to speak in a voice that, if not quite normal, was still soft and full of the love she felt.

"How did she throw you away? Were you abandoned, adopted...what?"

"Neither." He did twist away from her then, to lie on his back with his arm thrown up to cover his eyes. She mourned his loss, but gave him the distance he needed. Some things had to be faced alone, and perhaps this was one of them. "She threw me into the garbage when I was born. She didn't put me on the church steps or leave me at an orphanage so I could make up little stories about how much my mother had really loved me, but she had been really sick or something and had had to give me away so I'd be taken care of. All the other kids could make up stories like that, and believe them, but my mother made damn sure I was never that stupid. She dumped me into a trash can when I was a few hours old. There's not much way you can mistake an action like that for motherly love."

Anna curled into a little ball on her side, her fist shoved into her mouth to stifle the sobs that kept welling up, her streaming eyes fastened on his face. He was talking now, and though she had wanted to know, now she had to fight the urge to clap her hand over his mouth. No one should ever have to grow up knowing about such ugliness.

"She wasn't just trying to get rid of me," he continued in an emotionless voice. "She tried to kill me. It was winter when she threw me away, and she didn't bother to wrap me in anything. I don't know exactly when my birthday is, either January third or fourth, because I was found at three-thirty in the morning, and I could have been born either late on the third or early on the fourth. I almost died of exposure anyway, and I spent over a year in the charity hospital with one problem after another. By the time I was placed in an orphanage, I was a toddler who had seen so many strangers come and go that I wouldn't have anything to do with people. I guess that's why I wasn't adopted. People want babies, infants still wrapped up in blankets, not a thin, sickly toddler who screams if they reach for him."

He swallowed and took his arm down from his eyes, which stared unseeingly upward. "I have no idea who or what my parents are. No trace of my mother was ever found. I was named after the city and county where I was found. Saxon City, Malone county. Hell of a tradition to carry on.

"After a few years I was placed in a series of foster homes, most of them not very good. I was kicked around like a stray puppy. Social services got so desperate to place me that they left me with this one family even though I was always covered with a variety of bruises whenever the caseworker came around. It wasn't until the guy kicked in a couple of my ribs that they jerked me out of there. I was ten, I guess. They finally found a fairly good foster home for me, a couple whose own son had died. I don't know, maybe they thought I'd be able to take their son's place, but it didn't work, for them or me. They were nice, but it was in their eyes every time they looked at me that I wasn't Kenny. It was a place to live, and that was all I wanted. I made it through school, walked out and never looked back."

Chapter Five

What he had told her explained so much about the man Saxon had become and why it was so hard for him to accept any semblance of love. If the first eighteen years of his life had taught him anything, it was that he couldn't depend on what others called love but which he'd never known himself. As he had said, there was no fooling himself with pretty stories that his mother had loved him when her actions had made it plain that she not only hadn't cared, but she had deliberately left him to die. Nor had he received any real affection from the overworked staff of the charity hospital. Children learn early; by the time he had been placed in an orphanage, he had already known that he couldn't trust anyone to take care of him, so he had retreated into himself as the only surety in his life. He had depended on no one except himself for anything.

It was a lesson that had been reinforced by his childhood, shunted from one foster home to another, meeting with abuse in some of them and fitting in at none of them. Where did an outcast learn of love? The simple, heartbreaking answer was that he didn't. He had had to rise above more than simple poverty. He had needed to surmount a total lack of the most simple human caring. When she thought of what he had accomplished with his life, she was awed by his immense willpower. How hard had he had to work to put himself through college, to earn not only an engineering degree but to finish so high in his class that he'd had his choice of jobs, and from there go on to form his own company?

After the gut-wrenching tale of his childhood, they had both been emotionally incapable of probing any deeper. By mutual consent they had gotten up and gone through the motions of a normal day, though it was anything but. The past twenty-four hours had taken a toll on both of them, and they had retreated into long periods of silence, punctuated only by commonplace matters such as what they would have for lunch.

He was there. He showed no indication of leaving. She took that as a sign of hope and did no packing herself. Right now, all she asked for was his presence.

It was late afternoon on that rain-drenched day when he said flatly, "You never really answered my question this morning. Can we go on as we did before?"

She glanced at him and saw that though stress was still visible on his face, he seemed to have come to terms with it. She wasn't too certain of her own reaction, but she would rather bear the strain herself than take the risk of putting him off now at a time when that might be enough to drive him away again.

She sat down across from him, trying to marshal her thoughts. Finally she said, "For myself, I would like nothing better. It nearly killed me to lose you, and I'm not too certain I can go through that again. But I can't just think of myself. We can't just think of our own arrangement. What about the baby? At first, nothing will matter to it but Mommy and Daddy, but assuming that we stay together for years, what happens when it starts school and finds out that other mommies and daddies are married? This is Denver, not Hollywood. And though no one frowns on a couple living together, the circumstances change when a baby is involved."

He looked down at his hands and said very carefully, "How is it different if you move out? Its parents still won't be married, but you'll be trying to raise it alone. Is that supposed to be better for it? I don't know what kind of a father I'd make, but I think I'd be better than nothing."

Her lips trembled, and she fiercely bit down on them. Dear God, was she making him *beg* to be included in his child's life? She had never intended that, especially in light of what he'd told her that morning. "I think you'd be a wonderful father," she said. "I've never intended to prevent you from seeing your child. It's our living arrangement I'm not sure of."

"I am. I want you, and you…you want me." He still couldn't say that she loved him. "We don't have to do anything right now. Like you said, it'll be years before it's old enough to compare us with other parents. You still have a pregnancy to get through, and God knows I won't sleep at night if I don't know you're okay. At least stay until the baby's born. I can take care of you, go with you to those childbirth classes, be with you during delivery." Though his tone was confident, his eyes were pleading, and that was what broke down her resolve. If she pushed him away now, he might never recover.

"There's nothing I'd like better," she said huskily, and saw the lightning flash of relief in his eyes before he masked it.

"I'll move my clothes in tomorrow."

She could only blink at him in surprise. She had expected him to return to the status quo, sleeping almost every night with her but returning to his own apartment every morning to change clothes before going to work. The thought of his clothes hanging next to hers in the spacious closet made her feel both excited and a little alarmed, which was ridiculous, because she had never wanted anything as much as she had wanted a full, complete life with him. But things were changing so swiftly, and her life was already in upheaval with her pregnancy. Control of her body was slipping further from her grasp with every passing day, as the baby grew and demanded more of her. Though her early symptoms had been scant, she could now see definite changes.

She had been fighting one of those changes all day, and it was all suddenly too much. Tears welled in her eyes as she looked at him, and began to roll down her face. Instantly he was beside her, putting his arms around her and tucking her head against his shoulder. "What's wrong?" he demanded, sounding almost frantic. "Don't you want me to move in? I thought I could take care of you better."

"It isn't that," she sobbed. "Yes, it is. I'm happy, damn it! I've always wanted you to move in with me, or ask me to move in with you. But you didn't do it for my sake, you did it because of the baby!"

Saxon tilted her face up and used his thumbs to wipe away her tears. His black brows were drawn together in a scowl. "Of course I'm doing it for you," he said impatiently. "I don't know the baby. Hell, I can't even see much evidence of it yet! I don't want you to be alone any more than necessary." The scowl intensified. "Have you been to a doctor?"

She sniffed and wiped her eyes. "Yes, I didn't realize I was pregnant until I saw the doctor. I went because my last period was just spotting, and the one before that was really light. I've hardly had any symptoms at all."

"Is that normal?"

"As normal as anything else is. The doctor told me everything looked fine, that some women spotted for the first few months and some didn't, that some women had morning sickness and some didn't. All I've really noticed is that I get tired and sleepy and that I want to cry a lot."

He looked relieved. "You mean you're crying because of the baby?"

"No, I'm crying because of you!"

"Well, don't." He pulled her close and pressed a kiss to her forehead. "I don't like it when you cry."

There was no way he could know how it felt to be coddled and cuddled like that, how she had yearned for it. Love had been in short supply in her life, too, though she had never known the direct brutality Saxon had suffered. Her most cherished dreams had always been about having a home with him, just an ordinary home, with the sweet security of routine and the sure knowledge that he was coming home to her every day. In her dreams he had always held her and shown her how much he cared, while in reality he had offered her physical intimacy and an emotional desert. This sudden turn-around was so much like a dream come true that she was afraid to believe in it. Even so, she wasn't going to do anything to end it prematurely. For as long as he stayed, she intended to savor every moment.

True to his word, he moved in the next day. He didn't say anything to her about it, but a couple of phone calls, one from someone interested in leasing his other apartment and another from a utility company double-checking the address for the forwarding of his bill, made it obvious that he was completely giving up his official residence. That, more than anything, told her how serious he was about preserving their relationship.

She watched him closely for signs of edginess, because their relationship had changed in far more fundamental ways than simply that he no longer had dual residences. She had told him that she loved him, words that couldn't be erased or forgotten; by his reaction to their short estrangement, he had revealed a lot more about how much he cared than he ever had before. Though they had been physically intimate for two years, this sort of closeness was totally new to him, and she could tell that sometimes he didn't know how to act. It was almost as if he were in a foreign country where he didn't speak the language, cautiously groping his way about, unable to read the road signs.

He was increasingly curious about the baby and insisted on going with her to her next doctor's appointment, which was scheduled for only a few days after he'd moved in. When he discovered that an ultrasound photo later in her pregnancy might tell them the baby's sex, he immediately wanted to know when they would be able to do it, and how often the doctors were mistaken. Since it was the first interest he had shown in the baby's sex, she wondered if he was imagining having a son. He hadn't indicated a preference either way, and she had no decided preference, either, so they had somehow always referred to the baby as "it" rather than "he" or "she."

How would a son affect him? He would see more of himself in a boy, and it would be, in a way, a chance for him to correct the horror of his own childhood by making certain his own son never knew anything but love. In her mind's eye she saw him patiently showing a grubby, determined little boy how to swing a bat or field a pop fly. There would probably be years of attending a variety of ball games and watching with fierce pride every move the boy made. Every hit would be the best hit ever made, every catch the most stupendous, because the boy making it would be *theirs*.

Despite the dampening whispers of her common sense, she couldn't stop dreaming of a future with Saxon. One miracle had already happened: he hadn't disappeared when he'd learned of her pregnancy. She would continue hoping for another miracle.

Lying in bed that night, she nestled her head on his chest and listened to the strong, steady boom-*boom* of his heart. Her hand strayed down to her abdomen; the baby was hearing her own heart steadily pumping in the same rhythm, soothing and reassuring it just as Saxon's heartbeat soothed her. It was a wonderfully satisfying sound.

"You seemed really interested in the ultrasound," she said sleepily.

"Mmm," he grunted by way of a reply. Her head moved as she glanced up at him, though all she could see was his chin, and that not very well in the darkened room.

"Are you anxious to know what the baby is?"

He shifted restlessly. "I'd like to know, yeah. What about you? Do you have your heart set on a little girl?"

"Not really," she said, and yawned. "I just want a healthy baby, boy or girl, though it would be convenient to know ahead of time so we can have a name picked out and a nursery decorated without having to use greens or yellows."

"A nursery," he said in a faintly surprised tone. "I hadn't thought that far ahead. All I can picture is this little person about the size of a skinned rabbit, all wrapped up in a blanket. It'll stay where we put it and won't take up much space. Why does something that small need an entire room for itself?"

She grinned in the darkness. "Because otherwise the entire apartment would be cluttered with all the paraphernalia necessary for taking care of a baby. And where did you think it would sleep?"

The question startled him; then he laughed, the rare sound booming under her ear. "With us, I guess. On whichever arm you weren't using. I would say it could sleep on my chest, but I understand they aren't housebroken."

She snickered, and he laughed again. More content than she could ever remember being in her life, she snuggled even closer. "I imagine you want a boy. All day today I kept having daydreams about you teaching him how to play baseball."

Saxon stiffened, his body going rigid all along her

side. "Not especially," he finally said in a strained voice. "I'd really rather have a girl."

Surprise kept her silent, particularly because she didn't know what about the question had upset him. He didn't say anything for a while, and she began to drift off to sleep, but all drowsiness left her when he said quietly, "Maybe if it's a girl you'll love it more."

Chapter Six

"What about your family?" he asked carefully the next morning, as if wary of treading on unstable ground. In his experience, family was something other people had and, from what he'd seen at his foster homes, it wasn't desirable. But he wanted to know more about Anna, wanted to find out all he could about her in case some day he came home to find her gone. "Have you told them that you're having a baby, or anything about me?"

"I don't have any family," she replied as she poured skim milk over her cereal. Her manner was casual, but his interest sharpened immediately.

"No family? Were you an orphan?" He had seen a lot of orphans, sad and terrified children who had lost their entire world and didn't know what to do. Maybe his situation, dire as it had been, was preferable to theirs. At least he hadn't lost someone he loved. His mother hadn't died; she had simply dumped him in the trash. Probably both she and his father were still alive somewhere, though he sincerely doubted they were together. He was more than likely the result of a short affair, at best, and more probably a one-night stand.

"Yes, but I was never in an orphanage. My mother died when I was nine, and my dad said he couldn't take proper care of me, so he sent me to live with his half sister. To tell the truth, he simply didn't want the responsibility. From what my aunt said, he'd always been irresponsible, never holding down a job for long, spending his money in bars and chasing after other women. He died in a car accident when I was fourteen."

"What about your aunt?" he asked, remembering the "None" she had listed beside the next-of-kin information. "Do you still see her?"

"No. She died about a year before I went to work for you, but I doubt I'd ever have seen her again anyway. It wasn't a fond relationship. She and Uncle Sid had seven kids of their own. I was just an unwelcome extra mouth to feed, especially since she had never gotten along with Dad anyway. Aunt Cora looked as if she had posed for the painting 'American Gothic,' all prune-faced and disapproving, soured on life. There was never enough money to go around, and it was only natural that she provided for her own children first."

Anger swelled in him as he pictured her, a thin, lost little girl with big honey eyes, standing off to the side as he had often stood, never quite a part of a family unit. That had been the better part of his childhood, but it infuriated him that Anna had been subjected to such treatment. "What about your cousins? Don't you ever see them, or hear from them?"

"No, we were never close. We got along as well as most children who have been thrown together, but we never had much in common. They've all moved off the farm, anyway, and I don't know where they are. I suppose I could trace them if I wanted, but there doesn't seem any point in it."

Somehow he had never pictured Anna as being alone in the world, or of having a background in common with him. It shook him to realize that, in a different way, she had been just as deprived of nurturing as he had. She had never suffered the physical abuse, and perhaps that was why she was still able to reach out, to express her love. Even before he could remember, he had learned not to expect, or hope, or offer anything of himself, because that would leave him open to hurt. He was glad Anna hadn't known a life like that.

Even so, it couldn't have been easy for her to tell him that she loved him. Had she been braced for rejection? That was what he'd done, panicked and thrown her love back in her face. He had been terrified the next morning that she wouldn't be able to stand the sight of him after the way he'd run out on her. But she had taken him back, and thank God, she not only loved him, but she seemed to love his baby. Sometimes it seemed impossible.

"What about the foster family you stayed with?" she asked. "Do you ever call them, or visit?"

"No. I haven't seen them since the day after my high-school graduation, when I packed and left, but they didn't expect me to keep in touch. I told them goodbye and thanked them, and I guess that was good enough."

"What were their names?"

"Emmeline and Harold Bradley. They were good people. They tried, especially Harold, but there was no way they could turn me into their son. It was always there, in their eyes. I wasn't Kenny. Emmeline always seemed to resent it that her son had died but I was still alive. Neither of them ever touched me if they could prevent it. They took care of me, provided me with a place to stay, clothes, food, but there wasn't any affection there. They were relieved when I left."

"Aren't you curious if they're still alive, or if they've moved?"

"There's no point in it. There's nothing for me there, and they wouldn't be overjoyed to see me."

"Where did they live?"

"About eighty miles from here, in Fort Morgan."

"But that's so close! My cousins lived in Maryland, so it's at least reasonable that we haven't kept in touch."

He shrugged. "I left the state when I went to college, so it wasn't exactly convenient for me to visit. I worked two jobs to pay my tuition, and that didn't leave a lot of free time."

"But you came back to Colorado and settled in Denver."

"There's more demand for engineers in a large city."

"There are a lot of cities in this country. The point is, you're so close, but you never called them to tell them how college turned out, or that you were back in the state."

Temper edged into his voice. "No, I didn't, and I don't intend to. For God's sake, Anna, it's been fifteen years since I got out of college. They sure as hell haven't kept a candle in the window for me all this time. They knew I wouldn't be back."

She dropped the subject, but she didn't forget it. Harold and Emmeline Bradley. She committed their names to memory. Despite what Saxon thought, they had spent years raising him and were likely to be more than a little interested in what had become of him.

He left for work in silence, and returned that afternoon in the same brooding mood. She left him alone, but his silence made her quietly panic. Had her questions bothered him so much that he was considering terminating their arrangement? But he had started it by asking about her family, so he had only himself to blame. In the few days since she had told him of the baby she had become accustomed to thinking of him as more approachable, more *hers,* but suddenly she was very much aware of the wall that still surrounded him. She had knocked a few chinks out of it, but it was far from demolished.

Saxon hadn't liked all that talk about his foster family, but it had started him thinking. Unless he and Anna took steps to prevent it, this baby wouldn't have much of a family, either. He couldn't picture them having other children under their present circumstances, and to his surprise, he liked the idea of more children. He wanted them to be a family, not just live-in lovers who happened to have a baby.

He hadn't had pretty fantasies about his mother, but he had often wondered, with a child's bewildered pain, what it would be like to have a real family, to belong somewhere and have someone who loved him. It was a fantasy that hadn't lasted long under the merciless weight of reality, but he still remembered how he had imagined it, the feeling of security that was at the center of it and held everything together. He hadn't been able to picture parents, beyond tall shadowy figures that stood between him and danger. He never wanted his baby to have those kinds of fantasies; he wanted it to have the reality of a stable home.

Less than a week ago, just the idea of what he was now considering would have been enough to make him break out in a panicky sweat, but he had since learned that there were worse things. Losing Anna was worse. He hoped he never in his life had to live through another day and night like he'd endured then, because he didn't think his sanity could take it. In comparison, what he was thinking now was a snap.

Thinking it was one thing, actually putting it into words was another. He watched Anna with troubled eyes, though he knew it was useless trying to predict her answer. Behind her customary serenity she was deep and complicated, seeing more than he wanted her to see, understanding more than was comfortable. With so much of her thought processes hidden from him, he wasn't at all certain how she would react, or why. If she loved him there should be no hesitation, but that wasn't necessarily the case. She was capable of sacrificing her own happiness—assuming he could make her happy— for what she thought best for the baby.

It was strange what an impact the baby had had on their lives months prior to its birth, but he didn't regret the changes. It was frightening; he had the sense of living on the edge, where any false move could send him over, but at the same time the increased openness and intimacy he shared with Anna were, without a doubt, worth every minute of worry. He didn't think he could go back to the previous loneliness he had taken for granted, even embraced.

Still, it was a decision that racked him with nerves. In

the end, he couldn't say the words that would be an offer of himself, a statement of his feelings and vulnerability; instead he threw them out couched as a suggestion. "I think we should get married."

There was nothing he could have said that would have astounded her more. Her legs went weak, and she sat down heavily. "Marriage!" she said with a mixture of disbelief and total surprise.

He wasn't pleased that the solution hadn't occurred to her. "Yes, marriage. It makes sense. We're already living together, and we're having a baby. Marriage seems the logical next step."

Anna shook her head, not in refusal but in a futile effort to clear her head. Somehow she had never expected to receive a marriage proposal couched as "the logical next step." She hadn't expected a marriage proposal, period, though she had wanted one very badly. But she had wanted him to propose for different reasons, because he loved her and couldn't live without her. She suspected that was the case, but she would never know for sure if he never told her.

It wasn't an easy decision, and she didn't rush into speech. His face was impassive as he waited for her answer, his green eyes darkened and watchful. Her answer meant a lot to him, she realized. He wanted her to say yes. She wanted to say yes. The question was whether she was willing to take the chance that he did love her and marry him on blind faith. A cautious woman wouldn't want to make a hasty decision that would affect not only the two of them, but their child as well. A broken marriage inevitably left its scars on all concerned.

She had taken a leap of blind faith in quitting her job

to become his mistress, and she didn't regret it. The two years of loving him had been the best of her life, and she could never wish them undone. Pregnancy altered everything, she thought with a faint curving of her lips. She couldn't just think of herself now; she had to think of the baby. What was logical wasn't necessarily the best choice, even though her heart clamored for a quick acceptance.

She looked at him, her dark eyes grave. "I love you, you know," she said.

Once such a statement would have made his face go blank in a refusal to hear. Now he steadily returned her gaze. "I know." The knowledge didn't make him panic; instead he treasured it, savored it, as the most precious gift of his life.

"I want to say yes, more than anything I've ever wanted, but I'm afraid to. I know it was your idea for us to stay together, and you've been wonderful, but I'm not certain that you'll still feel the same after the baby's born. As the old saying goes, then it becomes a whole new ball game. I don't want you to feel trapped or unhappy."

He shook his head as if to forestall the answer he sensed was coming. "There's no way to predict the future. I know why you worry about the way I'll react, and to tell you the truth, I'm a little scared myself, but I'm excited, too. I want this baby. I want you. Let's get married and make it official." He smiled wryly. "The baby could have Malone for a last name. The second generation of a brand-new family."

Anna took a deep breath and denied herself what she had wanted more than anything else. "I can't give you an answer now," she whispered, and saw his face tighten. "It just doesn't feel right. I want to say yes, Saxon, I want that more than anything, but I'm not certain it would be the right thing to do."

"It is," he said roughly.

"Then if it is, it will still be the right thing a month from now, or two months from now. Too much has happened too fast—the baby…you. I don't want to make the wrong decision, and I think I'm operating more on my emotions now than on brainpower."

The force of his willpower shone out of his eyes, intensely green and focused. "I can't make you say yes," he said in a slow, deep voice. "But I can keep asking. I can make love to you and take care of you until you won't be able to imagine life without me."

Her lips trembled. "I can't imagine that now."

"I don't give up, Anna. When I go after something, I don't stop until I've gotten it. I want you, and I'm going to have you."

She knew exactly what he meant. When he decided something, he focused on it with a fierce tunnel vision that didn't let him rest until he had achieved his objective. It was a little daunting to think of herself as the object of that kind of determination.

He smiled then, a smile that was more than a little predatory. "You can take that to the bank, baby."

Chapter Seven

Marriage. The thought of it hovered in her consciousness during the day and crept into her dreams at night. Several times every day she started to throw caution to the winds and tell him yes, but there was a part of her that simply wasn't ready to take such an immense step. She had been willing before to settle for being his mistress, but now she was unable to settle for being his wife; she wanted him to love her, too, and admit it to both her and himself. She might be certain that he did love her, but until he could come to terms with his feelings, she couldn't rely on that. He could say "I want you," but not "I love you."

She couldn't blame him for having difficulty with the emotion. Sometimes when she was alone she cried for him, at first a discarded infant, then a lonely, frightened toddler, and finally an abused youngster with no one he could turn to for help. No one could have endured such a childhood without emotional scarring, without losing the ability both to give and accept love. When she looked at it clearly, she saw that he had reached out to her far more than could reasonably be expected.

She didn't really expect more, but she wanted it.

She couldn't get the Bradleys out of her mind. From what he had said, he had spent six years with them, from the time he was twelve until he was eighteen. Six years was a long time for them to keep him and not feel something for him. Was it possible that they had offered him more than duty, but at the time he hadn't been able to see it for what it was? And how had they felt at not hearing from him ever again?

Surely they had worried, if they had any hint of human warmth about them. They had raised him from a boy to a young man, given him the only stable home life he had ever known until Anna had become his mistress and made a sanctuary for him in the apartment. It was always possible that it had been exactly as he remembered it, that losing their son had prevented them from feeling anything for him beyond duty and a sense of pity. Pity! He would have hated that. If he had sensed that they pitied him, no wonder he hadn't gone back.

But though she fretted about it for several days, she knew that she wasn't accomplishing anything with her worrying. If she wanted to know for certain, she would have to drive to Fort Morgan and try to find the Bradleys. It might be a useless trip, since nineteen years had passed; they could have moved, or even died.

Once she made the decision to go, she felt better, even though she knew Saxon would be adamantly against the idea. However, she didn't intend to let his opposition stop her.

That didn't mean she intended to be sneaky about it.

After dinner that night she said, "I'm going to Fort Morgan tomorrow."

He tensed, and his eyes narrowed. "Why?"

"To try to find the Bradleys."

He folded the newspaper away with an angry snap. "There's no point in it. I told you how it was. Why are you worried about it, anyway? That was nineteen years ago. It's nothing to do with us now. You didn't even know me then."

"Curiosity, partly," she answered with blunt honesty. "And what if you're wrong about the way they felt? You were young. You could have misread them. And if you were wrong, then they've spent nineteen years feeling as if they lost two sons instead of just one."

"No," he said, and from the command in his voice she knew he wasn't refuting her suggestion but issuing an order.

She lifted her brows at him, mild surprise in her eyes. "I wasn't asking permission. I was letting you know where I'd be so you wouldn't worry if you called and I wasn't here."

"I said no."

"You certainly did," she agreed. "But I'm not your mistress anymore—"

"It sure as hell felt like you were last night," he interrupted, his eyes turning greener as anger intensified the color.

She didn't intend to argue with him. Instead she smiled, and her soft face glowed as she sent him a warm look. "That was making love." And it had been wonderful. Sex between them had always been hot and urgent, but since he had moved in with her it had taken on an added dimension, a shattering tenderness that hadn't been there before. Their lovemaking was more prolonged; it was as if, before, he had always been aware that he was going to have to get up and leave, and the knowledge had driven him. Now he was relaxed and leisurely in a way he hadn't been before, with increased pleasure as a result.

There was a flicker of tension across his face at the word "love," but it was quickly gone, with no lingering echoes.

"I'm not your mistress," she repeated. "That arrangement is over with. I'm the woman who loves you, who lives with you, who's having your baby."

He looked around at the apartment. "You may not think you're my mistress anymore," he said with soft anger, "but things look pretty much the same to me."

"Because you support me? That's your choice, not mine. I'll find a job, if it will make you feel better. I've never enjoyed being a kept woman, anyway."

"No!" He didn't like that idea at all. It had always been in the back of his mind that, if he kept her totally dependent on him, she would be less likely to leave. At the same time he had invested in stocks in her name to make certain she would be financially secure. The paradox had always made him uneasy, but he wanted her to be taken care of in case something happened to him. After all, he traveled a lot and spent a lot of time on construction sites, not the safest of places. He had also made a will a year ago, leaving everything to her. He'd never told her.

"I don't want you driving that far by yourself," he finally said, but he was grasping at straws, and he knew it.

The Way Home   73

"It's less than a two-hour drive, the weather forecast is for clear and sunny conditions tomorrow. But if you want to go with me, I can wait until the weekend," she offered.

His expression closed up at the idea. He had never been back, never wanted to go back. The Bradleys hadn't mistreated him; they had been the best of all the foster homes he'd been in. But that part of his life was over. He had shut the door on it when he'd left, and he'd spent the following years working like a slave to make himself into someone who would never again be helpless.

"They may have moved," she said, offering comfort. "I just want to know."

He made a weary gesture. "Then pick up the telephone and call information. Talk to them, if they're still there. But don't involve me in it. I don't want to talk to them. I don't want to see them. I don't want anything to do with this."

She wasn't surprised at his total rejection of the past; it was hardly the type of memory he would embrace. And she hadn't expected him to go with her.

"I don't want to talk to them over the telephone," she said. "I want to drive up there, see the house. I may not approach them at all. It depends on what I find when I get there."

She held her breath, because there was one appeal he could make that she wouldn't be able to deny. If he said, "Please don't go, for my sake," then she wouldn't go. If he actually asked for anything for himself, there was no way she could turn him down. He had been rejected so much in his life that she wouldn't add to it. But because of those prior rejections, she knew he wouldn't ask in those terms. He would never put things in the context of being a personal consideration for him. He would order, he would make objections, but he wouldn't simply ask and say, "Please don't."

He refused to talk about it anymore and got up restlessly to stand at the terrace doors and look out. Anna calmly returned to her own section of the paper, but her heart was beating fast as she realized this was the first normal domestic quarrel they had ever had. To her delight, they had disagreed, and nothing major had happened. He hadn't left, nor did he seem to expect her to leave. It was wonderful. He was already able to trust her enough that he wasn't afraid a disagreement could end their relationship.

She had worried that he would overreact to arguments, since they were part and parcel of every relationship. Normal couples had disagreements; probably even saints had disagreements. Two years ago, Saxon wouldn't have been able to tolerate such a personal discussion.

He was really trying, even though it was extraordinarily difficult for him to open up. Circumstances had forced him into revealing his past, but he hadn't tried to reestablish those protective mental walls of his. He seemed to accept that once the emotional boundaries had been crossed, he couldn't make them inviolate again.

She didn't know what she could accomplish by finding the Bradleys again. Perhaps nothing. She just wanted to see them, to get a feel for herself of what that portion of Saxon's formative years had been like. If they seemed interested, she wanted to reassure them that their foster son was alive and well, that he was successful and would soon be a father himself.

With his back still to her, Saxon asked, "Are you

afraid to marry me because of my past? Is that why you want to find the Bradleys, so you can ask them questions about me?"

"No!" she said, horrified. "I'm not *afraid* to marry you."

"My parents could be anything—murderers, drug users. My mother may be a prostitute. The odds are pretty good she was. There may be a history of mental illness in my background. *I'd* be afraid to marry me. But the Bradleys won't be able to tell you anything, because no one knows who my parents were."

"I'm not concerned with your parents," she said levelly. "I know you. You're rock solid. You're honest, kind, hardworking and sexy."

"So why won't you marry me, if I'm such a good catch?"

Good question, she thought. Maybe she was being foolish in waiting. "I don't want to rush into something that might not be right for either of us."

"I don't want my baby to be born illegitimate."

"Oh, Saxon." She gave a sad laugh. "I promise you I'll make a decision long before the baby is born."

"But you can't promise me you'll say yes."

"No more than you can promise me our marriage would work."

He gave her a brief, angry look over his shoulder. "You said you love me."

"And I do. But can you say that *you* love *me?*" she asked.

He didn't answer. Anna watched him, her eyes sad and tender. Her question could be taken in two ways. He did love her, she thought, but was incapable of actually *say-*

ing it. Maybe he felt that as long as he didn't say the words aloud, he hadn't made the emotional commitment.

Finally he said, "Is that what it'll take for you to marry me?"

"No. It isn't a test that you have to pass."

"Isn't it?"

"No," she insisted.

"You say you won't marry me because you don't know if I can handle it, but I'm willing to try. You're the one who's resisting making a commitment."

She stared at him in frustration. He was too good at arguing, agilely taking her previous arguments and using them against her. She was glad that he felt sure enough of her to do it, but she could see what she'd be up against in the future if they did get married. It would take a lot of determination to win an argument against him.

She pointed her finger at him, even though his back was still turned and he couldn't see her. "I'm not resisting making a commitment, I'm resisting making it *now*. I think I have a right to be a little cautious."

"Not if you trust me."

That turned back was making her suspicious. She gave him a considering look, then suddenly realized he had turned his back so she wouldn't be able to read his expression. Her eyes narrowed as she realized what he was doing. He wasn't as upset or even as indignant as he sounded; he was simply using the tactic as a means of maneuvering her into agreeing to marry him. It was all part and parcel of his determination to have his way.

She got up and went over to him, wrapping her arms around his lean waist and leaning her head against his back. "It won't work," she said softly. "I'm on to you."

To her surprise, she felt his chest expand with a low laugh; then he turned within the circle of her arms and looped his own around her. "Maybe you know me too well," he muttered, but his tone was accepting.

"Or maybe you need acting lessons."

He chuckled again and rested his cheek against the top of her head. But all humor was absent from his tone a minute later when he said, "Go see the Bradleys, if you have to. There's nothing there to find out."

Chapter Eight

Fort Morgan was a small town of about ten thousand people. Anna drove around for a little while to get her bearings, then stopped at a phone booth to look up the Bradleys' address. What she would do if they weren't in the book, she didn't know. It could mean they had moved or died, or it might just mean that their number wasn't listed.

She could have asked Saxon, but she hadn't wanted to ask him for information to help her to do something of which he didn't approve. Besides, it had been nineteen years, and there was no guarantee the Bradleys would still live in the same house, even if they had remained in Fort Morgan.

The phone book wasn't very big. She flipped through it to the *B*s, then ran her finger down the column. "Bailey…Banks…Black…Boatwright…Bradley. Harold Bradley." She wrote down the address and phone number, then debated whether she should call them to get directions. She decided not to, because she wanted to catch them unawares, as it were. People could mask their true reactions if they were given warning.

So she drove to a gas station, filled up and asked directions of the attendant. Ten minutes later she drove slowly down a residential street, checking house numbers, and finally stopped at the curb in front of a neat but unpretentious house. It looked as if it had been built a good forty or fifty years before, with an old-fashioned roofed porch across the front. The white paint showed signs of wear but wasn't at the point where one could definitely say the house was in need of repainting. An assortment of potted plants was sunning on the porch, but there weren't any ornamentals in the small yard, which gave it a bare look. A one-car, unconnected garage sat back and to the side of the house.

She got out of the car, oddly reluctant now that she was here, but she walked up the cracked sidewalk and climbed the three steps to the porch. A porch glider, with rust spots showing where the thick white paint had chipped, was placed in front of the windows. Anna wondered if the Bradleys sat out there during the summer and watched the neighbors go about their business.

There wasn't a doorbell. She knocked on the frame of the screen door and waited. A gray-and-white cat leaped up onto the porch and meowed curiously at her.

After a minute, she knocked again. This time she heard hurried footsteps, and her pulse speeded up in anticipation. With it came a wave of nausea that had her swallowing in desperation. Of all the times to have one of her rare bouts of morning sickness! She only hoped she wouldn't disgrace herself.

The door opened, and she found herself face-to-face with a tall, thin, stern-faced woman, only the thin screen separating them. The woman didn't open the screen door. Instead she said, "Yes?" in a deep, rusty-sounding voice.

Anna was dismayed by the lack of friendliness and started to ask for directions as an excuse for being there, planning to leave without ever mentioning Saxon. But the tall woman just stood there with her hand on the latch, patiently waiting for Anna to state her business before she opened the door, and something about that strength of will struck a cord.

"Mrs. Bradley?"

"Yes, I'm Mrs. Bradley."

"My name is Anna Sharp. I'm looking for the Bradleys who used to be foster parents to Saxon Malone. Is this the right family?"

The woman's regard sharpened. "It is." She still didn't unlatch the door.

Anna's hopes sank. If Saxon hadn't been exposed to any sort of love even here, where he had grown up, he might never be able to give or accept it. What sort of marriage could she have under those conditions? What would it do to her own child to have a father who always kept at a distance?

But she had come this far, so she might as well carry on. She was aware, too, of the compelling quality of the woman's steely gaze. "I know Saxon," she began, and with an abrupt movement the woman flipped the latch up and swung the screen door outward.

"You know him?" she demanded fiercely. "You know where he is?"

Anna moved back a step. "Yes, I do."

Mrs. Bradley indicated the interior of the house with a jerk of her head. "Come inside."

Anna did, cautiously, obeying an invitation that had sounded more like a command. The door opened directly into the living room; a quick look around told her that the furniture was old and threadbare in spots, but the small room was spotless.

"Sit," said Mrs. Bradley.

She sat. Mrs. Bradley carefully relatched the screen door, then wiped her hands on the apron she wore. Anna watched the motion of those strong, work-worn hands, then realized that it was more of a nervous wringing than it was a deliberate movement.

She looked up at her reluctant hostess's face and was startled to see the strong, spare features twisted in a spasm of emotion. Mrs. Bradley tried to school herself, but abruptly a lone tear rolled down her gaunt cheek. She sat down heavily in a rocker and bunched the apron in her hands. "How is my boy?" she asked in a broken voice. "Is he all right?"

They sat at the kitchen table, with Mrs. Bradley drinking coffee while Anna contented herself with a glass of water. Mrs. Bradley was composed now, though she occasionally dabbed at her eyes with the edge of the apron.

"Tell me about him," Emmeline Bradley said. Her faded blue eyes were alight with a mixture of joy and eagerness, and also a hint of pain.

"He's an engineer," Anna said, and saw pride join the other emotions. "He owns his own company, and he's very successful."

"I always knew he would be. Smart! Lordy, that boy

was smart. Me and Harold, we always told each other, he's got a good head on his shoulders. He always got A's in school. He was dead serious about his schooling."

"He put himself through college and graduated near the top of his class. He could have gone to work with any of the big engineering firms, but he wanted to have his own business. I was his secretary for a while."

"Fancy that, his own secretary. But when he made up his mind to do something, he done it, even when he was just a boy."

"He's still like that," Anna said, and laughed. "He says exactly what he means and means exactly what he says. You always know where you stand with Saxon."

"He didn't talk much when he was here, but we understood. The child had been through so much, it was a wonder he'd talk at all. We tried not to crowd him, or force ourselves on him. It about broke our hearts sometimes, the way he would jump to do every little thing we mentioned, then kinda hold himself off and watch to see if we thought he'd done it right. I guess he thought we were going to throw him out if he didn't do everything perfect, or maybe even kick him around the way they'd done in some of those other homes."

Tears welled in Anna's eyes, because she could see him all too plainly, young and thin and still helpless, his green eyes watchful, empty of hope.

"Don't cry," Emmeline said briskly, then had to dab at her own eyes. "He was twelve when we got him, bone-thin and gangly. He hadn't started getting his height yet, and he was still limping where the woman who had him before us knocked him off the porch with a broom handle. He twisted his ankle pretty bad. He had some long, thin bruises across his back, like the broom handle had caught him there, too. I guess it was a regular thing. And there was a burn mark on his arm. Mind you, he never said anything about it, but the caseworker told us a man ground out his cigarette on him.

"He never acted scared of us, but for a long time he'd get real stiff if we got too close to him, like he was getting ready to either fight or run. He seemed more comfortable if we stayed at a distance, so we did, even though I wanted to hug him close and tell him no one was ever going to hurt him again. But he was kinda like a dog that's been beat. He'd lost his trust of people."

Anna's throat was tight when she spoke. "He's still distant, to some extent. He isn't comfortable with emotion, though he's getting better."

"You know him real well? You said you used to be his secretary. Don't you still work for him?"

"No, I haven't worked for him for two years." A faint blush stained her cheeks. "We're having a baby, and he's asked me to marry him."

The color of Emmeline's eyes was faded, but her vision was still sharp. She gave Anna a piercing once-over. "In my day we did things in reverse order, but times change. There's no shame in loving someone. A baby, huh? When's it due? I reckon this is as close to a grandchild as I'll get."

"September. We live in Denver, so we aren't that far away. It'll be easy to visit."

A sad look crept over Emmeline's lined face. "We always figured Saxon didn't want to have nothing to do with us again. He said goodbye when he graduated from high school, and we could tell he meant it. Can't blame him, really. By the time we got him, his growing-up years had marked him so deep we knew he wouldn't want to think about any foster home. The caseworker told us all about him. The woman who gave birth to that boy has a lot to answer for, what she did to him and the living hell she caused his life to be. I swear, if anyone had ever found out who she was, I'd have hunted her down and done violence to her."

"I've had the same thought myself," Anna said grimly, and for a moment her velvet brown eyes didn't look so soft.

"My Harold died several years back," Emmeline said, and nodded in acknowledgment of Anna's murmur of sympathy. "I wish he could be here now, to hear how well Saxon's turned out, but I guess he knows anyway."

Her rough, simple faith was more touching than any elaborate protestation could have been. Anna found herself smiling, because there was something joyous in Emmeline's surety.

"Saxon said you lost your own son," she said, hoping she wasn't bringing up a source of grief that was still fresh. Losing a child was something a parent should never have to experience.

Emmeline nodded, a faraway expression coming over her face. "Kenny," she said. "Lordy, it's been thirty years now since he took sick that last time. He was sickly from birth. It was his heart, and back then they couldn't do the things they can now. The doctors told us from the time he was a baby that we wouldn't get to keep him all that long, but somehow knowing don't always help you prepare for it. He died when he was ten, poor little mite, and he looked about the size of a six-year-old."

After a minute the dreamy expression left her face, and she smiled. "Saxon, now, you could tell right off, even as thin and bruised up as he was, he was a strong one. He started growing the next year after we got him. Maybe it was having regular meals that did it. Lord knows I poked all the food down him I could. But he shot up like a bean pole, growing a foot in about six months. Seemed like every time we got him some jeans, he outgrew them the next week. He was taller than Harold in no time, all legs and arms. Then he started to fill out, and that was a sight to behold. All of a sudden we had more young gals walking up and down the street than I'd ever imagined lived within a square mile of this house, giggling to each other and watching the door and windows, trying to get a glimpse of him."

Anna laughed out loud. "How did he take being the center of attention like that?"

"He never let on like he noticed. Like I said, he was real serious about his schooling. And he was still leery about letting folks get close to him, so I guess dating would have been uncomfortable for him. But those girls just kept walking past, and can't say as I blame them. He made most boys his age look like pipsqueaks. He was shaving by the time he was fifteen, and he had a real beard, not a few scraggly hairs like most boys. His chest and shoulders had gotten broad, and he was muscled up real nice. Fine figure of a boy."

Anna hesitated, then decided to touch on the subject of Kenny again. Emmeline tended to get carried away talking about Saxon, perhaps because she had been denied the privilege for so many years. Now that she had finally met somebody who knew him, all the memories were bubbling out.

"Saxon told me that he always felt you resented him because he wasn't Kenny."

Emmeline gave her a surprised look. "Resented him? It wasn't his fault Kenny died. Let me tell you, you don't ever get over it when your child dies, but Kenny had been dead for several years before we got Saxon. We'd always planned to either adopt or take in foster kids, anyway, after Kenny left us. Kenny's memory laid a little easier after Saxon came to live with us. It was like he was happy we had someone else to care about, and having Saxon kept us from brooding. How could we resent him, when he'd been through such hell? Kenny didn't have good health, but he always knew we loved him, and even though he died so young, in some ways he was luckier than Saxon."

"He needs to be loved so much," Anna said, her throat tightening again. "But it's so hard for him to reach out to anyone, or let anyone reach out to him."

Emmeline nodded. "I guess we should have tried harder, after he'd had time to realize we weren't going to hurt him, but by then we were kinda used to keeping our distance from him. He seemed more comfortable that way, and we didn't push him. Looking back, I can see what we should've done, but at the time we did what it seemed like he wanted." She sat for a minute in silence, rocking back and forth a little in the wooden kitchen chair. Then she said, "Resent him? Never for a minute. Land sakes, we loved him from the beginning."

Chapter Nine

Saxon's face tightened when she told him Harold was dead, and the brilliant color of his eyes dimmed. She had expected him to refuse to listen to anything about the Bradleys, but he hadn't. If he was curious, though, he was hiding it well, because he hadn't asked any questions, either. The news of Harold's death jolted him into showing interest, though reluctantly. "Emmeline is still living in the same old house by herself?"

She told him the address, and he nodded. "It's the same house."

"She seems to be in good health," Anna said. "She cried when I told her I knew you." She took a deep breath. "You should go see her."

"No," he said shortly, dismissing the idea with a frown.

"Why not?"

She could feel him withdrawing, see his face closing up. She reached out and took his hand, remembering what Emmeline had said about letting him pull away when they should have pulled him closer. "I won't let you shut me out," she said. "I love you, and we're in this together."

His eyes were unreadable, but she had his attention. "If I had a problem, would you want to help me, or would you leave me to deal with it on my own?" she pressed.

There was a flicker of expression, gone too fast for her to decipher. "I'd take care of it for you," he said, and his hand tightened on hers. "But I don't have a problem."

"Well, I think you do."

"And you're determined to help me with it whether I think it exists or not, is that it?"

"That's it. That's the way relationships work. People butt in on other people's business because they care."

Once he would have thought it was an intolerable encroachment on his privacy, but though her determination was irritating him, at the same time it made him feel oddly secure. She was right; this was the way relationships worked. He'd seen it, though this was the first time he'd experienced it. Somehow their "arrangement" had become a "relationship," full of complications, demands and obligations, but he wouldn't have chosen to go back. For the first time in his life he felt accepted as he really was; Anna knew all there was to know about him, all the hideous details of his birth and childhood. She knew the worst, yet she hadn't left.

On a sudden impulse he lifted her astride his lap so he could look full into her face while they talked. It was an intensely personal position for talking, both physically and mentally, but it felt right. "It wasn't a good time of my life," he said in an effort to explain. "I don't want to remember it, or revisit it."

"The way you remember it is distorted by everything

that had gone before. You think of them as cold and resentful of you because you weren't their son, but that isn't at all the way they felt."

"Anna," he said patiently, "I was there."

She framed his face with her hands. "You were a frightened boy. Don't you think it's possible you were so used to rejection that you expected it, so that's what you saw?"

"So you're an amateur psychiatrist now?"

"Reasoning doesn't require a degree." She leaned forward and stole a quick kiss. "She talked for hours, telling me all about you."

"And now you think you're an expert."

"I *am* an expert on you," she snapped. "I've studied you for years, from the minute I went to work for you."

"You're pretty when you're mad," he said, abruptly enjoying this conversation. He realized with surprise that he was teasing her, and that it was fun. He could make her angry, but she would still love him anyway. Commitment had its advantages.

"Then I'm about to get a lot prettier," she warned.

"I can handle it."

"You think so, big guy?"

"Yes, ma'am." He cupped his hands on her hips and moved her suggestively. "I'm pretty sure I can."

For a moment her eyelids drooped heavily in response; then she opened her eyes wide and glared at him. "Don't try to distract me."

"I wasn't trying."

No, he was accomplishing, without effort. She was far from finished with her efforts to convince him, though, so she started to get up. His hands tightened on her hips and kept her in place. "Stay right where you are," he ordered.

"We can't talk in this position. You'll get your mind on sex, and then where will we be?"

"Probably right here on this couch. Not for the first time, either."

"Saxon, would you please be serious about this?" she wailed, then stopped in astonishment at what she had just said. She couldn't believe she had just had to plead with him to be serious. He was the most sober of men, seldom laughing or even smiling. She had probably seen him smile more in the past week or so than in the rest of the three years she had known him.

"I *am* serious," he said. "About this position, and about Emmeline. I don't want to go back. I don't want to remember."

"She loves you. She called you 'her boy,' and she said that our baby would be her grandchild."

He frowned a little, his attention caught. "She said that?"

"You should talk to her. Your memory is one-sided. They understood that you were wary of adults getting close to you, after the abuse you'd received, and that's why they didn't try to touch you. They thought they were making it easier on you."

A stark look came into his eyes as memories surfaced.

"Did you want them to hug you?" she asked. "Would you have let them?"

"No," he said slowly. "I couldn't have stood it. Even when I started having sex, in college, I didn't want the girl to put her arms around me. It wasn't until—" He broke off, his eyes unfocused. It wasn't until Anna that he had wanted the feel of arms around him, that he had wanted her to hold him close. With all the other women, he had held their hands above their heads, or he had been up on his knees out of their reach. But that had been sex; with Anna, from the very beginning, it had been making love, only it had taken him two long years to realize it.

He would never have allowed Emmeline or Harold to hug him, and they had known it.

Had his perceptions, and therefore his memories, been so distorted by his previous experiences? If what he had seen had been reflections in the carnival mirror of his mind, then nothing was as it had seemed. The beatings and general abuse he had suffered at the other foster homes had trained him to expect rejection, and he had been too young to be analytical.

"Can you really get on with your life unless you know for sure?" she asked, leaning closer to him. Those honey-dark eyes were pools he could drown in, and suddenly he pulled her tight against his chest.

"I'm trying to get on with my life," he muttered against her hair. "I'm trying to build a life, with you. Let the past go. God knows I've spent enough years trying to do that, and now that it's working, why dig it up again?"

"Because you can't let go of it! You can't forget your past. It's part of what made you the man you are. And Emmeline loves you. This isn't all for your sake. Part of it is for hers. She's alone in the world now. She didn't whine about it, or complain because you'd been gone for nearly twenty years and had never been back to see her. She just wanted to know if you were all right, and she was so proud to hear how well you've done."

Saxon closed his eyes, fighting to keep the images from forming in his mind, but it was a useless battle.

Emmeline had always been the stronger personality; Harold had been softer, gentler. He could still see her face, strong-boned, plain, as spare as a desert landscape. Never malevolent, but stern and upright. Her standards of cleanliness had been of the highest; for the first time in his life, he had always had good, clean clothes, clothes he hadn't been ashamed to go to school in.

He didn't want to think that she had spent twenty years wondering about him, worrying. No one had ever worried about him before, so the possibility simply hadn't occurred to him. All he had thought about was making a clean break with his past, making something of himself and never looking back.

Anna thought you had to look back, to see where you had been, as if the landscape changed once you had passed it. And maybe it did. Maybe it would look different now.

From habit he thrust emotion away from him, and the logic of the thing was suddenly clear to him. He didn't want to go back. He wanted Anna to marry him. Anna wanted him to go back. The three ideas fell into place, and all at once he knew what he would do.

"I'll go back," he said softly, and her head jerked up, her doe-eyes big and soft and questioning. "On one condition."

They faced each other in silence for a moment. He remembered the beginning of their relationship, when she had said she would be his mistress on one condition, and he had refused it, forcing her to take him on his terms. She was remembering, too, and he wondered if she would refuse on principle. No, not Anna. She was infinitely forgiving, and wise enough to know that the one instance had nothing to do with the other. He also accepted that he wouldn't always win, but that was okay, as long as Anna was the victor. As long as she won, he won, too.

"So let's hear it," she said, though she already knew. "What's the condition?"

"That you agree to marry me."

"You'd reduce our marriage to a condition that has to be met?"

"I'll do whatever it takes, use whatever argument I have to. I can't lose you, Anna. You know that."

"You aren't losing me."

"I want it signed and sealed, on record in the county courthouse. I want you to be my wife, and I want to be your husband. I want to be a father to our kids." He gave her a crooked smile. "This is kind of like a way for me to make up for my own lousy childhood, to give my kids something better and have a real childhood through them."

Of all the things he could have said, that one got to her fast and hard. She hid her face against his neck so he wouldn't see the tears welling up in her eyes and swallowed several times so she would be able to speak normally. "All right," she said. "You have yourself a wife."

They couldn't go to Fort Morgan immediately, because of his business commitments. Looking at the calendar, Anna smiled and made plans for them to go the following Sunday, and called Emmeline to let her know. It wasn't in Emmeline's character for her to bubble over with enthusiasm, but Anna could hear the pure joy in her voice.

The day finally came. As they made the drive, Saxon could feel himself tensing. He had been in foster homes all over the state, but he had lived in Fort Morgan the longest, so he had more memories of it. He could picture every room in that old house, every piece of furniture, every photograph and book. He could see Emmeline in the kitchen, dark hair pulled tightly back in a no-nonsense bun, a spotless apron protecting her plain housedress, while mouth-watering smells from the stove filled the entire house. He remembered that she had made an apple pie that was almost sinful, rich with butter and cinnamon. He would have gorged himself on that pie if he hadn't always been wary of anything he liked being taken away, so he had always restricted himself to one slice and forced himself not to show any enthusiasm. He remembered that Emmeline had baked a lot of apple pies.

He drove to the house without any difficulty, its location permanently etched in his mind. When he parked at the curb, his chest tightened until he felt almost suffocated. It was like being caught in a time warp, stepping back almost twenty years and finding nothing had changed. There *were* changes, of course; the porch roof was sagging a little, and the cars parked in the street were twenty years newer. But the house was still white, and the undecorated lawn was still as neat as a hatbox. And Emmeline, stepping out on the porch, was still tall and thin, and her gaunt face was still set in naturally stern lines.

He opened the car door and got out. Without waiting for him to come around, Anna had climbed out on her side, but she made no move to walk forward and join him.

Suddenly he couldn't move. Not another step. With only the small expanse of lawn separating them, he looked at the woman he hadn't seen in two decades. She was the only mother he'd ever known. His chest hurt, and he could barely breathe. He hadn't known it would be like this, that he would suddenly feel like that terrified twelve-year boy again, brought here for the first time, hoping it would be better than the others, expecting more of the same abuse. Emmeline had come out on the porch then, too, and he had looked up at that stern face and felt only the old rejection and fear. He had wanted acceptance, wanted it so much that his heart had been pounding in his chest and he had been afraid he would disgrace himself by wetting his pants, but he hadn't let himself show it, because not having it at all was easier than facing another rejection. So he had closed himself off, protecting himself in the only way he knew.

Emmeline moved toward the steps. She wasn't wearing an apron; she had dressed up in one of her Sunday dresses, but she was wiping her hands on the skirt out of habit. She stopped and stared at the tall, powerful man who was still standing at the curb. It was Saxon, without a doubt. He had turned into a breathtaking man, but she had always known he would, with that olive-toned skin, black hair and eyes like the clearest emeralds. She could see his eyes now, and the expression in them was the same as it had been twenty-five years ago when the caseworker had brought him to them, scared and desperate, and needing to be loved so much it had wrung her heart. He wouldn't come any closer, she knew. He wouldn't have back then, either, except for the caseworker's grip on his arm. Emmeline had remained on the porch rather than frighten him by rushing at him. And maybe it had been a mistake, waiting for him to be brought to her.

Saxon needed for people to reach out to him, because he didn't know how to make the first move.

Slowly her face relaxed into a smile. Then Emmeline, that stern, reserved woman, walked down the steps to meet her son, her mouth trembling and tears running down her cheeks, her arms outstretched. And she never stopped smiling.

Something broke inside him with an audible snap, and he broke, too. He hadn't cried since he'd been an infant, but Emmeline was the only anchor he had ever had in his life, until he'd met Anna. With two long strides he met her in the middle of the sidewalk, caught her in his arms, and Saxon Malone cried. Emmeline put her arms around him and hugged him as tight as she could, as if she would never let go, and she kept saying, "My boy! My boy!" In the middle of his tears he reached out to Anna, and she flew around the car and into his arms. He held them both tight in his embrace and rocked them together, the two women he loved.

It was the twelfth of May. Mother's Day.

Epilogue

Anna woke slowly from what seemed like the deepest sleep she'd ever had and opened her eyes. The first sight she saw kept her from moving for a long, long time, as she reveled in the piercing sweetness of it. Saxon was sitting beside her hospital bed, just as he had been beside her all during labor and delivery. She had seen his face taut with worry and torment over her pain, filled with jubilation when she finally gave birth, his green eyes brilliant with tears as he stared wordlessly at his tiny, squalling offspring.

He held the sleeping baby in his arms now, all his attention focused on the little creature. With infinite care he examined the tiny, perfect hands and minuscule fingernails, almost holding his breath as the little fingers folded over his big one in a surprisingly tight reflexive grip, even in sleep. He traced a finger over the almost invisible eyebrows, down the downy soft cheek, to the pink bud of a mouth. Their son fit almost perfectly in his big hands, though he had weighed in at a respectable seven pounds.

She eased around onto her side, smiling at Saxon when he snapped his attention to her. "Isn't he gorgeous?" she whispered.

"He's the most perfect thing I've ever seen." Awe was in his tone. "Emmeline has gone down to the cafeteria to get something to eat. I practically had to fight her to get him away from her."

"Well, he is her only grandchild. For now."

He looked incredulous, remembering her labor, but then he looked at the baby in his arms and understood how she could consider the result as being well worth the effort. Then he smiled at his wife, a slow smile that melted her bones. "As long as the next one is a girl."

"We'll try our best."

"We still haven't decided on a name for him," he said.

"You can pick out his first name. I've already decided on his middle name."

"What is it?"

"Saxon, of course," she said. "The second Saxon Malone. We're starting a new family tradition, remember?"

He reached out and took her hand, then eased himself onto the side of her bed, and together they admired their son.

* * * * *

THE PATERNITY TEST

Sherryl Woods

Prologue

Next Saturday's baby shower would be the fifth Jane Dawson had been invited to in the past three months. Every time she turned around, it seemed, another friend or another co-worker was having a baby. She was being overwhelmed by the sight of rounded tummies, radiant faces and silver rattles.

She'd become such a regular at Annie's Baby Boutique that Annie routinely called when something special came in. They'd become fast friends, and the boutique had become Jane's favorite after-school haunt for a cup of tea and some girl-talk.

As a result, Jane's biological clock was ticking so loudly, she was sure it could be heard throughout her hometown. She would be thirty in July, not so old for having babies these days, but definitely getting up there, especially with no prospective father in sight.

Once again back at Annie's, this time specifically to buy a present for Daisy Markham's shower on Saturday, Jane rubbed her fingers over the cheerful yellow gingham liner in an antique carved oak crib that was Annie's latest treasure and sighed heavily. She'd been sighing a lot lately. Wishing, too, and dreaming.

It was getting more and more difficult to hide her envy, as well. *Oohing* and *aahing* over one more hand-knitted pair of booties, one more tiny outfit, might send her over the edge. Today, she thought looking at the crib, could very well be the day.

"What do you think?" Annie asked, glowing with pride over the refinished piece. She still had streaks of wood stain and polish on her hands. Her no-nonsense short hair was mussed and she hadn't gotten around to so much as a dusting of powder across her face, much less any lipstick.

"Is that not the most beautiful crib you've ever seen?" she demanded.

Jane tried to hide her own yearning to possess that crib—to have a reason to possess that crib—and nodded. "It's lovely."

"Can you imagine?" Annie asked indignantly, buffing the already gleaming surface. "I found it stuck way back in a dim corner of an antique place out on Route 3. You should have seen it. It had been painted half a dozen times at least. Stripping it, I went through layers of white, blue, pink and several more of white paint. It was caked on so thick, it wasn't until I got almost down to the wood that I saw the carving."

The shop's owner rubbed her fingers lovingly over the intricate design. "A little angel. Have you ever seen anything so precious?"

"Never," Jane said, her yearning to claim it deepening.

Annie grinned. "Well, I know it's too extravagant for

a shower present, but I just knew of everyone who comes in here, you'd appreciate it the most. I had to call the minute I put it in the store. Sometimes the urge to share my finds overwhelms me. I hope you don't mind that I left a message at the school. It's not like I'm trying to make a sale. I know perfectly well you don't need a crib."

Something inside Jane snapped at Annie's offhand remark. "I'll take it," she said as if to prove her wrong. "Just the way it is with the yellow gingham liner and all. Put it on my account and send me the bill."

Almost immediately she regretted the impulsive words as Annie gaped.

"But—"

Jane cut off the shocked protest. "You can have it delivered to my place, right? John will bring it by Saturday morning, won't he?" she said, referring to Annie's husband, who frequently helped out with deliveries on weekends.

"Of course, but—"

"Thanks," she said, cutting off her friend's questions, logical questions for which she obviously had no rational answers. "I've got to run. I have a PTA meeting tonight. All the teachers have to be there early to greet the parents. We're trying to butter them up so they'll help us raise the money to upgrade the cafeteria. Don't forget to wrap up that little pink sweater and bonnet for Daisy's shower. It's Saturday afternoon. You can send the package along with the crib."

"Of course."

Jane felt Annie's puzzled, worried gaze follow her as she left the store and walked up the hill toward the old brick school.

Not until much later, after the PTA meeting, after she was back home and sipping a cup of tea, did she concede that Annie might have cause to wonder what an unmarried, uninvolved woman was going to do with a baby crib. Hopefully she could come up with a plausible explanation before everyone in town concluded that she'd turned into an eccentric old spinster whose hormones required serious adjustment.

Annie's devoted husband, still handsome and fit at fifty, delivered the crib at 9:00 a.m. on Saturday. He set it up in Jane's spare bedroom and never once asked why in the world she'd bought it. Jane swore her undying gratitude to the man for that.

After he was gone, she made herself a cup of raspberry tea and sat down in the tiny bedroom to admire the crib. She dreamed of the day when she'd have a baby of her own sleeping on the pretty yellow sheets, when she could decorate the walls of the room with bright paper and a border of ducks and rabbits and put a rocker in the corner. The image was so clear, she felt an incredible pang of longing to make it real.

"But it's not real," she told herself sternly, forcing herself to leave the room and close the door firmly behind her. The purchase of that crib suddenly seemed foolish. She was months, if not years, ahead of herself.

This time it was her friend Daisy who was having the baby, her third. She already had two boys and had discovered that this one would be a girl. She and her husband were over the moon about it, even though the boys were teenagers already and this baby had been a huge surprise.

Jane told herself that the sharp stab of envy she felt was normal, the alarm going off on her biological clock, so to speak. Buying a crib, however, was a bit of an overreaction. Maybe she should call Annie, admit she'd made a ridiculous mistake and have John pick up the crib and take it back to the store. She even reached for the phone, but she couldn't seem to make herself dial.

If only…

She brought herself up short. There was no sense looking back. Mike Marshall, the love of her life, was in her past. They had made a rational, mature decision together to end the relationship nearly a year ago when he'd been offered an incredible job in San Francisco. A clean break, they had decided. No looking back.

Mike had always dreamed of the kind of opportunities this new company would give him. He'd craved the recognition it could bring him as an engineer, the financial stability of the salary a big firm could offer.

Jane's dreams were different, simpler—a home, a family, roots in a community where neighbors knew each other and cared about each other. It was almost the way she'd grown up, the way she wanted her own children to be raised, quietly and with a greater sense of stability in their lives than she had had with a father who'd always been running off.

Since Mike had gone, she'd told herself a thousand times that they'd made the right decision, the sensible decision. Love sometimes meant letting go. If they'd been meant to be together, they would have walked down the aisle years sooner, but Mike had always held back, needing the proof that he could support a family in a style his own background had never provided.

But Jane still cried herself to sleep thinking about him. Being sensible, she'd concluded, sucked.

Since he'd gone, she'd hidden her favorite snapshot of him deep in the bottom of her drawer, but every now and then she stumbled across it and each and every time it brought tears to her eyes. The sale of his old house, right next door, had made his move final and the permanency of it had left her shaken for months. Lately she'd told herself she was over him, that she *had* to be over him. But she wasn't, not by a long shot.

Once they had talked about a future, about having babies and growing old together, but that golden opportunity in California had been too powerful for Mike to resist. She wouldn't have let him turn it down, even if he'd wanted to.

And she hadn't been ready or willing to leave the town and the job that suited her so perfectly. Both of them had dug in their heels, unable to see any way to compromise. And so a relationship that had once meant the world to both of them had ended.

By now he'd probably found someone new, someone more suited to a big-city lifestyle, someone whose social life revolved around more than baby showers and picnics and an occasional movie. She hoped he had. She didn't want him to be as lonely and miserable as she was.

What if he was, though? What if he missed her as desperately as she missed him? If that were the case, though, wouldn't he have called?

No, of course not, she told herself, not if he took their agreement as seriously as she did. Not if that famous Irish pride of his had kicked in as viciously as hers had. When it came to pure stubbornness, they were a perfect match.

She opened the door to the spare room and stared at the crib again, imagining her baby there, hers and Mike's. A chubby, strong little boy with round cheeks and thick black hair just like Mike's. Or maybe a rosy-cheeked little girl with glints of red in her hair just like Jane's.

Had she closed the door on that dream too soon? Had she accepted Mike's departure too readily, conceding defeat when she should have been fighting tooth and nail to find a way to make it work?

Finding that crib at Annie's had forced her to face emotions she had convinced herself were dead and buried. If she still loved Mike as deeply as ever, didn't she owe it to both of them to see him again, to see if there was anything left now that he'd had a chance to test his wings in the kind of job and city he'd always dreamed of?

Spring break was just around the corner. So was Mike's birthday, though she'd always been more sentimental about such occasions than he had been. After she paid for the crib, her savings account was going to be low, but there was enough left for a trip to San Francisco without dipping into the rainy day money her mother's small insurance policy had left her. Could there be a better investment of her savings? She couldn't think of one.

Maybe they would fall in love all over again. Or maybe they would sleep together one last time for old times' sake.

Maybe by some glorious fluke they would make a baby, she thought wistfully. Okay, it was highly unlikely, but what a joyous blessing it would be! Whether their relationship resumed or faltered, she would treasure a child of theirs, raise it on her own, if need be.

The decision to go to San Francisco was made as impulsively as the purchase of that crib. It took an hour on the phone with the travel agent to nail down all the arrangements. By the time she was finished she was late for Daisy's shower.

The party was in full swing when she arrived, the laughter and teasing audible from outside. When she walked in, the group fell silent and stared.

"Where on earth have you been?" Daisy demanded, hefting her bulky figure from a chair and rushing over to hug Jane. "You're never late."

"We tried calling the house a half-dozen times but the line was busy," Ginger added. "Donna was about ready to drive over there."

"So? What happened?" Daisy prodded. "Don't tell me Mike showed up on your doorstep after all these months."

"Nothing like that," Jane said. "I just lost track of the time."

"You never lose track of the time," Daisy protested.

"Well, this time I did," she said, a defensive note in her voice that clearly startled them.

Donna, who'd known her since first grade, studied her intently. "Okay, maybe he didn't show up, but it has something to do with Mike, doesn't it? Did he call?"

"No, he didn't call."

"But it does have something to do with him?" Donna persisted with the unerring accuracy of such a longtime friend.

Jane wasn't ready to discuss her plans with anyone, not even her closest friends. She forced a brilliant smile. "Hey, forget about me, okay? I'm here now and I want to see the presents." She handed her own to Daisy to add to the pile beside her. "Get busy. You look as if that baby could pop out any second now. I want you to finish opening all these before it does."

With some reluctance, everyone finally turned their attention back to the gifts. Jane *oohed* and *aahed* with the rest of them, but her mind was already somewhere else, in a city she'd never seen, with a man who was part of her soul.

Chapter One

Engineer Mike Marshall had had more adventures than most men twice his age. Most of the riskiest had come in the past twelve months, since his move to San Francisco. Until today—his thirty-second birthday—it hadn't occurred to him to wonder why he was suddenly so willing to put his life on the line.

The truth was, he'd always been eager to take risks. As a kid, he took every dare ever offered. Now, though, he didn't even wait for the dare. If an overseas assignment for his company didn't satisfy his hunger for adventure, then he scheduled a trek up Mount Everest or a rafting trip on the Snake River. It had been months since he'd had a spare minute, much less a moment's boredom.

And yet, something was missing. He knew it, just the way he knew when a design for a bridge or a dam wasn't quite right. He stared out his office window at the Golden Gate Bridge emerging from a thick fog and tried to put a name to what was missing from his life.

Not excitement, that was for sure. Every day was packed with it.

Not companionship. He'd met a dozen women, beautiful, successful women, who shared his passion for adventure.

Not money. His salary was more than adequate for his needs, more than he'd ever dreamed of making back in Virginia. For the first time in his life, he felt financially secure, able to support a wife and family if the right woman ever came along.

Not challenges. The partners in his engineering firm only took on the most challenging jobs.

What, then? What was the elusive something that made him feel as if the rest hardly mattered? What was behind this vague sense of dissatisfaction? It irked him that he couldn't pin it down.

To his relief, the buzzing of his intercom interrupted the rare and troubling introspection.

"Yes, Kim. What is it?"

"You have a visitor, sir. She doesn't have an appointment," she added with a little huff of disapproval.

Mike grinned. Kim Jensen was a retired army drill sergeant with close-cropped gray hair and the protective instincts of a pit bull. She maintained his schedule with the precision of a space shuttle flight plan. Flexibility was not part of her nature.

"Does this visitor have a name?" he asked.

"Jane Dawson, sir."

The clipped announcement rattled him as nothing else could have. His heart slammed to a stop, then took off as if he'd just been advised that it was his turn to bungee-jump from the penthouse floor of a Union

Square office building. The reaction startled him almost as badly as the mere thought of Jane in San Francisco. Jane, who'd never flown in her life, had come clear across the country, out of the blue, with no warning? He had to see it with his own eyes.

"Send her in, by all means."

"Are you sure, sir? You have an appointment at fourteen hundred hours. Sorry, sir. I mean in ten minutes."

"Send her in," he repeated and stood up, wondering at the astonishing sense of anticipation that was zipping through him.

"Just plain Jane," as she'd been known a dozen years ago, was in San Francisco? The woman who'd vowed never to leave their small Virginia hometown had braved her first flight on a whim, just to say happy birthday, perhaps? The concept was so out of character he found it almost as impossible to grapple with as the design for a sturdy, yet inexpensive bridge in some third world country.

But unless he'd imagined Kim's announcement, Jane was here, on his turf, and his heart was beating as rapidly as it had the day he'd stolen his very first kiss from her. At the same time a long-missed sense of calm settled over him.

The door to his office opened, Kim stepped aside and Jane walked past her. His mouth dropped open. He'd known her his whole life and he almost didn't recognize her. Her old high school nickname was hardly appropriate anymore. There was nothing plain about the woman before him. She was wearing a lime green suit that flattered her coloring and slinky heels that flattered her long legs. Her hair was shorter, with a sassy, trendy cut that feathered against her cheeks, then skimmed to her shoulders in layers. The red highlights glinted brighter than ever. She looked more sophisticated than he remembered. Sexier, too. Then her familiar sweet, shy smile came and went and his heart flipped over, just as it always had.

"Hello, Mike. Happy birthday."

His own grin broadened. "I can't believe it. Come here, you."

He opened his arms and, after an instant's hesitation, Jane stepped into the embrace. When she was settled against his chest, her head tucked under his chin, the oddest sensation crept over him. It was as if he knew, at long last, what had been missing.

But, of course, that couldn't be. He'd put Jane Dawson firmly in his past when he'd made the move to San Francisco. He'd given her his word that the break would be clean and he'd kept it. With his parents dead, his brothers and sisters scattered and the family home sold, there'd been no reason to go home again. He hadn't looked back, not once. Well, hardly more than once.

He stepped back eventually and looked her over. "You look fabulous. Sit down. Tell me what you're doing in San Francisco. Is it a teachers' convention of some kind? Why didn't you let me know you were coming? How long are you staying?"

She laughed at the barrage of questions, the sound as clear and melodic as a bell. "Last question first. I'm here for a week. I didn't let you know because I didn't know myself until the last minute. Spring break crept up on me and I decided not to spend it cleaning the house the way I have every other year since I started teaching. This is pure vacation."

She regarded him uncertainly. "I hope you're not about to take off on an assignment or something. Will you have time to have dinner at least? We haven't missed celebrating your birthday together since we were kids."

"Dinner will be a start," he agreed, thinking of all he could show her in a week, imagining her excited reaction. That was the thing he had loved about Jane. She brought such enthusiasm to every discovery, whether it was finding an arrowhead in the clay banks of the Potomac River or seeing the first crocus pop up in the spring. It was the quality that made her such an excellent teacher. She was able to communicate that enthusiasm to her students.

She'd always been able to communicate it to him, as well. Maybe that was why they'd been so good together, even though her pursuits were far more sedate than those he might have chosen for himself. Once they'd toured Stratford Hall, Robert E. Lee's birthplace, together. When she'd suggested it, Mike had shuddered at the prospect. He'd been barely into his teens and a whole lot more interested in playing ball than touring a musty old plantation.

Afterward, to his amazement, he'd felt as if he'd been caught up in the middle of an incredible family drama that had eventually played itself out on a Civil War battlefield. There was no denying that Jane had a gift for teaching, a gift for firing the imagination.

At the moment, with her looking the way she did, his imagination was taking off in a much more provocative direction, remembering the feel of her in his arms, the burning of her lips on his.

His intercom buzzed way before he was ready for the interruption.

"Sir, your appointment's here," Kim announced with a touch of triumph and the obvious expectation that he would promptly shoo his unscheduled visitor out of his office.

"Get him a cup of coffee or something and tell him I'll be right with him," Mike told her. He turned back to find Jane staring out the window, her eyes wide and shining with excitement.

"It's something, isn't it?" he asked, moving up behind her to gaze at the Golden Gate.

"Better than the pictures," she agreed. She turned. "I can see why you were drawn here. The Golden Gate always did inspire you. Even when we were kids, that was your favorite picture in the encyclopedia. You must have sketched it a million times. Now it's right outside your window."

For a few weeks that had awed him, too. Then he'd begun to take it for granted, just as he once had the love of the woman standing here with him now. The sound of his buzzer reminded him that he had a prospective client waiting and an impatient secretary who wasn't likely to let him forget it.

He touched Jane's cheek with regret. "I do have to take this meeting. Where are you staying?" he asked. "I'll have Kim clear my schedule this week. I'll be by at six to pick you up."

"Are you sure? I don't expect you to drop everything for me."

"I'm sure," he said with no hesitation at all.

In fact, he hadn't been more sure of anything in a very long time.

* * *

Jane still couldn't believe it. Her first flight had been a real nail-biter even before the first pocket of turbulence, but it was nothing compared to walking into Mike's office, staring down that snippy, protective secretary of his, then actually seeing him again. She'd been stunned by the surge of old feelings, startled by an unfamiliar rush of uncertainty until she had seen the warm welcome in his eyes.

Now, a few hours later, she realized that their very first date hadn't shaken her nearly as badly as dressing for this one nearly sixteen years later. Of course, she'd never before prayed so intently for a date to wind up in bed. For once in her life, she wanted to make something happen, to risk everything to make her dream come true. She'd been obsessing on having his baby ever since the possibility had first crossed her mind. She wanted desperately for it to happen, wanted him to want her as he once had. But as badly as she wanted his baby, she wanted him more.

Her hands shook as she fumbled with the clasp on the gold locket. Would he remember? Mike had given her the locket on her sixteenth birthday. His picture was still inside. Glancing in the mirror as the locket settled between her breasts, she wondered if it was the wrong touch. Was she counting too much on sentiment and old yearnings, instead of the here and now? If so, her presents were all wrong, too, chosen to remind Mike of all he'd left behind.

If only she could be cold and calculating, intent only on getting pregnant by a man who had once been her best friend, as well as her lover. But five minutes alone with Mike in his office had told her that, for better or worse, she was still in love with him. It remained to be seen how he felt about her or whether they would be any better at compromise now than they had been a year ago.

Her fingers faltered when she heard the impatient knock on her door. She almost dropped the tiny, very expensive bottle of French perfume she'd indulged in. She managed one last dab of the scent between her breasts, then went to the door.

Mike never failed to startle her when he was all dressed up in a suit and tie. Used to seeing him in jeans and T-shirts for so many years or even in a dress shirt with the sleeves rolled up and his tie askew as he had been in his office earlier, she wasn't prepared for the full impact of a light gray suit, white shirt and teal-and-gray silk tie with Mike's dark hair and perpetually tanned skin. When she wasn't looking, the boy next door had turned into a sophisticated man. Odd how she'd never noticed that before he'd left, even though he'd been thirty-one by then.

His approving gaze swept over her, heating her flesh. An impudent grin spread across his face and the boy next door was back. "Did you buy an entire new wardrobe for this trip?" he asked.

"Of course not," she lied, unwilling to let him see just how much she'd invested in this supposedly impromptu visit. She wondered if he'd guessed that her new haircut and the glistening highlights were courtesy of a San Francisco stylist to the tune of over two hundred dollars. She'd turned pale when she'd seen the bill, but one glance in the mirror told her it had been money well spent.

"I've never seen that dress before," he insisted. "I definitely would have remembered."

"You've been gone a year. Naturally I've bought a few new things in all that time."

His gaze narrowed perceptibly. "Was the dress for a special occasion?"

Jane couldn't prevent the laughter that bubbled up. "Mike Marshall, you're jealous."

He looked appalled by the suggestion. "Don't be ridiculous."

"You are. You have never made such a fuss about my clothes before."

"Because you were always in sedate little outfits suitable for teaching fifth-graders," he muttered. He gestured toward the dipping neckline and clinging silk. "This is something else."

"Want me to change?" she asked.

"Oh, no. You can wear that dress for me anytime."

"Just not for anyone else."

"I didn't say that."

She grinned. "You didn't have to." She linked her arm through his. "Come on. Let's get out of here before you start getting ideas."

"Honey, if you don't want me getting ideas, you'd better pull a sweatshirt on over that dress."

Jane shook her head, deciding she liked this newly discovered power she had to turn him on. "Not a chance. I'm all dressed up with a handsome man at my side. I want to go out on the town. I'm not wasting a single minute of this trip. I want to see and do everything."

"Then we'd better get started. This isn't our hometown, where we could cover everything in a weekend.

San Francisco will take a little more time to explore."

They started with dinner across the bay in Sausalito, followed by a stroll along Fisherman's Wharf and an Irish coffee on the waterfront. Jane fell in love with the twinkling lights, the riot of sights and sounds and smells. Questions tumbled out so quickly that Mike had a hard time keeping up with the answers.

It was almost two in the morning by the time they made their way, exhausted, back to her hotel. He paused at the door to her room.

"I should say good-night here," he said, his knuckles resting against her cheek as he toyed with a strand of her hair.

Familiar, never-forgotten sparks shot through her at his touch. "You should," she agreed, then stood on tiptoe to brush a kiss across his lips. "But I hope you won't."

"Jane—"

"Don't argue. Besides, I haven't given you your birthday presents yet."

It was exactly the right incentive. Despite his claims of indifference, Mike had never been able to resist a present. When they'd first met as kids, he'd been uncomfortable with the way her mom went all out on special occasions, especially birthdays. His own family barely acknowledged birthdays, maybe because there were so many of them and so little money for extras.

Jane had always treated Mike's birthday as if it were a national holiday. She'd baked a cake, found half a dozen small, special treats and wrapped them as if they were solid gold trinkets. She'd done the same this year. She'd even arranged for the hotel to deliver a birthday cake to her room while they were out. A bottle of champagne was on ice beside it. Mike stared at it as if she'd ordered a feast.

"How did you manage this?"

She grinned. "It is San Francisco, after all. Anything's possible. Isn't that what you told me when you were trying to convince me to move here with you?"

"I'll bet the cake's not my favorite," he said, already poking a knife speculatively through the thick coating of whipped cream frosting.

"Oh, but it is. Chocolate with raspberry filling," Jane confirmed.

He turned and smiled at her. "You're amazing."

"So you've always told me. I suppose I'll always have to go to extraordinary lengths to live up to my reputation." She opened a drawer and extracted three small, brightly wrapped packages. "These first, then cake."

As he always had, he opened the smallest one first. It was a gold key ring with a bright beach design enameled on it and Virginia written in bold red letters.

"Afraid I was going to forget home?" he asked, laughing.

She gazed at him, then said quietly, "I was afraid you already had."

His laughter died and his gaze locked with hers. "Never."

Jane swallowed hard, then looked away. She couldn't read too much into that, she didn't dare. "Open the biggest one next," she insisted.

"But I always save that for last."

"Not this year."

"Okay, okay," he said, picking up the flat, ten-by-twelve-inch package. As if to taunt her, he took his own sweet time with the ribbon and paper. When he finally had it open, she saw the heat rise in his cheeks as memories tumbled back. He glanced at her, his astonishment plain.

"It can't be."

"Oh, but it is," she assured him. "It's a picture of your car, that old blue convertible you loved so much." She paused, then added softly, "The one we made love in the first time."

"Where on earth…? I thought for sure this was on the junk heap long ago."

"Nope. I was walking through town one day and heard the sound of that engine—"

"Who could ever mistake that?" he asked, chuckling. "It sounded like a lawn mower on speed. The word clunker was coined for that engine."

"Maybe so, but that clunker still runs, and a teenager, one of Velma Scott's boys, has it now. He thinks he's the hottest kid in town."

"Just the way I did."

"You were the hottest boy in town," Jane said softly. "Anyway, I asked him if he'd take me over by the river and let me take a picture for you."

"I hope you didn't tell him why," Mike said.

She chuckled. "Didn't have to. He figured that part out all on his own. He said he remembered watching the two of us in that car when he was just a kid."

"Hopefully not while we were parked by the river."

Jane laughed at his horrified expression. "It was ten years ago when you sold it. He was maybe eight at the time. I doubt he was allowed out at midnight."

"Thank God for that." He ran his fingers over the

glass as lovingly as he once had touched the finish on that beloved car. He met her gaze. "Thank you."

"You're welcome."

"Can I ask you something?"

"Sure."

"Why the trip down memory lane?"

She shrugged, trying to feign indifference. "I don't know. I suppose I was feeling nostalgic when I realized it was your birthday and it would be the first one in years we hadn't shared."

"Have you missed me, Jane? Is that it?"

She forced herself not to look away, not to skirt the truth. If ever an occasion called for honesty, this was it. "I missed you, yes. More than I'd imagined possible."

"Oh, baby," he whispered, gathering her close. "I've missed you, too."

He tilted her face up, then slowly—inevitably— lowered his mouth to hers. And with the touch of their lips, passion raged and a lifetime of memories came flooding back.

Chapter Two

No one back in Virginia would have called Jane plain if they could have seen her tonight, Mike thought as his touch brought color to her cheeks and a flare of heat to her eyes. He'd always thought she was pretty, but tonight he was certain he'd never seen any woman more beautiful.

Cupping her face in his hands and gazing directly into her eyes, he asked, "Are you sure? We promised we wouldn't do this again. You said—we agreed—it would only drag things out, complicate them."

"I haven't had a decent complication in my life in a long time now. I'll take my chances," she said, her gaze steady. "Please, Mike, I want you to make love to me again. I've missed being in your arms. I've missed the way I feel when you touch me."

"Like this?" he asked, caressing her. "And this?" His hand slid lower, caught the hem of her skirt and lifted it as he stroked the inside of her thigh above the sexy black hose she wore.

Her familiar whimper of pleasure was his answer.

Teasing and taunting, he came closer and closer to the hot, moist place between her thighs, never touching it, until she was arching against his hand, demanding more. In bed, her natural shyness had always vanished. She let him know what she needed, provoked him into giving it to her, then shared every bit of her pleasure with him. She was doing the same thing now.

His own pulse was racing, his body hard, but still he concentrated on Jane. He took her to the edge, then retreated, until she was gasping and pleading with him to come inside her.

He wanted to. Oh, how he wanted to, but he hadn't come prepared. Making love had been the last thing he'd imagined them doing tonight, because they'd both so vehemently declared the relationship over. He'd figured he'd be lucky if she allowed him to steal the kiss he'd been wanting since she'd waltzed into his office earlier.

"Mike, please," she whispered against his ear. She reached between them, sought his erection and almost jolted him off the bed with her cleverly wicked touches.

"We can't. I don't have anything with me," he said, sorrier than he could say.

"It's okay," she insisted, arching against him.

He regarded her doubtfully. They'd never taken chances before. "You're sure?"

She shoved his clothes aside and feathered kisses across his belly, then lower. "I'm sure," she insisted, then touched her tongue to the tip of his arousal. "I'm sure."

Mike never questioned her sincerity after that. This was the first woman he'd ever loved, the woman whose body and responses were as familiar to him as his own. Urgency wiped out all rational thought as he stripped away his clothes and then the last scraps of hers. Her skin was hot and damp when he finally poised above her. Slowly, savoring every sweet sensation, he sank into her, sheathing himself in slick velvet heat.

For a moment that was enough, just being inside her again, just feeling the stirring of his body, the pounding of his heart. Then he wanted more, so much more. Jane's cries echoed in his head as each thrust went deeper and deeper, joining them in a frenzy that went beyond lust.

It had never been like this before. They'd never made love with such uninhibited abandon, as if each sensation were wild and reckless and new. No dare he'd taken since leaving her had been this exciting, this thrilling. Maybe he'd always held back something, knowing that one day the right job would come along and he would leave. Maybe she'd always held back, knowing she would stand aside and watch him go.

Now, though, it was as if they had reached that hurdle and pushed past it. Whatever happened to them, the chemistry between them would triumph. This was the proof of that. The past, the future, neither mattered. It was now, this moment they were living in.

Thinking of it, Mike smiled. Jane caught him. Entwined in his arms, their bodies slick with sweat, she tilted her head and assessed him curiously.

"Something about this amuses you?"

"It's you," he said at once. "You amuse and delight and thrill me."

"Prove it," she dared, wriggling her hips provocatively.

"You just wait," he taunted, rolling until he was on his back and she was astride him. "I'm going to let you have your way with me."

He linked his hands behind his head and leaned back against a pile of pillows. "I'm all yours, Janie."

Her eyes widened. "But—"

"Just use your imagination. Anything goes."

A grin spread slowly across her face. "Big mistake, Mike. I have a very inventive imagination and months alone to let it run wild."

To his astonishment and delight, she pretty much exhausted him proving it.

When they'd finally collapsed and were nestled in each other's arms again, Mike listened to the soft sound of her even breathing, then sighed. "Oh, Janie," he murmured. "How am I ever going to let you go a second time?"

He would have to, too. There wasn't a doubt in his mind about that. He loved San Francisco and his job, the life he'd built for himself, the sense of security that had been such a long time coming. And as much as he wanted to, he couldn't deny that Jane belonged in the town where they'd grown up. Her roots ran deep, her feelings for the place and her friends ran even deeper. In a few short days she would go back and he'd be left to make do with these new memories and a cold, lonely bed.

Waking up to find Mike still beside her, his breath on her shoulder warm, his arm across her middle heavy, Jane smiled contentedly. It wasn't over between them, not with such powerful chemistry exploding at the slightest touch. They had six more days to figure out a solution that would keep them together. She felt more hopeful than she had since the night he'd told her he was leaving.

"You look awfully smug," Mike murmured, his voice gravelly with sleep.

"Do I? Maybe that's because I actually managed to distract you not only from opening your third present last night, but from your birthday cake and champagne."

"And you consider that a coup?"

"I consider it a miracle."

"Where is that present?"

She shrugged. "On the floor somewhere, I suppose."

"I hope to heaven it wasn't breakable."

She grinned as she thought of what the box contained—glow in the dark condoms. They'd been meant as a joke...and as a last resort if the picture of his old car hadn't gotten him into bed. Mike was a healthy, virile male, unlikely to resist such a blatant message. And, as he'd said the night before, they'd never taken chances. She hadn't deliberately set out to take one last night. The condoms, she reassured herself, were proof of that.

Even so, she couldn't help whispering a little prayer that she had gotten pregnant. Not to trap him, never that, but to give herself the child she wanted so desperately. Mike's baby.

"Jane?"

"Hmm?"

"The present. It's not breakable, is it?"

"That's definitely something you don't need to worry about," she assured him. "These are guaranteed not to break."

"These?"

She scrambled off the bed and found the box, then tossed it to him. He shook it, obviously intrigued by the light weight. When he ripped off the paper and saw what was inside, he chuckled.

"Insurance?"

"There are twelve of them. As I recall, there was a time you would have considered that a dare."

He winked at her. "Still do. Order up a huge breakfast so I'll have the strength for it and we'll try to make a dent in the supply."

They saw very little of San Francisco that day or the next, but Jane couldn't have been happier. She had come to see Mike, not the city. This was the honeymoon they'd never had, the one she'd been envisioning since she first knew what the word meant. It didn't seem to matter that the wedding she'd also envisioned had never happened. If anything, their appetites for each other were more insatiable than ever. They talked, made love, ate, made love, slept and made love again. It couldn't have been more perfect.

On her fourth day in San Francisco, she awoke to hear Mike in the shower, humming an off-key rendition of an old Johnny Cash song. The sound was so familiar, had once been so much a part of her daily life that she had to remind herself sharply that it might be only temporary. Sooner or later they were going to have to talk about something besides what to order from room service and which color of condom to try next. She picked up the box and shook it. There were none left. That pretty much eliminated one of their favorite topics.

She slipped out of bed and crept into the bathroom. When she opened the shower curtain, Mike grinned at her.

"Lonely?"

She nodded. When he beckoned, she stepped under the shower. Mike's hands, slick with soap, began to explore. It took only a heartbeat for both of them to become as steamed up as the room and thoroughly aroused. Her body was sensitive to the slightest brush of his fingers. In the blink of an eye he was lifting her, guiding her until he was deep inside and her legs were wrapped around his waist, her back pressed against the cool tile.

"Oh, yes," she murmured, as the hot spiraling need slashed through her yet again.

Mike's head was thrown back, his muscles tensed as yet another climax tore through them both.

When the aftershocks were over, he released her slowly. Her body slid along his until her feet touched the tile floor. Jane was shaken by how quickly he was able to shatter her, how attuned her body was to his. She had always enjoyed sex with Mike, thrilled to his touch, but in the past few days, they had moved to some new level of neediness. She couldn't believe what he was able to do to her with little more than a slow, seductive look.

"I can't believe what you do to me," Mike said, echoing her thoughts, looking at her with amazement once they were back in the bedroom dressing. "We were always good together, but this…"

"I know. It's astonishing."

"Scary, too," he said.

Jane stilled, gazing at his reflection in the mirror in front of her. "Scary? Why?"

"What will happen when you go home again in a few days? This intensity isn't something you can just walk away from and forget." He studied her intently. "Or is it?"

So, she thought, they were going to have this conversation now. She'd hoped to put it off a little longer, hoped to have time to put her own feelings into perspective.

"What are you asking me?"

"I suppose I'm asking what happens next. Do you just go back home and pretend that this was just a romantic interlude, a spring break to remember, something you can tuck away in a mental scrapbook? Or does it mean something to you?"

Hands and knees trembling, Jane sank down on the edge of the bed. "Do you want it to mean something, Mike?"

He came and sat beside her and took her icy hand in his. "Yes, I want it to mean something," he said fervently. "I want it to mean that this time we'll figure out a way to make things work. I want our love to last this time. I want it to mean that you'll stay here and marry me."

Jane swallowed hard. It was what she wanted, what she'd prayed for…almost. "Here," she repeated, unable to hide the note of defeat that crept into her voice.

"Yes, here," he said, the old familiar defensiveness promptly coloring his words. "Why not here? It's a beautiful city. It's exciting. There are thousands of people who would give anything to be able to live here, especially in the style I can afford." He frowned. "But you're not one of them, are you? You won't even give it a chance."

"That's not true. I came here, didn't I? It's not entirely my fault that we've barely left the hotel."

Mike sighed. "You have a point, which is why I'm already dressed, instead of taking you back to bed again. I want you to see the city, see my place. I want you to meet my friends. I want to take you sight-seeing and shopping until you fall in love with it all the way I have."

Jane's spirits sagged. Couldn't he see that she was in love with him? Wasn't that enough? Why did San Francisco have to be part of the bargain?

"Please," he said softly, as if he'd read her mind. "Just give it a chance, keep an open mind. That's all I'm asking."

It was only fair, she supposed. She reached up and touched his cheek. "I'll give it a chance," she promised, then turned away before he could see the tears gathering in her eyes as she saw part of her dream already slipping away.

Chapter Three

Jane dedicated herself to getting to know San Francisco, to giving it a fair chance. Mike could see the grim determination in her eyes when she sat down with a guidebook over lunch on Fisherman's Wharf and chose the spots she wanted to visit. She mapped out a rigorous, dutiful schedule his secretary would have admired.

Once they'd started, though, her attitude began to change. As he'd anticipated, she was entranced with everything, almost despite herself. The transition over the next couple of days was slow, but unmistakable. She peppered him with more questions than he could answer, delighted in the strange and exotic food, the sightseeing ride on a boat on San Francisco Bay, the opening day ball game he'd committed to attending with clients he couldn't offend. Jane charmed them and cheered as if she'd been a loyal Giants fan her whole life.

But there was no mistaking the sense that she was on vacation, enjoying an interlude, rather than settling into a new routine. Maybe that was his fault. Maybe he shouldn't have taken the time off. If he'd left her to her own devices, maybe she would have begun to adapt as if she lived there, instead of taking it all in as a tourist.

As it was, there was a sinking sensation in the pit of Mike's stomach as Sunday rolled in. He sensed that she would leave and nothing at all would have been resolved by this visit. He was at a loss over what else he could possibly do to win her over.

There was no question in his mind that their love was as strong as ever, even after a year's separation. The sex was extraordinary. Their thoughts meshed on so many topics, disagreements were rare. It was just that the one subject about which they disagreed was a doozy, the kind that could make or break their future.

They awoke at dawn on Sunday, this time in his bedroom, rather than her hotel. When he pulled her into his arms, when he made love to her, he couldn't hide the fierce desperation in his heart. It was in his every frantic, possessive touch, in every kiss.

And in hers.

When it was over and he held her, he felt the dampness of her tears falling on his chest and knew that he had lost the battle once more.

"You're going to leave, aren't you?"

"Of course," she said briskly, then added with a catch in her voice, "school starts again tomorrow. You knew that."

"It'll be out in June," he said, struggling to keep his tone even. "Will you be back then? Can't you at least give it a three-month trial run? You could move in here with me, really get to know the city. We could spend weekends exploring all of California. Don't we deserve that much?"

She looked at him briefly, then her gaze skittered

away. "Maybe. I don't know, Mike. What would be the point? Your life is here. Mine's there. Teaching matters to me. My friends matter. And we can't do this to each other over and over again. It's not like this is around the corner from home. We can't exactly commute."

"There are teaching jobs here. You liked my friends. They adored you. Okay, maybe there's not the long history you share with Donna, Ginger, Daisy and the others, but these are good people, too. You loved the museums, the restaurants. I don't get it. What's the problem?"

Tears clung to her lashes. "It's not home," she said.

For her it was as simple—and as complex—as that. Anger ripped through him. Unreasonable fury stripped away any pretense of calm. He stood up and began to pace. It was happening all over again. She was throwing away what they had as if it had no importance whatsoever. He tried telling himself that she was throwing it away, not him, but it felt the same.

"You could come back," she suggested tentatively. "Obviously your company respects your work. Maybe you could make some sort of an arrangement with them. It would mean traveling, but you do that now, right? You're not even in San Francisco most of the time."

"That's not the point. This is where the headquarters are, where clients meet with us. If I'm not underfoot, I won't be the one they think of when a big job comes in. I'll get the leftovers. Then one day they'll wake up and discover they don't need me anymore at all." He'd been through enough firings and downsizings with his father to know what emotional devastation that wreaked on everyone around. He would wind up resenting Jane for having put him in that position.

He and Jane had been over the same ground a hundred times before he'd left for San Francisco the first time. Nothing had changed…in her position or his. And it broke his heart.

If only this visit had gone badly, if only the feelings had died. Instead they were stronger than ever. He loved Jane. He wanted her as his wife. He wanted their children. He just couldn't see any way to make it work, not when she was so totally unyielding, not when he couldn't see any way to bend.

"We'd better be getting to the airport," he said finally. "You wouldn't want to miss your flight."

He refused to acknowledge the hurt in her eyes. It didn't make sense that they both had to be in this much pain. There had to be an alternative, one they hadn't thought of, but damned if he could see it.

They rode to the airport in silence. Inside the terminal, as she prepared to go to the gate, he pulled her into his arms and kissed her with a hunger that left them both shaking.

"I love you," he said fiercely, as if she needed the reminder.

"I love you," she whispered. "Will you call?"

He hesitated. "I don't know. I don't know if I can go through this again, if you should go through it again. We're just making each other miserable."

A tremulous smile quivered on her lips. "Only when we say goodbye. The rest is magic."

"But we seem doomed to keep saying goodbye," he told her with regret. "Maybe this should be the last time."

Tears spilled down her cheeks. "Or maybe we just need to learn to believe in the magic," she whispered, and then she was gone.

Maybe she was right, he thought as he watched her go. Maybe the magic would come through for them yet, but he was far too practical a man to count on it.

When the phone rang at ten o'clock on Sunday evening after she'd gotten home, Jane's heart began to race. It was Mike. It had to be. No matter what he'd said about making this latest goodbye the last, he hadn't meant it. He couldn't have. Her hand shook as she reached for the receiver.

"You're back," Donna said, sounding relieved. "How was your spring break? Was it wonderful? Are you going to tell me now where you went?"

"Not tonight," Jane said, trying to hide her disappointment at the sound of her best friend's voice. "I'm beat. It's been a long day."

"Are you okay? You sound funny."

"I'm fine, just a little tired."

"Then we'll go out after school tomorrow. Dinner's on me. Darryl's coaching Little League tomorrow night and I can't wait to hear all about this mysterious adventure of yours."

When Jane was about to beg off, Donna said, "No excuses. If you say no, I'll know something's wrong."

"Okay, fine. Dinner will be great." All she had to do was get through it without bursting into tears.

The next day after the last of the kids had cleared out and Jane had done every last bit of paperwork she could find to delay the inevitable, she looked up and spotted Donna in the doorway to her classroom.

"The kids have only been back one day. You can't possibly have any more papers to grade," she told Jane.

"No, I suppose not," Jane said with regret, glancing around just to be sure.

"Then let's get out of here. It's a beautiful day, or haven't you noticed?"

"I noticed." The damp morning fog had drifted away by noon, leaving behind a sky so blue it made her eyes ache looking at it. It reminded her of the days she'd spent in San Francisco.

"Where do you want to eat?" Donna asked.

"Doesn't matter. You pick."

"Emilio's, then. I'm in the mood for Italian with lots of cheese and garlic."

"And cholesterol," Jane teased.

"I lived on little more than trail mix for an entire week," Donna countered. "Darryl takes his camping seriously. I deserve real food."

Jane thought of all the excellent meals she'd eaten on her own vacation, every ethnic variety imaginable, each one more delectable than the one before. "Well, not me. I should be dieting for the next month."

Donna grinned. "Then you went someplace with terrific restaurants. Now we're getting somewhere."

Whey they arrived at Emilio's, Donna led the way into the restaurant and picked a table in the corner. "More privacy back here, so you can tell me all the details."

Emilio brought them both huge glasses of iced tea, took their orders, then vanished into the kitchen to shout orders at the chef, who also happened to be his wife.

"One of these days she's going to chase after him

with a butcher knife," Donna observed, just as the debonair Italian came scooting back into the front.

"Maybe she just did," Jane said, chuckling at his chagrined expression as he retreated to his post at the door.

Her gaze was still on poor Emilio, when Donna asked casually, "How's Mike?"

Jane's head jerked around. "Mike? What made you bring him up?"

"That's where you went, isn't it? To see Mike in San Francisco?"

"Where would you get a crazy idea like that?"

"Oh, give it up, Janie. You've got that wounded look in your eyes again, just the way you did when you two split up last year. I take it it didn't go well."

"You're wrong."

"Wrong about where you spent spring break or wrong about how it went?"

Jane sighed. "Can't I have any secrets?"

"Not from me," Donna said easily. "I've been your friend for too many years now. Now, spill it. I want to hear everything. Is Mike spectacularly successful?"

"So it seems," Jane said with a trace of bitterness.

Donna stared. "Hey, what's that all about?"

"I'm sorry. I'm pleased for him, really I am. It's just that it would be so much easier if he hated it, if he wanted to come home again, but he doesn't. The job is a dream come true. He loves everything about San Francisco."

"And you don't, I suppose."

"It's a wonderful city. I had a terrific time," she claimed, but even she could hear that her tone was flat.

"But?"

"This is home."

"Jane, aren't you being the teensiest bit stubborn?"

"Ornery as a mule, to hear Mike tell it," she admitted.

"Well, maybe you should give a little."

"And do what? Go out there, marry Mike, then discover that I'm so homesick I can't stand it?"

"Were you homesick this week?" Donna asked.

"Of course not, but it was just a week." She smiled. "And Mike did keep me very busy." There was enough innuendo in her voice that no one could have mistaken her meaning, especially not someone as attuned to her as Donna.

"And you still walked away," Donna said with a shake of her head. She regarded Jane with a genuinely puzzled expression. "Are you crazy or what?"

The pressure of the week in San Francisco, the still-unresolved conflict with the man she loved and now Donna's unsympathetic reaction were all too much. Jane snapped.

"How can you even ask me that?" she demanded angrily. "You of all people know what it was like in my family. My dad had the world's worst case of wanderlust. He took off whenever the mood struck him. When he was here, he felt trapped and we all paid for it with his foul moods. When he was gone, it was no better, because then my mom was miserable. I won't set myself or Mike up for the same kind of anguish."

"Fine. I see where you're coming from, but have you ever explained all of that to Mike? Maybe he's never made the connection."

"How could he not have made it? He lived next door. He saw it."

"He was a kid," Donna argued. "Do you have any idea how oblivious kids can be? You should. You're a teacher. Besides, unless I miss my guess, you were as tight-lipped then as you are now. You probably never let him know what was going on." Her gaze was penetrating. "Did you?"

Jane sighed. "Probably not. I would have felt as if I were betraying my dad if I'd talked about it. In those days, I only wanted to please him so he'd stay."

"Then tell Mike how you felt, why you're afraid going to San Francisco could turn out the same way. He deserves to know what's going on in your head. All of it. Right now he probably just thinks that he's not important enough for you to take a risk that seems perfectly reasonable to him. He's offered you marriage, right?"

Jane nodded.

"And you turned him down?"

"Yes."

"Again."

"Yes."

"Can't you see what that must do to his ego?"

"Yes, but—"

"But what?" Donna countered impatiently. "No excuses, Janie. You have to tell him everything or else close the door on the best thing that ever happened to you. In the end how happy will you be here if the man you love isn't in your life?"

"I thought you weren't all that crazy about Mike," she said, confused by her friend's sudden defense of him, this unexpected push into his arms.

"I wasn't, not when I thought he was the one totally

at fault, but I'm seeing another side to this now. Tell him, Janie."

"There still won't be a way to compromise."

"Maybe there shouldn't be a compromise," Donna suggested carefully. "Maybe just this once you should give in and follow your heart. I know how much a home means to you, but that house of yours isn't a home, not unless you manage to fill it with love. Last time I checked the love you want is several thousand miles away."

"Why do I have to be the one to put everything on the line?" she asked plaintively. "Why is it my sacrifice to make?"

"It's not a contest," Donna countered. "If you look at it that way, you're both bound to lose. In this case, you're the one with the options. He has a job there that he can't equal back here, at least for now. You could teach there, as well as here. Mike's ready to make a home for you there. Isn't that really what you've always wanted—a house, kids, a man who really loves you?"

The idea was tempting. It always had been. "He said the same thing," she admitted.

"Then maybe it's time you listened to him." Donna regarded her intently. "Or is the real truth that he just doesn't matter enough?"

"How can you say that?"

"Because, sweetie, actions speak louder than words, and you're still here."

Chapter Four

Mike wasn't going to call Jane. He made a solemn vow to himself about that. She was the one who'd walked away…again. The door to their future had slammed closed when she'd gotten on that plane.

It was amazing, though, how the color had gone out of his life when she left. San Francisco had had its own unique charm before she'd come. Now, having seen it all over again through her eyes, he should have been doubly enchanted by all it offered. Instead it felt empty and lonely and bland.

The excitement had gone out of his work, too. His boss had offered him a plum assignment just that morning and all he'd been able to do was nod and take notes on the details. The job meant spending two months in Canada planning a new bridge project. He should have been elated. Instead he saw it only as a way to escape the bittersweet memories San Francisco now held for him. Even at that, he debated turning it down. He'd promised his boss an answer before the day ended.

It was hard to believe that just over a week ago he'd been wondering what was missing in his life. Now he knew and he couldn't think of a single way to change things and get what he wanted, what he needed.

No, that wasn't entirely true. He could quit his job and go back to Virginia. Jane would marry him then, but he would wind up restless and bitter, just the way her old man had been.

Oh, he'd seen what a hell Johnny Dawson had put his family through, though Jane had done everything in her power to hide the dissension from him. For a long time he'd ached for the little girl whose life had been turned upside down every few months. He'd done as well as any kid could to offer the stability she didn't have at home. That's when the bond between them had been forged. He'd been so sure it would last a lifetime.

He'd seen the look in her eyes when he'd told her about San Francisco, the hurt and betrayal. At that moment, she had lumped him in with her father and that had been that. She couldn't see how different it would be for the two of them. He would have to travel, yes, but he would always come home. He would never leave her in any doubt about that, not the way her father had.

He wondered if it would do any good at all to tell her that, then concluded that it wouldn't. If she couldn't see it, then all the words in the world wouldn't convince her. And she wouldn't take the risk necessary for him to convince her with actions.

Which meant there were no answers, not now, anyway. He walked down the hall and told his boss he'd take the Canada assignment. He was on a plane the next day, grateful to be running from the memories that now haunted him everywhere he turned.

Jane hadn't needed the home pregnancy test or the visit to her doctor to confirm that she was pregnant. She had known it for weeks. Her body was as reliable as a clock. When she missed her period, there wasn't a doubt in her mind about the reason. Joy flooded through her, though, when the doctor actually said the words.

"You're going to have a baby," Dr. Laura Caine said. "Right after the first of the year."

Tears slid down Jane's cheeks. "You're sure? There's no mistake?" She didn't think she could bear it if she got her hopes up, only to discover there'd been an error in the lab.

"No mistake," Dr. Caine assured her. "I take it, despite the tears, that you're happy about this."

"Oh, yes," Jane breathed, cradling her stomach. "Oh, yes."

"There will be complications."

Jane's heart slammed against her ribs. "Complications? What sort of complications?"

"With the school. Parents might object to having an unmarried woman teaching when she's carrying a child."

"I don't care," Jane said, chin tilted defiantly. "I'll take a leave of absence, if I have to. I want this baby, Doctor."

"Can you manage a leave of absence financially?"

"If I have to," she said, thinking of the money her mother had left her. If ever there was a rainy day need for it, this was it. "You'll get paid. Don't worry about that."

"For heaven's sakes, Jane, I'm not concerned about your bill," the doctor said, clearly insulted. "I'm worried about the stress you'll be putting on yourself and the baby."

"Oh." She flushed. "I'm sorry."

"Don't worry about it. Look, if there's anything I can do to make it easier for you, if you need a letter for the school, whatever, let me know."

"Thank you."

"What about the father?"

"What about him?"

"Will you tell him? He could help out if you're out of work."

"No," Jane said quietly. "I won't be asking him for help."

That night, though, as she sat in the room she already thought of as a nursery and contemplated her wonderful news, an image of Mike kept intruding. He would be happy about this. She knew he would. And he had a right to know. Common decency told her that. It didn't have to mean marriage or child support or any of those things. He just had a right to know he was going to be a father.

It took her a week to work up the courage to call. When she'd left three unanswered messages at his apartment, she guessed that he was off on an assignment. She finally took a deep breath and forced herself to call his office, bracing herself for an inquisition from that ogre who answered his phones and guarded his door.

"Mr. Marshall is out of town," Kim told her, giving away nothing about his whereabouts.

"Can he be reached?"

"In an emergency."

"This qualifies as an emergency," Jane insisted. "Ask

him to please call Jane Dawson as soon as possible. He has the number."

"I'll give him your message when I hear from him."

Jane lost patience. "Is that how you handle an emergency? You just sit around and wait for him to check in?"

"Those were his instructions."

Suddenly Jane was a twelve-year-old girl again. She'd fallen from a tree and broken her arm. She remembered desperately wanting her daddy, needing him, crying for him, only to be told by her mother that they had no way at all to reach him. It wasn't going to be that way for her child. She would see to that.

"Never mind," she said dully. "Don't bother telling Mr. Marshall I called."

That night, for the first time since she was twelve, she cried herself to sleep over a man who was too far away to care.

The Canadian project took forever, far longer than anyone had anticipated. Mike could have left someone else in charge once the work was underway, but his boss agreed with him that the client deserved Mike's personal attention. And Mike had no reason to go back to a lonely apartment in a city that had lost its luster. It was early December before he finally returned to San Francisco.

Spring, summer and fall had passed in a blur. Not a moment had gone by, though, that he hadn't thought about Jane. He'd missed her, longed for her and cursed himself for the weakness.

Obviously, though, she hadn't been thinking about him. If she'd called, Kim would have given him that message.

On his first night home, he knew he would be too

restless to sleep. He drove straight from the airport to the office and found himself faced with a mountain of files and old message slips. He was about to toss the messages, when Jane's name popped out at him. He glanced at the date: *May 27.* Cold fury ripped through him. Why the hell hadn't he gotten the message way back then? Why had it been left on his desk all these months?

He noted that Kim had first written "emergency" in the message space, then crossed it out and written, "never mind."

Dear God in heaven, what sort of emergency had there been? Why hadn't Jane been given his Canadian number at once? Oblivious to the hour, he called his secretary at home, waking her from a sound sleep.

"Kim, I'm at the office. There's a message here from last May from Jane Dawson. Why wasn't I told about this? She said it was an emergency. What kind of emergency?"

"Wait, let me think," she said, instantly alert. "It was right after you left. Oh, yes, I recall. When I told her you'd left instructions that messages were to wait until you called in, she told me to forget it. I should have just thrown the message slip away, sir. I'm sorry."

"No, what you should have done was give me the damned message," he shouted. "Never mind," he said, slamming the phone down, then dialing Jane's number. His heart pounded, thinking of her needing him and then being brushed off.

It had to be nearly dawn in Virginia, but Jane's phone rang and rang. Not even her answering machine picked up. At least the number hadn't been disconnected, he told himself, but that was small consolation.

He had a bad feeling about this, a very bad feeling. He

called the airlines, then left the office. At home he heard
three more messages from Jane, probably left months
ago, as well. More panicked than ever, he threw some
clean clothes into a suitcase and headed straight for the
airport. He would be on the first flight out in the morning.

On the long drive from the airport to the riverfront
town about eighty miles away, he told himself over and
over that there was no reason to worry. Her answering
machine was probably just broken. She'd probably just
left the house earlier than usual that morning. He would
find her at home when he arrived.

As he drove into town, he tried to see it through her
eyes, tried to imagine it as a safe haven. True, the streets
were clean and lined with large homes with gracious
front porches. The old oaks were bare now, but in spring
and summer their shade would provide welcome relief
from the penetrating glare of the sun. Instead of being
gray and choppy as it was now, the river would be a glistening blue.

The downtown section was barely more than a half
dozen blocks of tidy storefronts and blinking neon
signs. In summertime, the sidewalks were bustling with
locals and tourists, but at this time of year, with the
wind bitingly cold off the river, they were practically
empty. One shopper, head lowered against the wind,
rushed toward the blinking lights of the small gift shop,
intent on Christmas shopping, no doubt.

Why didn't all of this beckon to him, as it did to
Jane? It wasn't that he hated it or held bitter memories.
Simply put, it had never been enough. It had lacked the
opportunities he'd craved.

A few minutes later he was sitting in front of Jane's

house, staring at the drawn blinds and remembering the first time he'd seen the little girl who lived there. She'd been his shadow from that first meeting.

He never even glanced next door at the house that had been his home for most of his life. He was too stunned by the bleak darkness of her house. There were no signs of life at all, no indication of Christmas preparations inside. Jane had always decorated and baked with a fervor for the holidays. That sick feeling in the pit of his stomach intensified.

What if something had happened to her? What if she'd been ill and needed him? A thousand *what ifs* ran through his head, each one worse than the one before.

The school, he thought finally. There would be answers at the school. He drove the few blocks without even noticing what he passed. He was tearing up the walk, when he ran smack into Donna Iverson exiting the building. He'd known her almost as long as he'd known Jane, but she'd never much liked him. Now she stared at him incredulously.

"Mike?"

He grabbed her shoulders. "Where is she?" he demanded, not even trying to hide his worry. "Where's Jane?"

He saw the caution spread across her face. "Dammit, Donna, tell me. Has something happened to her?"

"It's taken you long enough to get around to asking that question," she said heatedly. "It's been months since she called you."

"I just got her message last night. I've been in Canada for months. You have to believe me—if I'd known she was looking for me, I'd have gotten back to her." He ran his fingers through his hair as he thought of how Jane must have felt when he didn't return her calls. Compassion threaded through his voice as he imagined her pain. "She must have felt so abandoned when I didn't call."

"She did," Donna agreed, regarding him evenly, clearly not intending to give an inch.

He felt the need to defend himself to her. "But I didn't know she needed me. I swear I didn't. I would have called—hell, I would have been here—if I'd had any idea she needed me."

Something softened in her expression then. "You love her, don't you? You really love her?"

"Always have."

Donna nodded, clearly accepting it as the truth. "I thought so. I told her there had to be some sort of mix-up, some reason you hadn't called. I begged her to keep trying, but she refused."

"Then tell me where she is. Let me try to straighten this out."

"Come on over to my house," she said. "We need to have a talk."

He wanted answers here and now, but he could tell he didn't have a choice. Donna intended to do this her own way. He followed her to a small brick house with black shutters, went inside and accepted the cup of coffee she offered him. "You are going to tell me where she is, right?"

"After we talk. I want to be absolutely sure I'm doing the right thing."

Mike grinned despite himself. "I always knew I was going to have to ask permission to marry her. I never figured you were going to be the one I'd have to ask."

"Oh, there's a whole slew of us around here who care

about Jane. You're just lucky I'm the first one you ran across. Darryl wants to cut your heart out."

She said it with such cold-blooded sincerity, he shuddered. "Then I'll be sure to steer clear of Darryl."

"Maybe not. I married him six months ago. He'll be home any minute now."

Mike had an image of Darryl Smoot left from high school. The boy had been as big as a house and mean to boot, at least on a football field. Off the field, he'd cultivated the same image, but the rumor had been that it had all been for show. Mike prayed that the rumors were true.

He and Donna were still skirting the subject of Jane's whereabouts when Darryl came through the door. He was still huge, but he was all muscle now and the scowl that spread across his face when he recognized Mike was intimidating enough to give Mike a few bad seconds. Then Darryl turned his back on him as if he didn't exist and gave his wife a resounding kiss.

"What's the story, sugar? When did he turn up?" He gestured in Mike's direction.

"He's looking for Jane."

Darryl turned a fierce look on him. "Maybe Jane doesn't want to be found, same way you didn't when she called looking for you."

"That was all a big mistake," Mike explained again.

"So you say."

"It's the truth, dammit. Just tell me where she is. Is she okay? What the hell is going on?"

Donna snagged her husband's arm, then shot a look at Mike. "Excuse us a minute, please."

He heard their whispered exchange outside the kitchen door, but he couldn't make out a single word.

He guessed they were debating how much to tell him. If the circumstances had been different, he'd have told them what they could do with their games, but they were his best hope for getting at the truth in a hurry. If anyone knew Jane's secrets, it would be Donna. And like it or not, he'd rather tangle with her and Darryl than try to get information out of the principal of Jane's school.

Finally, when he was about to lose it, the kitchen door swung open and Darryl came back alone. He held out a piece of paper.

"Here's her address." He positioned himself so he was in Mike's face, literally and figuratively. "You do anything to hurt her again and you'll deal with me. Is that understood?"

"Understood," Mike agreed, then moved around the man. When he was at the door, he glanced back. "I'm glad she's had you in her corner all this time," he said with absolute sincerity.

"Should have been you."

Mike sighed heavily. He could see Darryl's point. "Yes," he agreed without reservation, without even knowing what it was Jane had been left to face alone. "It should have been me."

Chapter Five

Jane had baked ten dozen batches of Christmas cookies since dawn. She'd only burned the first three dozen, trying to get the timing down in the ancient oven in the tiny furnished apartment she'd rented until the baby was born. The apartment itself wasn't bad, with its huge windows overlooking the river and its bright curtains and overstuffed furniture. The appliances, however, were a very different story. The stove was turning her holiday baking into an adventure.

She'd taken a leave of absence for an entire school year, rather than battle the board of education over her suitability to teach. She had enough money left from her mother's insurance policy to cover her expenses, including this apartment in a town just far enough from home to protect her reputation. Maybe it was a foolish, old-fashioned ruse, but she had to try to give her child a start that didn't include speculation about his or her paternity.

She had debated just staying in her own house and weathering the gossip, but in the end she'd concluded she and the baby would both be better off if they just turned up again in the spring. Maybe she was only postponing the inevitable questions, but she'd felt she would be better able to cope with them after she'd gotten through the pregnancy and had a healthy baby.

There was an ironic twist to her decision, of course. In the end, she'd done exactly what she'd refused to do for Mike. She had left the hometown she loved.

But it wasn't as if it was going to be forever, as it would have been if she'd married Mike. And she was still close enough to have lunch every couple of weeks with her friends. They met at a restaurant midway between the two towns, caught her up on all the news and brought her anything she needed from her house. They were scheduled to get together again on Saturday and she intended to have her usual packages of Christmas cookies ready for them since it was likely to be the last time she saw them before the holiday.

The apartment smelled of cinnamon and sugar and ginger and echoed with the sound of Christmas carols being played at full volume. In fact, the CD player was so loud, she barely heard the knock at the door. She turned the sound down, then listened just to be sure.

"Who on earth…?" she murmured, wiping her hands on a paper towel and grabbing the last batch of cookies from the oven before going to the door. It was probably a neighbor complaining about the volume of the music or her landlord coming to beg a couple of cookies. The man had an insatiable appetite for sweets and a constantly—and futilely—dieting wife who refused to bake them for him.

With her cheeks flushed from the heat of the oven

and probably streaked with flour, Jane suspected she was quite a sight. Judging from the impatient pounding on the door, though, she didn't dare pause to make any improvements in her appearance.

"Okay, okay," she muttered under her breath, throwing open the door. Her mouth gaped. "Mike? How on earth did you find me?"

He shook his head, still staring. "Doesn't matter."

No, she supposed it didn't. The point was, he was here. She wasn't sure which of them was the most stunned. His gaze went from her face to her unmistakably huge belly in the blink of an eye, then remained there as all the color drained out of his face.

"You…you're…"

"I'm going to have a baby," she said, supplying the words that eluded him. She regarded him intently. For a rugged man, he looked awfully shaken. "You aren't going to faint, are you?"

"Of course not," he said at once. "But—"

"I think you'd better come in and sit down," she said, though that was the last thing she wanted. For months she'd dreamed of finding Mike on her doorstep, but the dream had eventually died. Now her own reaction was nothing like what she'd anticipated. She felt nothing, or so she swore to herself. She was just surprised, that explained the sudden racing of her pulse, the lurch of her heart.

To give herself a little time to gather her composure, she left Mike in the living room and went into the kitchen to pour him a cup of coffee and herself a glass of milk. She added a handful of cookies to the tray and carried it back into the living room. Mike still looked dazed.

"What? When?" he asked, apparently incapable of forming a coherent sentence.

If she'd imagined him sweeping her up and dancing around at the sight of her body swollen with his child, this stunned reaction would have been a serious letdown, but she'd stopped counting on anything from Mike Marshall. Still, she had no intention of lying to him.

"The baby's due in three weeks, right after New Year's. I got pregnant in April."

"April," he repeated, then his gaze shot to hers. "You mean?"

She tried not to be hurt that he hadn't guessed it at once. "Yes, the baby's yours, Mike."

The confirmation snapped him out of his daze. "Why the hell didn't you tell me?" he demanded angrily.

So much for the joy she'd hoped for. Jane stared him down, then said quietly, "I tried."

"Well, you didn't try hard enough."

"I left messages at your apartment," she said pointedly. "I called your office, only to be told you were away and weren't to be bothered. What more would you have had me do?"

"Write me a letter, keep calling." He ran a hand through his hair in a familiar gesture of frustration. "Dammit, Janie, you should have found a way."

"Did it ever once occur to you to call me?" she retorted. "You knew we'd taken chances. Maybe you should have been responsible enough to check to see if there were any consequences."

"So now it's my fault for not checking with you? Don't you dare try to pull that, Janie. You know perfectly well you told me there was no risk."

She flushed at that. "That's not exactly what I said," she argued, but without much spirit.

"It's sure as hell what you implied."

She couldn't deny that was exactly the impression she'd meant to give him. "Mike, it doesn't matter, not now. I'm having the baby in a few weeks. I don't expect anything from you. Not a thing. You're off the hook. You can hop the next flight to San Francisco and forget all about this."

He stared at her as if she'd lost her mind. "And what if I don't want to be off the hook? What if I want to be a father to this baby?"

She fought the little frisson of hope stirred by his words. He was just feeling territorial.

"Then we'll work something out," she said evenly. "I would never try to keep you from your child. That's why I called you in the first place."

"But you still won't marry me?"

"Now? Under these circumstances?" she asked incredulously. "No, of course not. A baby doesn't solve the problems we were having. It's just an added complication."

"That's how you view our child, as a complication?"

"No, never," she said fiercely. "That wasn't what I meant at all."

"What, then?"

"Just that it was difficult enough figuring out what to do when it was just the two of us involved."

"A baby should simplify it. We should both be thinking about what's best for our child."

"But we obviously don't agree on what that would be. We never have."

"How the hell do you know that? I only found out about this baby a few minutes ago. I don't even know what I think." He stared at her in frustration. "Jane Dawson, you are the most pigheaded woman I have ever known in my life."

"That kind of attitude will certainly win me over," she said dryly.

"I'm not trying to win you over. Obviously I've lost that battle. But I'll tell you one thing and make no mistake about it," he said, his voice climbing, "I am going to be a father to this baby and you can damned well get used to the idea."

"Well, that's just fine," she shouted back.

In the silence that followed, another CD slid into place on the player and the pure, clear notes of "Joy to the World" filled the air. Jane couldn't help it... she began to chuckle. When she glanced at Mike, she saw the fierce expression on his face begin to give way to a smile.

He sighed, then said softly, "Merry Christmas, Janie."

"Merry Christmas, Mike."

"Think we can discuss this rationally?" he asked.

"Maybe in the spirit of the season, we can try," she conceded, then gave a little gasp as the baby walloped her with a ferocious kick.

"What is it?" Mike demanded at once. "Are you okay?"

"It's nothing, just a little reminder that your kid's getting restless. The baby gets a little rambunctious around this time of day, probably because it's time to eat. A couple of cookies aren't going to do the trick."

"We'll go out," Mike said at once.

"I can fix something here."

"Do you have to argue about everything?"

She grinned. "Pretty much."

"Well, just this once give in gracefully, okay?"

His gaze settled on her stomach and a look of such yearning came over his face, that Janie felt something inside her shift. She had always imagined Mike looking at her with exactly that expression of awe when she was carrying his child. She had always imagined them sharing the wonder of it. Impulsively she moved across the room and stood in front of him.

"Give me your hand."

He stared at her. "Why?"

"Do *you* have to argue about everything?" she teased, echoing his accusation against her.

He held out his hand and she placed it against her stomach. The baby didn't disappoint her. The kick was another solid wallop. Mike's eyes widened and he stared at her incredulously.

"Oh, my God, that was him, her, whatever?"

Jane nodded.

"Do you know which it is?"

She shook her head. "I didn't want to know." The truth was it would have hurt too much to know if it was going to be the little boy she'd dreamed of giving Mike. She hadn't wanted to deal with that until she had to.

"It's a boy," Mike said with utter confidence. "If it's not, we're never going to have to worry about anybody messing with our daughter. She'll blow 'em away." His gaze on her softened. "You're okay? No problems with the pregnancy?"

"I'm healthy as a horse," she assured him.

"I want to know every detail," he said fiercely. "And I want to go to your next doctor's appointment with you."

Jane stared at him in shock. "You'll be here that long?"

"Honey, you couldn't get me out of town now if you wanted to. I'm here for the duration."

When she opened her mouth to argue, he cut her off. "Get used to it, Jane. I'm here to stay."

"But your job…"

"I've worked nonstop ever since you left San Francisco. I'm due for some time off. I'll call tomorrow and make the arrangements."

The thought of Mike being around for the birth of their child left her feeling shaken. If he stayed that long, if he took care of her as he obviously intended, if he reminded her of how deeply she loved him, how would she ever manage to say goodbye again?

Mike didn't sleep a wink that night. Only a part of his restlessness could be blamed on the too-short, lumpy sofa in Jane's living room. There hadn't been any question of him sharing her bed. When they'd gotten back from dinner, she'd walked into the bedroom and shut the door. A moment later she'd emerged and tossed some sheets and a pillow in the direction of the sofa. He'd gotten the message. What he hadn't gotten was a moment's sleep.

He was still wrestling with the idea that he was going to be a father. He and Janie were going to have a baby. The thought boggled his mind. Over dinner he had pumped her for every single detail of her pregnancy, trying to hide his resentment over having already missed so much of this miraculous process.

To think that she could have had this child and he might never have learned of it. The very idea of that made him so furious he wanted to break things. When he got past wanting to throttle her for not seeing to it he was informed, he thanked God over and over that she had decided to go through with the pregnancy. His next hurdle was to convince her to marry him so their child would bear his name.

He could hardly wait to hear the explosion likely to greet that plan. He'd spent the whole night trying to come up with the right words to convince her. In the end he'd concluded he would just drag her off to a church and let a minister persuade her that her child deserved to be born within the sanctity of marriage. He liked that. It was exactly the right button to push.

However well she might seem to be coping, it was obvious to him that she'd left her home because she didn't want the stigma for herself or her baby of being an unwed mom. That stigma wasn't likely to go away just because everyone back home missed the actual pregnancy. The only way to make things right for all of them was to get married. He just had to get the timing perfect.

Jane was a morning person. She always had been. He figured she'd be up with the birds, which meant he had to get busy. He dug around in the kitchen cupboards and came up with the best china the place had to offer. He found a couple of candles tucked in a drawer and put them in the middle of the table in the apartment's tiny dining alcove. Then he went to work in the kitchen.

He made biscuits and an omelet and squeezed fresh juice from the oranges he found in the refrigerator. He had coffee perking and a glass of milk poured by the time he heard the first stirrings in her room.

A few minutes later, she wandered into the dining area, barely covering a yawn. She stared at the fancy table and the huge breakfast, then sank into a chair.

"You've been busy," she said, regarding him warily.

"You told me to make myself at home. Do you want jam for your biscuits?"

"Yes, please." She toyed with the food on her plate. "Mike?"

"Yes."

"You can't keep doing this."

"Why not?"

"I'll be big as a barn."

"Maybe a bungalow," he said, grinning. "Never a barn. It won't matter anyway. I'll still think you're beautiful."

"That's only because you haven't seen my swollen ankles," she said, holding out her feet. She was wearing fluffy blue slippers. "Look. And this is at the beginning of the day. They'll only get worse."

"That's because you've been on your feet too much. That's going to stop, now that I'm here. You can keep them propped up."

"And do what?"

"Watch TV, read a book, crochet little booties."

"I don't think so."

"Jane, I intend to pamper you." He glanced at her plate. "Finish your omelet. The baby needs protein."

"How do you know?"

"I read that book you left by the sofa. Milk and protein for the baby's bones, plus plenty of fruits and vegetables."

She regarded him with amusement. "Mike, I'm eight and a half months pregnant. I know what to eat. I know how to take care of myself. If you're going to hover, you can leave now."

"I'm going to hover," he said, then added with a touch of defiance, "And I'm not going to leave. Get used to it."

Chapter Six

Mike was very big on routine. He always had been. Growing up in his household of rambunctious brothers and sisters, order and routine had been in short supply. He had always craved it. Jane suspected that was one of the reasons he'd been drawn to the calm and serenity in her house. Now he'd taken that need for order to new heights.

By the third day of his visit, Jane was fairly sure he'd missed his true calling...drill sergeant. When he wasn't stuffing her with food, promptly at 7 a.m., noon and 6 p.m. with a couple of snacks thrown in at precisely 2:30 p.m. and 8 p.m., he was pushing the latest child care books on her to read. Judging from the stack he'd accumulated, she doubted there was a single title on parenting or prenatal care left in the local library.

And then there were the walks. Not the sort of strolls she'd grown accustomed to taking every afternoon, no. These were more like forced marches. By the time Saturday rolled around, she could hardly wait to get out from under his watchful gaze for a few hours while she met her friends for lunch.

When she appeared in the living room wearing her favorite maternity dress, the only outfit that didn't make her look like a blimp, he popped up out of his chair.

"Where are you going?"

"I'm meeting Donna and some others for lunch."

"Where?"

"At a little restaurant and craft shop in Lottsburg. I doubt you've ever been there."

He looked horrified. "But I know where Lottsburg is. It's on a back road in the middle of nowhere. You can't drive over there by yourself. I'll take you."

"Mike!"

"Stop arguing. I drive or you stay here."

"Dammit, Mike, I am not helpless."

"No, but the baby's due any second. What if you go into labor while you're on that country road all alone? Or what if there's an accident? The steering wheel could hurt the baby." He shuddered visibly. "No, I'm going and that's that."

"Mike, if you'd been this bossy when we were together, I'd have thrown you out on your ear."

"You weren't having a baby then," he said, as if that were explanation enough for his overprotectiveness.

Jane sighed and followed him to the car. "You'll sit at a separate table," she informed him as they drove.

"Whatever."

"In fact, you could wait in the car."

He grinned at her. "Don't push your luck, angel."

"Okay, a separate table will do."

Naturally, though, it didn't work out that way. All of

the women she knew were well acquainted with Mike. They had all pretty much guessed that he was the father of her expected baby, even if they hadn't said as much to her face. The minute she and Mike walked in the door together, the others crowded around, assuming that his presence meant a wedding was just around the corner. Jane guessed from Donna's satisfied expression that she was the one who'd steered Mike to Jane's apartment.

"Feeling smug?" Jane inquired, choosing a seat by her friend.

"Hopeful," Donna replied. "He's still around. That's a good sign, isn't it?"

"Depends on your point of view," Jane grumbled. "He's fussing over me as if I were the first woman on earth to have a baby."

"And your complaint about that is?"

Jane sighed. "It's not going to last. Sooner or later, he will go back to San Francisco."

"You don't know that. He looks content enough to me. This could be just what he needs to decide he wants to stay in Virginia."

"He spends an hour or more on the phone to his office every day when he thinks I'm taking a nap. Doesn't that tell you something?"

"It tells me there are twenty-three hours he's devoting to you. Be grateful. Most husbands don't give their wives that much attention, ever."

"You don't understand," Jane said. "I can't let it matter. I just can't."

"You still love him, don't you?"

"Yes, but…"

"Then use this time with him to come up with a

workable arrangement." She regarded Jane slyly. "Maybe you should think about the fact that you've been living away from home and away from teaching for months now and it hasn't been as awful as you feared it would be."

"Because I still talk to all of you and see you. And at first I was so exhausted, I slept all the time. I wasn't awake long enough to miss teaching."

"Honey, that's why they invented long-distance phone lines and airplanes. As for the exhaustion, wait till you have a toddler around the house." She patted Jane's hand. "Think about it, okay? Promise me."

Jane nodded. "I promise."

Donna grinned. "Good. Now, then, let's get this party underway."

"Party?"

"Annie?" Donna called. "Are you hiding back there?"

"I'm here," Annie called back and wheeled in a cart laden with packages as all the others shouted, "Surprise!"

"A baby shower. I can't believe it," Jane whispered, tears in her eyes. Mike made his way to her and put a hand on her shoulder and squeezed. She looked up at him and caught the way he was eyeing all the presents. She was probably going to have to fight him for the right to open them.

"After all the baby showers you've attended for the rest of us, it was the least we could do," Daisy said.

Jane thought back to Daisy's shower the previous March. That was the event that had triggered all of this. That was when she'd realized just how desperately she wanted a baby of her own. That was when she'd bought that wonderful antique crib from Annie.

It was also when she'd begun thinking of Mike again, wishing that they were together just like this. Well, almost like this. She'd hoped for a more traditional arrangement, but she was having his baby and he was here at her side. That counted for a lot.

As she opened the presents, *oohing* and *aahing* this time over her own gifts, a feeling of absolute contentment stole over her. She wouldn't have done a thing differently, she realized now. Whatever difficulties lay ahead, she wanted this baby—Mike's baby—with all her heart. If she couldn't have Mike with her for the rest of her life, at least she would have a permanent reminder of the love they'd once shared.

When the last present had been opened, and the last crumb of cake had been devoured, she made a decision. She turned to Mike. "I want to go home," she whispered.

"Okay. I'll get all of this stuff in the car and then we'll go back to the apartment."

She shook her head. "No, I mean I want to go home, to my own house. I want to put these things in the nursery. I want to stay there. I want to spend Christmas in my own place, to be there when I go into labor."

He studied her worriedly. "Are you sure? You've gone to this much trouble to hide your pregnancy. Do you really want to go back now?"

"I'm sure. I don't want to hide out anymore. Will you come with me?"

"You know I will." He knelt down and brushed a strand of hair back from her cheek. "In fact, if you want we can stop at St. Mary's on the way and see about getting married."

"Married?" she said as if she'd never heard the word

before, never heard him propose the same thing a dozen different times. Sneaking it in again now, when she was so clearly vulnerable, was a low-down, dirty trick. She wavered.

"If you won't do it for yourself or for me," he added, "let's do it for the baby."

She wanted to. Oh, how she wanted to, but a marriage that from the very start wasn't meant to last? Wouldn't that be worse than no marriage at all?

"Think about the baby," Mike persisted, when she remained silent, repeating a now-familiar refrain. "The baby deserves to have the father's name, my name. We've loved each other our whole lives. Surely we can do this one thing together for the baby we've created."

It was the right thing to do for the baby. Jane could see that. But was it right for the two of them? How much heartache could they bear? The time would come when Mike would leave. It was inevitable.

"Darling, stop thinking so hard. Stop trying to gaze into a crystal ball and figure out what will happen tomorrow or a month from now. Right now all that matters is the baby and what's best for his or her future."

He made his case passionately and persuasively. If he couldn't say the exact words Jane wanted to hear, if he couldn't promise to stay in Virginia, well, that wasn't the only thing that mattered under the circumstances.

"We can talk to the minister," she said at last and wondered if she'd just made the best decision of her life...or the worst.

It took some doing, but when Mike wanted to make something happen, he pulled out all the stops. By nightfall, they had moved Jane's belongings back into her own home, met with the minister and arranged for a quiet, private ceremony to take place two days before Christmas. Donna and Darryl had agreed to stand up for them.

On the morning of the wedding, they found the church already decorated for Christmas with huge baskets of poinsettias. The candles were lit, giving off a soft glow around the altar. Jane had bought a new, cream-colored silk maternity dress and shoes to match. Mike was wearing a black suit with a crisp white shirt and black tie.

Even though the marriage would be only temporary, little more than make-believe, Jane couldn't help trembling as she looked around at the beautiful old church. It was just as she'd always imagined her wedding would be, except in most of those daydreams she hadn't been almost nine months pregnant.

Just before the ceremony was to begin, Mike gave her a bouquet of a single white poinsettia surrounded by white roses and tied with white satin ribbons. He tilted her chin up and gazed into her eyes.

"Everything okay?"

Jane managed a wobbly smile. "Everything's fine," she assured him, thinking to herself if only…

If only it were for real, if only it were forever.

When the minister read the vows, she repeated them in a voice that trembled, while Mike's rang out clear and sure. It almost sounded as if he meant every word, but she knew better. This was for the baby, nothing more. Pride should have kept her from saying yes, but for once pride had mattered less than doing what was best for her child. And she would have a few days or weeks with Mike that she could cherish forever.

In a few weeks it would all be over, the baby would be here and Mike would leave. Her life would go on. Tears tracked down her cheeks as the minister pronounced them man and wife. Other brides had surely cried, she thought, but none from the sort of heartache she was feeling.

When Mike bent and kissed her and tasted the salty dampness on her lips, he regarded her with surprise. Instantly concerned, he whispered, "Oh, baby, it's going to be all right. I promise."

Jane wanted to believe him. He'd always made good on his promises. This one, though, seemed to be beyond his capabilities.

Donna and Darryl gave them a moment alone, then swept in and announced they'd arranged for a wedding lunch.

"That wasn't necessary," Jane said, touched by their attempt to make this occasion seem real and special, even though both of them knew the circumstances were anything but normal.

"Of course it was," Donna insisted. "Come on. We even have a limo waiting and sparkling grape juice in the back so we can toast the newlyweds on our way to the restaurant."

They were halfway to Fredericksburg when Jane's back began to ache. They were almost on the doorstep of the restaurant when the first contraction hit. She doubled over and clasped Mike's hand.

"Dear heaven, what is it?" Mike said, the color draining out of his face. "Janie, talk to me. What's wrong?"

When the hard grip of the contraction loosened, Jane managed a smile. "I'm not sure, but I'd say we got married in the nick of time. Unless I miss my guess, this baby's coming now."

"Now?" Three voices echoed with shock.

"Oh, yeah," Jane said as she was seized by another contraction.

Donna patted her hand as Mike guided her back into the limo. "Don't you worry about a thing," she told Jane. "The hospital's practically right around the corner and years from now you can tell your kid that he made the trip in a limo instead of an ambulance."

"As long as he's not delivered in the back seat of a limo," Jane said. She glanced at Mike. "How are you holding up?"

He swallowed hard. "To tell you the truth I'm feeling just the slightest bit superfluous. You're the one who's got to get the job done."

"Oh, no, you don't," Jane muttered. "You're not running off with Darryl to buy cigars or something. You're going to be in that delivery room with me."

"But I trained as your coach," Donna protested. "Are you sure you want to change at the last second like this? Does Mike even know how to do the breathing exercises?"

"Don't go getting territorial on me," Jane said. "You can coach. Mike can hover. It's something he does very well."

Darryl grinned. "I guess that leaves me to pace and buy the cigars."

The limo screeched to a halt at the emergency room entrance and Mike and Donna butted heads trying to be the first one out. Darryl took off out the other side. It was several seconds before anyone noticed that Jane was still inside.

"Hey, guys," she called out plaintively. "You can't do this without me."

Mike scooped her up and carried her inside. An orderly swooped down on them and took them straight up to labor and delivery, where less than two hours later black-haired, blue-eyed, David Michael Marshall entered the world screaming his head off to protest the indignity of it all.

By nightfall Donna and Darryl were gone and Jane and Mike were alone with their son. They regarded the six-pound-three-ounce baby with awe.

"How did we ever create anything so beautiful?" Mike wondered.

"He started out with a pretty decent gene pool on his daddy's side," Jane said pointedly.

"Better on his mother's."

"Do you want to hold him?"

There was no hesitation at all. Mike reached for him eagerly and settled into the rocker beside the bed. As Jane drifted off, the last thing she heard was Mike explaining to his son that he would always, always be there to protect him.

"You can count on it, son." He glanced at Jane. "So can you."

But she had already fallen asleep.

Chapter Seven

Mike couldn't seem to take his eyes off of his son. From the moment he'd held the baby in his arms at the hospital, he'd felt an incredible mix of love and pride and joy. Nothing had prepared him for the overwhelming sense of protectiveness that had washed through him.

David was so tiny, so astonishingly fragile, yet the boy could bellow loud enough to be heard from the hospital nursery all the way to Jane's room. He was clearly going to be a kid who would make his displeasure known.

Staring down into that tiny face, Mike wondered if his father had felt the same way after the birth of each of his kids. It made him think about the way his father had struggled over the years trying to support his family, trying to protect them, always falling just a little short. He'd seen how defeated his father had looked every time he failed to be promoted, every time another job ended.

Mike had watched, felt his father's pain and vowed never to let that happen, to always go the extra mile for his employers, to be so good at what he did that he'd be indispensible. He knew that was what was driving him now, that it was behind his refusal to give up the opportunity he'd been given in San Francisco. That job enabled him to give Jane and his son anything they wanted or needed. How could he walk away from it?

And yet that job was the very thing that seemed destined to keep them apart.

He sighed, glanced over at Jane and smiled. She was finally asleep. She had shown amazing strength and bravery in the delivery room. He'd been in awe of her. She deserved to sleep for a month and he intended to see to it that she got all the rest she needed for as long as he could. He just wasn't sure how long that would be.

He'd told his bosses he'd be back in San Francisco after the baby's birth. He'd assumed that would be sometime in late January. Since the baby was a few weeks early, they would expect him sooner, probably right after the first of the year.

He couldn't help wondering what Jane's reaction was going to be when he said he had to go. He wanted desperately for her to come with him, but nothing in the past couple of weeks had indicated she'd softened her stance against leaving her home. And he knew that jobs as satisfying and challenging as the one he had in San Francisco were too few and far between to walk away from.

Was he being selfish to want to hold onto that kind of career satisfaction and financial security for his family? Or was it Jane who was at fault? One thing was for certain: Neither of them seemed willing to break the stalemate. Love, which supposedly conquered everything, couldn't seem to make a dent in this.

The door to Jane's hospital room opened and a nurse

stepped in just as the baby began to whimper in his arms again.

"Just in the nick of time, I see," the woman said, reaching for the baby. "I'll take him for his bottle and put him down in the nursery so you and your wife can get some rest."

Mike relinquished his son with reluctance.

The nurse grinned. "Don't worry. I'll bring him back first thing in the morning. I promise. Believe me, you'll be glad you've had a full night's sleep tonight, once you get him home. This may be the last you have for some time to come."

Mike sighed when they'd gone. She had no way of knowing that his sleepless nights would be over in a couple of weeks at most. Then Jane would be left with the full burden of 2 a.m. feedings and pacing the floor with a cranky baby.

How could he let that happen? How could he possibly leave the two of them behind and go back to San Francisco? What kind of pleasure and satisfaction could he take from a job that had cost him his brand-new family? What good was financial security if it cost him the very family he was trying to protect?

He was still struggling with that when he realized Jane was awake, watching him. His mouth curved.

"Hey, you, why aren't you sleeping?"

"Where's the baby?" she asked.

"Back in the nursery, so you can sleep. The nurse suggests we both take advantage of the peace and quiet while we can."

"He's okay, though?" she asked, gazing worriedly toward the door.

"He's perfect."

"You're sure?"

"Janie, you saw him. He couldn't be healthier or more beautiful."

She struggled up. "I want to see him."

He recognized the stubborn jut to her chin and gave up the fight. "Let me get you a robe. Donna ran out and brought one back from the mall. She said you'd want to wander out of here in the middle of the night and you couldn't do it with your backside showing through that indecent hospital gown."

"I knew there was a reason she was my best friend."

Mike wrapped the robe around her, then tucked his arm around her waist. "Ready? Do you want me to get a wheelchair?"

As he'd anticipated, she frowned at the idea.

"I can walk," she insisted, setting out a little stiffly.

Outside the nursery window, she scanned the bassinets until her gaze fell on their son. "There he is, Mike. Look, he's blowing little bubbles in his sleep."

"Just like you," he teased.

She regarded him with indignation. "I do not."

"Sure, you do. I was just sitting there watching you. You're both adorable when you sleep."

"Mike Marshall, you are a bald-faced liar."

He chuckled. "Okay, maybe I was wrong about the bubbles, but you do snore."

She swatted him. "You're just saying that so you won't feel so bad about the fact that I haven't let you in my bedroom."

"I was in your bedroom not five minutes ago," he reminded her. "That's how I know for a fact that you snore."

"If you want me to believe that, you'll have to tape-record it."

"Then you'll have to let me move into your room with you. It could take several nights to get convincing documentation."

"Oh, no, you don't. If you can't get it in one night, right here in the hospital, then it doesn't happen."

"Come on back to bed. I'll get one of the nurses to come in and witness it firsthand. Will you believe an impartial observer?"

"Not likely," she said, after taking one last look at the baby. "You can charm those women into saying any-thing you want them to. I saw you wheedle a dinner tray out of one of them."

"That was for you," he protested, walking her slowly down the hall. "I knew you had to be starved."

"The point is you were able to get your way, even though it was way past dinnertime."

"If I'm so good, how come I can't talk you into com-ing back to San Francisco with me?"

For just an instant, he thought he saw pure longing in her eyes, but then it was gone. She crawled gingerly back into the bed without answering.

"Jane?"

"I can't," she whispered. "I want to, but I can't."

"Couldn't you just give it a try?" he pleaded. "Maybe for a few months? They're not expecting you back at school this year anyway, right? Come home with me and see how it goes. Let me give you the perfect life we always imagined we'd have."

A tear spilled over and washed down her cheek. Mike relented. "Never mind. It's not the time to talk about it."

"I'm sorry."

"Don't be," he said, trying not to blame her for feelings that were so entrenched they might never get past them. He tucked the covers back around her, then brushed a kiss across her forehead. "Get some sleep."

Her eyes drifted closed, then struggled back open. "Mike—"

"Hush. It's okay."

"No, you don't understand. I just wanted to say thank you."

"For what?"

"For being here. For my baby."

"Our baby," he said fiercely. "He's our baby, Janie."

But she was already asleep.

The baby's homecoming was as triumphant as if he'd been royalty. It might not have been marked by media attention, but all of Jane's friends were there when Mike drove up.

Inside, Jane found the house decorated for the holidays and the nursery filled with all the supplies the baby could possibly need. Everything was perfect, or would have been if she hadn't had this sick feeling that it was all about to end. She forced a smile when Donna came over with outstretched arms.

"Let me hold my godson," she said.

"Don't go getting any ideas," Darryl warned, coming up behind her. "We've agreed to wait another year."

"I know. That's why I need to hold this one as much as Jane will let me," Donna said.

Mike joined them. "Hand him over," he said. "You'll get your turn when I'm gone."

Jane felt the salty sting of tears at the reminder that this whole homecoming was bittersweet. It marked a new beginning for her and the baby, but the clock was already ticking toward the end of her brief marriage to Mike. No doubt he'd want to set a divorce in motion before he left. What was the point of staying married when there was going to be an entire continent between them? The baby carried his father's name and that was what this whole sham of a marriage had been about in the first place.

Suddenly she couldn't bear it another minute. She ran from the room. As she let the kitchen door slam behind her, she was dimly aware of Mike's muttered curse, then pounding footsteps chasing after her.

"Jane!"

He caught her heaving shoulders and turned her around. "Oh, baby, don't cry. Dammit, I keep getting it all wrong."

She looked up and caught the tormented expression on his face. "It's not you. It's us. One minute I can almost believe that all of this is real, that we really are a family, just the way I always dreamed we would be. The next I realize it's make-believe."

"It's not make-believe," he said. "It doesn't have to be. I love you, Janie. And you love me. I know you do."

"Yes," she agreed, her voice ragged. "But that doesn't change anything. You're going to leave. You have to do it. I understand that."

He stared deep into her eyes. "Do you? Do you really understand it?"

She nodded. "Yes, but I hate it, Mike. I really hate it."

He gathered her close. "I know, baby. I know. It's just like it was when your dad used to go away, isn't it?"

Startled, she met his gaze. "You know that?"

"Well, of course. Remember, I was the one you used to run to every time he'd go. Not that you ever talked about it, but I could see the hurt in your eyes, the fear that he wouldn't come back. I hated him for doing that to you." He sighed. "And now I'm doing the same damned thing. Telling you I love you one minute, then saying goodbye and walking out the door."

He tucked a finger under her chin and tilted her face up. "There's one difference, though."

"What's that?"

"You can count on me coming back."

Hope stirred inside her. "You'll be back?"

"Whenever I can. Our boy is not going to grow up wondering if his father cares about him. It may not be a perfect arrangement, but I promise you we'll make it work."

Something died inside Jane as she realized what he meant, that the separation would go on forever. "I guess we'll be no different from a million other divorced couples," she said bitterly. "Shipping our child back and forth on a plane."

He stared at her. "Who said anything about a divorce?"

"You did."

"No, what I said was we would make this arrangement work."

She stared at him, appalled by the suggestion. "You expect me to just hang around here, waiting for the moments you can spare us? I don't think so, Mike Marshall. I do not intend to live my life in the same sort of emotional limbo that my mother did. Go or stay, it's your choice. But let me be very clear about one thing, if you go, it will be the end for the two of us. I'll file for divorce the day you get on the plane."

She whirled around and went back inside, making very sure that she was always in the middle of a throng of friends, so Mike couldn't challenge her about her threat. She knew that a confrontation was inevitable. She couldn't ask her friends to hang around all night to prevent it, but for once she felt she was in charge of her own destiny.

If Mike chose to go—and she told herself she was prepared for that possibility—then he was the loser. There would never be anyone who could love him as she did, never be anyone to compare with his firstborn son. Her life was here, and so was his, if only he could recognize it in time.

Chapter Eight

Christmas came and went, then New Year's. On the second day of January, Jane was sitting in the nursery rocking the baby, when she caught a glimpse of Mike in the doorway. She could tell from his expression that the time had come and he was going to say goodbye. Tears flooded her eyes and streamed down her cheeks. He saw them and was by her side in an instant.

"Janie, don't cry." He pulled out a handkerchief and dabbed at the dampness on her cheeks.

She shrugged off his touch. "It's okay. Just roller-coaster hormones."

"Is that all?" he asked, watching her worriedly.

She forced a smile. "Of course." She met his gaze evenly. "What about you? You seem upset."

"We can talk about it later." His gaze settled on his son. "How's my boy doing?"

"Your boy has a full tummy and is sound asleep," she said. "I should put him in his crib, but I love sitting here holding him in my arms and rocking him. I still can't quite believe he's real."

A ghost of a smile passed over Mike's face. "Yeah, I know what you mean."

"Want to trade places?"

"Sure."

He said it so eagerly that she laughed. "Here, then. I'll go do the latest mountain of laundry. I never imagined that a guy this little could generate so many dirty clothes."

Mike traded places with her, settling Davey against his chest and humming to him. She would have given anything for a picture of the two of them, but her camera was out of film. They'd gone through three rolls in the past week and she'd neglected to pick up more. She'd have to remind Mike to get some when he picked up the prints later.

Unless he was going to leave before that. That was what he'd been about to tell her. She was sure of it. She wouldn't cry when he said the words. She wouldn't. Why make it harder than it had to be? They'd both known this day was coming.

But knowing it intellectually and facing it were two very different things. She listened in dread for the sound of his footsteps coming from the nursery. When he finally walked into the kitchen a half hour later, she was dry-eyed.

"We need to talk," he said, gesturing toward a chair. When she was seated, he asked, "Want some tea?"

Jane shook her head. Her stomach had knotted the moment she saw him. Tea wouldn't help. Nothing would.

Mike sat down opposite her and drew in a deep breath. "I'm leaving tomorrow."

Even though she'd anticipated the words, shock rippled through her. "I see."

"But I have a request before I go."

She regarded him warily. "What kind of a request?"

"A few days back you threatened to file for divorce the minute I left. I'd like you to wait."

"Why, Mike? Why wait?"

"Because I don't think we should throw our marriage away like this."

"We're not throwing it away," she said angrily. "It never had a chance."

"And whose fault is that?" he demanded, then closed his eyes, visibly struggling for calm. "I'm sorry. I know it's not your fault or mine. This goes deeper than pure stubbornness. I know that, too. We both have reasons for feeling the way we do."

"Reasons that won't change over time," she said. "We were apart for a whole year and nothing changed."

"Because neither of us made the effort."

"What's different about now? What kind of effort are we supposed to make?" she lashed out. To her shock, she thought she saw tears in his eyes.

"Please, Janie, don't write us off yet," he pleaded. "There has to be some way to make it work. I have to leave here believing that."

"I wish I could say I agreed with you, but I don't. Some impasses just can't be broken. Why prolong this?"

"Because we made vows," he said fiercely. "Despite the circumstances, those vows meant something to me. If they meant anything at all to you, then you have to give us more time." He gazed at her intently. "Did they? Did they mean anything at all to you?"

"You know they did," she said in a whisper. "They meant everything."

He stood up and gathered her into his arms. "Then you have to wait. Don't file those papers, Janie. Please."

Engulfed by the pure masculine scent of him, surrounded by his heat and his strength, she couldn't have refused him anything at all.

"I'll wait," she said at last. "For whatever good it will do, I'll wait."

If there was any shred of hope at all for the three of them to be together always, she would cling to it.

In the middle of March, Jane had a call from the principal of her school. The teacher who'd taken over her classes was ill. The principal wanted to know if there was any chance that Jane could come back to finish out the school year.

"Of course," she said eagerly. Staying home was driving her batty. Davey didn't need her attention every second. And if she was going to be a single working mom, the sooner she set the pattern for it, the better. "When do you need me?"

"Monday will be fine."

"Thank you. I'll be looking forward to it," Jane said. Only after she'd hung up did she realize that in accepting the job, she was conceding that she would never leave home to join Mike.

Donna stopped by later that afternoon. "I hear you're coming back to work on Monday."

"The grapevine in that school always was remarkable."

"What's Mike going to say about it?"

"Mike doesn't have anything to do with it. He's in

California. I'm here. I always intended to go back to work. This is just a little sooner than I planned."

"But you still haven't filed for divorce and neither has he. Shouldn't you talk this over?"

"No. It's only a matter of time. We talk almost every day but nothing's really changed. He keeps holding me to the promise I made before he left, that I wouldn't file for a divorce until we agreed that there was no chance we could make it work."

"Is he coming back any time soon?"

"He hasn't mentioned it and I haven't asked."

"Do you miss him?"

Jane sighed. "My heart breaks every time I hear his voice. I want him here with me more than anything in the world. And I know it's crazy, but I think Davey misses him, too. He's been fussier since Mike left, as if he knows he's lost someone important."

Donna regarded her sympathetically. "I hate this. I really do. You two belong together."

"I always thought so," Jane agreed. "But maybe Fate had something else in mind."

Jane went back to work the following Monday and quickly settled back into a routine that had once been as familiar to her as breathing. Because it was such a small school, she already knew many of the kids in her class. The substitute teacher's gradebook and detailed progress reports on each student filled in what she didn't know.

By the end of the first week, she felt as if she'd put her life in order and resigned herself to the idea that Mike would never be a part of it. She even dropped by Annie's Baby Boutique after school on Friday just as she had before she'd gotten pregnant with Davey. Now, though, she could shop to her heart's content for her own child.

At home, the minute she stepped inside, she sensed that something was different even before she spotted the pile of suitcases in the hallway. Her heart slammed against her chest, then began an unsteady rhythm.

"Mike?" She hurried down the hall toward the nursery, knowing instinctively that was where he would be. "Mike?"

He was in the rocker with the baby in his arms. The sight of the two of them made her breath catch in her throat.

He glanced up. "Hey, pipe down, will you? I've just gotten him settled down."

"And what have you done with the baby-sitter?"

"Sent her home. The kid and I don't need any help."

She grinned at him. "Is that so? Did she, by any chance, feed and change him before she left?"

"Of course."

"No wonder you're so confident, then." He did look confident, too. He also stared at her as if he couldn't wait to devour her. She felt the heat of that look all the way across the room.

Finally she dared to ask, "How long will you be here?"

His gaze locked with hers. "For good."

This time she was pretty sure she stopped breathing altogether. "For good?" she repeated in a shaky voice. "Why? How?"

"Later," he said. "Right now, how about getting over here and giving your husband a proper welcome-home kiss?"

Dazed, Jane crossed the room and bent down to brush a quick kiss across his brow.

He scowled at her. "You call that a proper kiss?"

She grinned. "That's exactly what I call it—very, very proper."

"Then I guess what I'm after is something else entirely." He reached up and curved his hand around her neck and drew her back down. When their lips were barely a hairbreadth apart, he paused. "I love you, Janie."

And then he kissed her and there was nothing the least bit proper about it. In fact, the kiss devoured, sending heat and need flooding through her. When he finally released her, she frowned at him.

"You'd better have meant it," she said.

"Meant what?"

"You'd better be staying for good, because I'd have to slug you if you were kidding around."

"No kidding," he vowed. "In fact, I think I'll just put Davey here in his crib so I can take his mommy to her bed and prove just exactly how serious I am."

The minute he had their son settled in for his nap, he turned and the fire in his eyes set off butterflies in Jane's stomach. When he swept her into his arms and headed across the hall to her room, she pushed aside every last reservation she had and let the sensation of being in his arms overwhelm her.

Explanations, everything could wait until later, she thought as she gave herself up to the tender glide of his hand over her flesh. His caresses, the heavenly feel of his mouth on her breasts, the wicked demand of his fingers probing her moist, secret places, all of it carried her off to a place where everything was perfect and love was eternal.

Slick fire raged between them as their bodies joined. Each thrust lifted her higher until she was crying out for release, crying out for Mike, then shuddering as he took her over the top and beyond.

Tears streamed down her cheeks when it was over, tears of joy, but Mike stared at her with concern.

"Janie, what is it? Did I hurt you?"

He started to move away, but she held him tightly. "No, please. It's just that we've never made love like this before. It's never felt like this."

"Like what?"

"Like the start of forever." She searched his face. "That is what it meant, isn't it?"

He brushed the damp tendrils of hair back from her cheeks. "Yes, that's what it meant."

She sighed then and fell asleep. For the first time in months, she slept peacefully.

Mike stared down at the woman in his arms and wondered how he could ever have convinced himself to leave her. This was where he belonged. It had taken some ingenuity on his part and a whole lot of understanding and cooperation on the part of his bosses, but he'd finally found a way to get back to her.

Jane sighed contentedly and opened her eyes. She reached for his face and touched her fingers to his cheek, then smiled.

"You are here. This is real."

"It's real."

"You aren't going back to San Francisco?"

"I'll have to go occasionally, but this will be home."

"You didn't quit your job?"

"I threatened to." He described the scene in which he'd told his bosses that he was going to have to make the most difficult—most impossible—choice of his life. "Then I offered them an alternative. I suggested we open an East Coast office. We're getting more and more business on this coast anyway. It made perfect sense."

A smile of pure joy spread across her face as she grasped the implications. "And it made perfect sense to put you in charge of it," she guessed.

"That's pretty much it. The office will be in northern Virginia, but the commute's workable. Once in a while I may have to stay over up there if a meeting's going to run very late, but they'll be paying me enough that we could even get a small apartment if we wanted to." He grinned at her. "Our own private little love nest."

"Now that's an interesting spin to put on a place you'll need because you're tied up in business meetings," she teased.

"I figure that's only one use we can put it to. Once we have a bunch of kids underfoot, we're going to need a little privacy every once in a while. We can go to the Kennedy Center, have a late-night supper, then spend all night making love and come back to our kids like a couple of rejuvenated newlyweds. What do you think?"

She knelt on the bed beside him and peppered his face with kisses. "I think that you are the most inventive, smartest man on the face of the earth. You've done the impossible."

He traced a line from the pulse at her throat down between her breasts and on beyond. "Just wait till you see what I can do with the possible," he said.

The first sparkle he'd seen in ages lit her eyes. "Dare you to show me," she said at once.

So he did.

* * * * *

A STRANGER'S SON

Emilie Richards

Chapter One

No one in his right mind would choose to rekindle childhood memories during the worst blizzard in twenty years. But Devin Fitzgerald had often done the unthinkable. He had left Yale Medical School three months into his second year to join a struggling rock band with the unlikely name "Frozen Flame." And he had left Flame at the peak of their extraordinary and undeserved success to strike out on his own. Four years into the runaway success of his solo career, he had made a decision to limit touring so that he would have more time to compose and record. Now he was considering a new career entirely.

But none of those decisions seemed as risky tonight as driving the back roads of picturesque Holmes County, Ohio, in a car without chains and a body clothed in nothing warmer than a lightweight leather jacket.

As Devin tapped his brakes to slow his Jeep Cherokee to a crawl, he hummed a few bars of the melody that had been plaguing him for days. Most of his songs started this way. An interval, a rhythm, a melodic mood that expanded in his head one measure at a time until he had enough to whistle and eventually to pick out, one-fingered, on the piano. This particular melody was more elusive than most, but he suspected the finished composition might be his best. Already it made him think of soft summer nights in America's heartland, of fragrant moonflowers on split-rail fences and the winking of fireflies in knee-high acres of corn.

He had needed to come home.

He had needed to come home, but *not* at midnight in the middle of a blizzard.

Devin tapped his brakes again. The Cherokee resented his interference, and the powerful engine sighed in protest. He was barely moving now, but the snow was so thick that he still couldn't see exactly where he was. He knew he was on the right road. It had been years since he had been to Farnham Falls, but little had changed. Before the snow had thickened, he had recognized an old gray farmhouse that had once been the last landmark before the turnoff. There were other houses just beyond it now, but not many. This was still farm country, a stronghold of the Amish and Mennonites, and rural to the bone. The road he was looking for would appear on his right before too long, and if he was lucky and the Cherokee made the turn, he would be home soon.

Home. Devin almost smiled at the thought. He had been everywhere, lived everywhere, for the past eight years of his life. He was an adaptable man, as comfortable in Sri Lanka or Sicily as Seattle. He hadn't missed Farnham Falls particularly. There had been little here for a restless youth with a Fender guitar, a thirty-watt amplifier and delusions of grandeur. Every day of his adolescence he had dreamed of leaving. But in the past months he had dreamed only of coming back.

He was alone on the road. He hadn't seen a headlight in thirty minutes, and there were no Amish buggies clip-clopping their way home. Everyone with sense was at home asleep, with an extra quilt thrown over them for good measure. The snow crunched under his tires and licked at his windshield wipers. He hadn't been this alone in years; he hadn't experienced silence in quite this way since he was fourteen and slogging his way through the January snow to his aunt's barn to feed the resident animals. Something very much like peace was descending with the snowflakes. He knew he should be concerned for his own safety. If his car stalled he could be in trouble. He had tried his cellular phone just a little while ago, only to discover that it was crackling with static. He wasn't worried. The snow was glorious, and for the first time in months he was feeling almost whole.

The giant oaks that marked the turn seemed smaller now, but the turn led to the same narrow, unpaved lane he remembered. He fishtailed and slid perilously close to a ditch before he steered the car out of the spin. He had another mile to go, maybe two, and he would be home. His cousin Sarah had promised that the house still looked much the same as he remembered it. Sarah, her husband and two children had lived there in the years since aunt Helen's death, but now they were out on the West Coast, and the house belonged to Devin. Sarah hadn't understood why he wanted it. "You could live anywhere in the world, Dev," she'd said when he'd offered to buy the house from her. "You hated Farnham Falls. You haven't been back since high school."

"But I don't hate it anymore," he'd explained. And he didn't. Ohio represented a time in his life when he had been filled with dreams and the delicious innocence of youth. He wanted to find that place inside himself again.

If it was still there.

He kept his foot off both the accelerator and the brake and concentrated on the middle of the road. The house would be warm. His manager had found someone to clean and ready it for him, stock the refrigerator with food and the shed with firewood. There was no telephone, no television. He had seen to that himself. He was looking forward to a month of quiet nights and quiet days. A month when he could think without interruption. Once he got to the house, the blizzard would make everything that much sweeter. No one would visit. No one would even know he was there.

Unless he stopped just ahead to help the occupants of the car that was half in, half out of the ditch.

Devin tapped his brakes, and the Cherokee began to slide again. He cursed the other idiot who—like him—hadn't known enough to stay off the roads tonight. He couldn't see the car clearly, since it was shrouded by snow, but it appeared to be small, a compact model that probably looked better when it wasn't nose down, belly exposed. He steered to the right until the Cherokee was under control, then tapped his brakes again. He was twenty yards beyond the other car when he finally came to a halt.

For a fraction of a second he considered not going outside to check on the car's occupants. He didn't want to leave the warmth of the Cherokee or announce his presence in town. He told himself a rapid series of lies even as he began to button his jacket. The car was smothered in snow, so it had been there for some time. Whoever had been driving it had already gone for help. There was nothing to indicate an accident so serious that anyone might be injured. But he had already slammed the car door behind him by the time the last excuse had begun to form. He might be world-weary, cynical even, but in the very depths of his soul he was a Farnham Falls boy, raised to care about the people around him and to offer help when needed. Eight years of rock bands and groupies, of incomprehensible adulation and life lived under a microscope, hadn't erased the values his aunt Helen had instilled in him.

Someone needed help. He had help to give.

Devin had left his headlights on, but they did little to illuminate the accident scene, since the Cherokee was so far ahead and aimed in the wrong direction. Two feet into the storm, the wind nearly knocked him off his feet. He shoved his hands in his pockets and leaned into the wind, but it stabbed at his cheeks and neck and sifted through the worn denim of his jeans. He wasn't wearing socks, and he regretted that now. His loafers sank into each drift, and snow packed his shoes. By the time he was ten yards from the car his feet were on fire, which was only slightly better than the inevitable numbness that would quickly follow.

"Is anybody in there?" He shouted the words, but the wind twirled them back at him. He caught snowflakes on his tongue the moment he opened his mouth and swallowed them in a burst of sensation. He repeated his shout as he closed in on the ditch, but he didn't expect a reply. He wasn't going to find out if anyone was still in the car until he was peering in a window.

What if a passenger was injured? He wondered if he remembered any first aid. He supposed that his months in medical school had been wiped away by now. In the past years he hadn't been called on to do anything more than perform, compose and give interviews. There had always been someone at his side to take on anything resembling an emergency. He told people what to do and they did it, no matter how foolish or complicated his orders. But no one was nearby to take orders now.

Lord, he was glad there wasn't. He was so glad to be on his own that even the thought of freezing to death in the middle of nowhere had appeal. It seemed almost justified. Devin Fitzgerald, formerly of Frozen Flame. He had been frozen inside for so long that he liked the symbolism.

"Is anybody in there?" He was close enough to the car now to see into the windows—if the windows hadn't been cloaked with snow. Another blast of air shoved him forward. The wind was howling, a demented, witchy shriek that would have made his skin crawl if it hadn't been nearly frozen. He leaped over a mound that a snow-plow had piled there in the last storm and started inching his way down an incline toward the ditch.

The car was in worse trouble than he'd thought. The back wheels were completely off the ground, and the front of the car was more accordion than hood. The driver had probably spun the steering wheel as the car slid off the road, because the weight had shifted toward the driver's side as the car had come to rest. There was no hope of getting in or out that way. He would have to try the passenger's side.

As he had expected, the ditch bottom was ice under

snow, inches of it that might or might not hold his weight. Devin gritted his teeth and tested the ice with one foot. He thought it shifted, but there was nothing to be done about it even if it wasn't frozen solid. He had to get to the bottom of the ditch to open the door.

He skidded across the ice and reached up for the door handle just as the ice cracked beneath him. He hung on, but the handle couldn't stop him from sinking nearly a foot. Ice water took the place of snow in his shoes, and he grunted with shock.

"Is anybody in there?" He had sounded more concerned the first time, but this time he was just glad his voice was working. He listened, but the wind was his only answer.

He scrubbed at the window with his hand, but there was still a layer of ice beneath the loose snow. He scratched at it with his fingernails and pressed his face against the window. It took his eyes a moment to adjust to the nearly complete darkness of the car interior.

There *was* somebody there.

"Hey!" He banged on the window with the heel of his hand, then tried to open the door. But the handle wouldn't give. "Hey!"

He couldn't tell if the shadowy figure inside the car was a man or a woman, but he saw movement. A head turned at the sound of his voice.

"Let me in!" he shouted. "You've got to get out of there. You're going to freeze!" He wondered how badly the person had been injured. He saw a head loll back against the seat. "Can you unlock the door?"

There was no signal that indicated the person inside could do anything at all.

Cursing like a roadie with a hangover, Devin let go of the door handle. He could try to find something to break the glass, but that might injure the driver. He tried the back door instead, but it was locked, as well. He scraped that window clean and peered inside again. There was nothing to indicate that the opposite door might be unlocked, but it was worth a try.

He gauged the safety of scrambling across the trunk and decided it was safe enough. The car seemed wedged in place, and his weight wasn't going to disturb it. He hefted himself up and slid across the back window to land on his feet on the driver's side. The back door here was high enough that, despite the car's angle, he could probably slide in if it was unlocked. He reached up and pulled on the handle. Nothing happened.

Frustrated and growing numb, he squatted beside the driver's window and began to scratch the ice away. "Can you turn and unlock the door behind you?" he shouted. He could just make out the straight slope of a nose, short dark hair and the glint of eyes, open eyes that were staring in his direction.

When the driver didn't move, he shouted again. "I'm going to have to break the glass to get to you, if you can't open it yourself."

"Go away."

For a moment he thought the sound he heard was the wind. But the wind didn't speak in syllables. He was so cold that it took him another moment to put the sounds together. Then he knew what he'd heard. The driver was a woman, and she was conscious enough to speak, even if she wasn't making sense.

"Unlock the damned door!" He slapped his palm

against her window. "I'm not going to hurt you. I'm trying to save your life! You're going to freeze to death!"

She turned her head away from him.

She had to be injured to act so irrationally. As he watched helplessly, she fell forward toward the steering wheel and her body jerked. It was so dark that he could see only shadows and movement. He shouted to her again, hoping he could convince her to help. "Listen! It's zero degrees out here, and the temperature's falling. You could freeze before I can get help. Please. Help me help you!"

He thought he was going to have to break the window. He was contemplating which window would be safest when she spoke again. "Go. Please…"

He felt around in the snow for help. He needed a rock, and even then he imagined the glass would take a couple of mighty blows to break. He had already decided on the window behind the driver when he heard her sobbing.

He felt like a criminal. He didn't even know what to say to reassure her, but he tried his best. "Honey, it's okay. It really is. I'm a Farnham Falls boy, born and raised. I wouldn't hurt you for anything. I'm going to get you out of there in a few minutes and get you to a hospital."

She was sobbing harder. He stood to broaden his search for a rock or stick when he heard the sound of a window screeching in protest as it was lowered.

With a prayer of thanksgiving on his lips he squatted again and reached inside her window to unlock the door behind her. Then, before she could say a word, he opened the door.

"The car might shift when I get in," he warned her. "But don't worry. It's not going to turn over. It's wedged too tight. I'm going to get in and unlock the other side.

Then I'm going around to get you out the passenger side. But you're going to have to trust me and do what I say, or we're both going to freeze before I get you back to my car."

She was still crying, but he glimpsed something like a nod.

A minute passed before he made it back around to the other side and got the passenger door open. "Okay, now. I'm going to get in and pull you out this way. How badly are you hurt?" He wished that he had asked her that before. The possibility existed that he could make matters worse by moving her, despite the cold.

"I hit...my head." She grunted the answer as if she was in pain.

"Okay. Anything else hurting?"

"Please... Just get me out."

"That's exactly what I'm going to do. Just relax and let me do the worrying."

She groaned and bent forward again. He knew better than to panic, but the temptation was there. He lifted a foot to the open doorway and hauled himself up and into the passenger seat. Then he reached for her.

There was a lot more of her than he had bargained for. He released her immediately and leaned away. He managed to dispense with profanity, despite the call for it. "You're pregnant!"

She groaned again and rested her head against the steering wheel, which rested taut against her swollen abdomen.

A terrible thought occurred to him. "Are you in labor?"

She groaned again, and that was the only answer he needed. He touched her cheek in comfort, but she jerked her face away from his hand. "Just...get me out!"

"Right away. Just don't drop that kid in the snow."

She didn't dispense with profanity, although her vocabulary was sadly limited. Despite himself, Devin grinned. His own shock was quickly giving way to a sense of omnipotence. He was going to get her out of here, and he was going to save her and the baby. For months he had wondered if there was anything more to Devin Fitzgerald than flash and hype. Now he was about to find out.

He put his arms around her again. "Wedge your feet against the side door," he instructed, "and push while I pull. We're going to get you on this seat first, then I'm going to help you out of the car. I'm going to try to carry you up the embankment to mine."

"You…can't!"

"Oh yes I can." He began to slide her toward him. With gratitude he realized she was taking his suggestion. When she was suspended between the two bucket seats, he slid off his seat and down into the ditch, pulling her steadily as he went. When she was settled on the passenger seat he rested a moment before he spoke.

"Okay, swing your legs around to the floor. I'll put one hand under your knees and one around your back."

"You're going to drop…me." The last word was followed by another groan. He suspected it signaled the onset of another contraction.

"We'll wait until that one's finished," he said, as calmly as he could. "Let me know when it's done. But they're coming pretty fast. We've got to get you to a hospital immediately. And I'm not going to drop you. Not on your life!"

Time seemed suspended as he waited. He wished he could see her face, but the light in the car wasn't working—damaged, he guessed, in the accident. Even if there was a moon tonight, it was blocked by storm clouds. The darkness was as thick as the snow. He had only the impression of a small-boned woman, delicate features and shining dark hair.

"Ready?" he asked, when the struggle seemed to be subsiding.

She nodded.

He slid his arms beneath and around her. His feet were wet and quickly growing numb, but compared to what she was about to endure, he supposed frostbite was nothing. He took a tentative step backward and swung her into the air. With relief he realized that he probably *was* going to be able to carry her. She wasn't as light as a feather, but even with the extra weight she was toting, she was a small woman. If he could get up the embankment without slipping and over the mound of snow to the road, they would make it.

"What's your name?"

"Just…get me out of here!"

"Well, Get-me-out-of-here, hang on tight." He started forward. All he could see of her now was shining hair. Her cheek was against his chest, but he thought she was sobbing. "We're going to get you to the hospital. Was that where you were heading?"

"Yes. No. My doctor…"

He tested his path, one careful step at a time. The embankment was slippery, but not the problem he had feared it would be. "You were trying to get to the hospital but couldn't make it?"

"The storm knocked out…my phone. My doctor lives… I was trying…"

"To get to him," he finished. "Bad luck all the way around. Is he close by? I sure as hell hope he's close by." He gripped her harder as she groaned again. He was very much afraid that she was having another contraction.

"Down this road…"

"Where's your husband? Shouldn't he be with you?"

"Bastard!"

So it was like that. Devin wasn't surprised. Men were famous for abandoning women who got pregnant unexpectedly. Something akin to rage filled him. He would like to find the man who had done this to her, then left her alone to have their baby in the middle of a blizzard. "Look, don't you worry." He gripped her tighter and took another step. "I'll stay with you if you want. I'll see you through this. I'm going to make sure you're fine."

She was sobbing loudly now. If he gripped her any tighter he would bruise her badly. He didn't know how to comfort her. They both needed comfort, so he began to sing. Softly. To the top of her head. He made it up the embankment before he realized what song he'd chosen. Not one of his greatest hits. Not one of Frozen Flame's. It was the lullaby his mother had sung to him every night until her death early in his childhood.

The song that he had been hearing in his head for the past weeks.

He spoke without thinking. "I'll be damned…."

"You *are* damned…Devin…Fitzgerald."

He was poised with one leg over the snow mound when she spoke. He was frozen for a moment. Not from the brutal gusts of wind that could turn a man to ice. But from her words and a terrible revelation.

He swallowed an answer and a question. He stepped over the mound and nearly stumbled, but somehow he managed to keep them both upright. Then he started across the road and down to his car. He was silent, and the only parts of him that seemed to be working were his legs. The rest of him was suspended and waiting.

He made it to the car, balancing her against it as he opened the passenger door. Then he settled her inside.

And in the beam of the overhead light he finally saw her face.

He couldn't remember her name, but she had remembered his. "Get me down this road, then get…out of my life!" she said between gritted teeth.

He squatted beside the open door, squatted in the snow and the wind and the near darkness. But the car light shone clearly on her face. "Is this my baby?" he whispered.

"Not…in a…million years!"

But Devin knew the truth, even as she began to cry again. The child this woman was carrying belonged to him, as surely as the woman had belonged to him for one magical spring night the previous year.

He remembered that April night as clearly as if it were yesterday. He wondered if she was remembering it, too.

Chapter Two

A sea of daffodils danced in a light spring breeze outside the town-house window, and somewhere nearby a blue jay squawked displeasure at a tabby cat curled up in the sunshine. April was in full bloom in Ohio, but Robin Lansing didn't have time to notice.

"So you think I should wear the green dress?" Robin held up two dresses for her best friend to examine.

Judy McAllister frowned and shook her head. "The red. Sexier. And wear your hair down."

"I'm not supposed to be sexy. I'm supposed to be professional. I'm representing the paper. I'm trying to get Devin Fitzgerald to give me an interview, not a back rub."

"You'll have a better chance at both in the red dress," Judy said wryly. "First you have to get him to notice you."

"I have as much chance of speaking to him as the man in the moon." Robin held the red dress against her chest and decided Judy was probably right. It was worth a chance.

"Look, the guy—or at least his press agent—sent the

paper two tickets to his concert and the party afterward. Apparently he's still got a soft spot for his old hometown. You've got an in. Now you just have to use it."

"I'm glad you're coming with me."

"You'd better get dressed or neither of us will make it to Cleveland on time."

Robin finished dressing while Judy closed up the apartment and fed the cat. At the last minute Robin shook out her hair, which had refused to go into a smooth knot at the top of her head, and let it hang loose below her shoulders.

"You know, that dress ought to come with a printed warning." Judy's blue eyes were sparkling. She was dressed up herself, but no matter what Judy wore, with her curly brown hair and round face she managed to look like Miss Wholesome Ohio, the title she had garnered in their senior year of high school.

Robin smiled at her friend. "I'm glad you came to see me. You're good for my ego."

"It's a short trip from Cincinnati. And besides, I'm just glad to see you coming out of mourning."

Robin's smile didn't even falter. It had been two years now since Jeff, her husband, had died. Life had gone on, as Jeff had insisted it would. She was almost ready to step back on board. "Jeff would have liked this dress."

"You know, if you get an interview with Devin Fitzgerald, it could lead to a job on a larger paper."

"I know." Robin had left a job on a larger paper at the beginning of Jeff's final hospitalization. After his death she hadn't been able to face a busy newsroom every day. She had come to the *Farnham Falls Gazette* instead, to take a job as editor and begin the healing process. The job had been perfect for the two years she had held it, but getting free tickets to Devin Fitzgerald's concert was the only exciting thing that had ever happened. It probably was time to move on.

The two women chatted casually on the drive north, but Robin could feel her excitement building. She was an admirer of Devin Fitzgerald's, not precisely a fan, since her tastes ran more to classical and jazz; but Devin hadn't abandoned melody or poetry in his work, as so many rock artists had. He was part James Taylor, part Mick Jagger. Despite the driving beat of drums and the shiver of electric guitars, there was a purity, a raw emotion, to his songs that never failed to touch her.

He was a handsome man by anybody's standards, with golden-brown hair that nearly touched his shoulders, ice-blue eyes, a square jaw and a high forehead. Robin knew from watching his videos that he was large enough to dominate a stage. With his wide shoulders and long legs he looked like a New Age prophet when he performed. She was anxious to see him in person.

She wondered if she would get close enough tonight to even tell Devin who she was and what paper she was from. The tickets and backstage pass had been a big surprise to everyone at the paper. Devin Fitzgerald had spent most of his youth and adolescence in Farnham Falls, but his connections over the years since had been tenuous. The aunt who had raised him had died a long time ago, and even his remaining cousin had moved to the West Coast. Devin contributed sets of compact discs or generous checks to any fund-raiser in town, but he hadn't been back in years.

By the time the two women arrived in Cleveland and

had parked at the hotel where they would spend the night, Robin was almost feeling young again. She was only twenty-seven, but some of those years had been agonizing. She knew plenty about pain, and she supposed that was part of the reason that Devin's music appealed to her. He knew something about pain himself. While she had been losing a husband, he had been losing a wife to infidelity and divorce. Robin's pain had been silent and unheralded, but Devin's had been dissected in public.

"I've read every article about Devin Fitzgerald that I could find, in case I get a chance to interview him," Robin told Judy as they walked amid a swelling mass of young and old toward the downtown arena where the concert was going to be held. "But there hasn't been much written in the past year about his personal life."

"Maybe it's taken him time to recover, too."

"Do you suppose someone like Devin Fitzgerald is allowed to take that kind of time? The pressures on him must be fierce."

"He's got more money than God and probably more women than a sultan. I'm having trouble working up sympathy."

Robin smiled, but she wondered if Judy was right. Fame and fortune didn't protect anyone from the realities of life. As she and Judy found their seats at the front and settled in to watch the opening act, she wondered if Devin Fitzgerald had been changed by misfortune in the same ways that she had. Now she understood how short life could be, and how capricious. She intended to fully live each day that was given to her and to savor with gratitude the good things that came her way. If anything positive had come from Jeff's death, it was that.

* * *

Devin had braved the first wave of well-wishers right after the concert, but the second wave had been forced to wait until after he showered. Now he dried himself and slipped on a clean pair of jeans and a freshly ironed white shirt.

The concert had gone well. It was one of only half a dozen he would do that year, and all the tickets had been snapped up the first day they had gone on sale. His manager hadn't understood why he'd insisted on a performance in Ohio, but Devin knew he owed something to the state where he'd been born. He wished that he had time to go back to Farnham Falls, to sneak in on some back road and revisit his childhood there. He had almost convinced his cousin Sarah to sell him the house where he had been raised. Maybe then he could go back, dig his roots deep in the county's dark soil and try to remember who he was.

At the same moment he went in search of his shoes the door to his dressing room opened. "We've got a roomful of people waiting to shake your hand." Harry Bagley, Devin's manager, stuck his head through the opening. "You about ready?"

Devin considered refusing. He was bone weary. He had put more of himself than usual into the concert, performing three encores with his backup band and one by himself with nothing but a spotlight and a guitar. But this was Ohio, and he owed these people. "About. You been hiding my shoes?"

Harry shook his head in exasperation. "You need me to hire somebody to dress you, Dev? Is that what you need?"

Devin collapsed on a plaid couch and rested his head

against the back. "I need about six months away from you and everybody else. Then maybe I could find my own shoes."

"You need to get laid."

Devin opened his eyes and stared at Harry. It was an old argument. Harry believed that everything could be cured by money or sex. Since Devin had plenty of one, the root of all his problems must simply be a lack of the other.

Harry held up his hand to stop Devin's inevitable reply. "I'll find the shoes. I'll put them on and tie the damn things if that's what it'll take to get you there."

"Get out. I'll be there in a few minutes."

Harry snorted. "If you're not, I'll be back."

"You come back and you're fired."

"Yeah, yeah." The door slammed behind him.

Devin sat up and began looking for his shoes again.

The party was in full swing by the time he joined it. He was mobbed immediately, which exhausted him immediately. He had used up most of his energy onstage. The suite was brightly lit and noisy, exactly what he didn't want tonight. At the beginning of his career he had craved both. After a performance his adrenaline had flowed so fast and furiously that he'd needed this excitement so that he could come down slowly. But more often now he only wanted peaceful conversation, soft music and the warmth of friends.

One look around the room told him that friends, real friends, were in short supply tonight. His band had already come and gone. The best of the myriad people who traveled with him weren't here. The place was filled with strangers and people he didn't want to know better.

Harry took his elbow and led him across the room to

introduce him to a small group of men in business suits. He was still making the rounds ten minutes later, listening politely and commenting when it was called for. Someone had gotten him a drink; someone else had given him a plate of food, which he'd had to set down somewhere in the middle of the room to shake a hand.

He was hungry, his head hurt, and his ears rang from all the noise. As he smiled and conversed he backed slowly toward the door, signaling his bodyguard and driver to go for his car.

A soft, warm body stopped his progress.

"Oh, I'm sorry."

He heard the woman's voice before he saw her. He was apologizing as he turned. "No, it's my fault. I..."

Pale ivory cheeks turned pink at his words. He hadn't seen a woman blush in years. For most of the women he knew, it would have been pointless. This one did it naturally, but then, everything about her seemed natural. She was a dark-eyed beauty with long hair that was as black and shiny as a raven's wing. She wore very little makeup, just enough to enhance the delicate features that Mother Nature had blessed her with. She was tiny. The top of her head barely came up to his chin, but she was no child. In a hip-hugging dress the scarlet of tulips, she was every inch a woman.

"I'm clumsy." He recovered quickly. He had met a million women at parties like this one, and too many times he had been disappointed.

"No, I was in the way." She smiled. "I liked the concert."

Liked, not loved. She liked it. She wasn't gushing with praise. She liked it. "Did you?" he asked. "I'm glad."

"I have a neighbor who claims that when he was a boy he could hear you playing the guitar in your aunt's barn all the way from his house."

He tilted his head to get a better look at her. "Really?"

She held out her hand. "I'm Robin Lansing. From the *Farnham Falls Gazette*. Thank you for sending us tickets."

He absorbed it all. She was from Farnham Falls. She knew an old neighbor, someone who had known him as a child. "Us?"

"Yes. My friend Judy. She's here somewhere."

Someone put a hand on his shoulder to get his attention, but Devin ignored it. "Do you like the party as well as the concert?"

"I don't like it at all." She smiled. Her entire face lit up, and he felt bathed in sunshine. "Not until now, anyway. I'm glad I got to meet you."

"Is that why you came?"

"I came to see if I could get an interview, but I can see that's going to be impossible."

"Why?"

"Because this is a zoo. We'd have to shout at each other."

"You're not nearly pushy enough to do what you do for a living."

"Probably not. But most people seem to want to talk to me, anyway."

He wanted to talk to her. Devin suspected this woman might be the only sane person in the room. He had become an excellent judge of character in the years of his career, particularly since his divorce. This woman believed in old-fashioned virtues like honesty and concern. He knew that after one minute in her company.

And she was as lovely and fresh as an Ohio spring. He wanted to know more.

"I'm starving," he said. "And I'm tired. I want something to eat and a friend to talk to. Would you like to be that friend?"

He saw the first tracing of wariness cross her features. "To talk to? Is that code for something else?"

This time he smiled. "Talk's what I'm asking for. *All* I'm asking for. You can tell me all about Farnham Falls. Are you willing?"

"May I take notes?"

"I'll tell you when."

"All right. But I need to let Judy know."

"I'll wait right here."

"We've got two choices," he told her, when she rejoined him and they threaded their way through the arena complex toward the place where his limo would meet them. He took her hand and ignored the security trio who trailed behind them. "We can try to find a restaurant that's open and hope I won't be recognized, or we can go back to my hotel and order from room service in my suite."

"Are you ever not recognized?"

"Nope."

"Then we'll go to your suite."

She was silent as they got into the limo and silent as they drove past a squad of cheering fans who had figured out where he would exit. She was silent in the hotel, too, as security whisked them through gathered crowds. She was silent until they got to his suite and closed the door behind them. "I'm beginning to get a feel for the way you live," she said.

"Daunting, isn't it?"

"Do you get used to it?"

"More or less. Less, tonight. I'm not in the mood to be a god."

"Are you ever?"

"Not really." He gestured toward the comfortable leather sofa, and she sat down. He smiled when she took off her shoes and tucked her feet under her skirt. "What do you want to eat?"

"A hot fudge sundae."

"A woman who knows her own mind."

"After you've had to make a few crucial decisions in your life, the little ones are a piece of cake."

He thought about that as he dialed and gave their order. Then he joined her on the sofa, sprawling an arm's length away. He wanted to ask her what crucial decisions she had made, but it seemed too personal. "Are you from Farnham Falls? Should I remember you?"

"No. I grew up outside of Columbus. I graduated from Ohio State."

"Ohio University for me."

"I know. I'm sorry I know so much about you, really. I'd like to hear it all from you, instead."

He would like to tell her, too. She was right. She was easy to talk to. She was certainly easy to look at. "Start with your childhood, and when we've finished your life we'll do mine. Then I want to hear all the Farnham Falls gossip."

"You must be a remarkably patient man, or a masochist."

"I'm just a man hungry for small-town life." Or for one particularly lovely small-town woman. Devin wasn't sure which, and right now it didn't even matter. He smiled lazily and settled in for the evening.

Robin didn't know how she ended up in Devin's arms slow dancing to an old Frozen Flame ballad. He had put on the compact disc to illustrate a point he'd been making about early nineties rock, and the next thing both of them knew, they were moving to the music together. The hour was late. Very late. In fact, it was nearly dawn, and they had been talking without a pause.

She had told him about herself, and he had filled in the things about himself that she hadn't learned from her research. They had laughed together, each delighting in the other's sense of humor. But as the hours had passed they had gotten more personal. She had told him about Jeff and the diagnosis of leukemia that had come just one month after their marriage. He had told her about his brief marriage to Wendy, a blues diva who sang with great conviction about love and in real life had no convictions about it at all.

She couldn't imagine a woman so cold that she couldn't love Devin Fitzgerald, if given the opportunity. Either he was the worst of charmers, the one-in-a-million phony who could get through Robin's personal radar screen, or he was one of the most genuine men she had ever met. She had watched him relax as their time together passed into hours. He was starved for this kind of conversation and intimacy, and she had realized just minutes into the conversation that she was, too.

She had also watched the expression in his eyes warm, and noticed the subtle shifts of his body so that little by little they drew closer. She knew he was attracted to her. She had tried from the moment he bumped into her not to be attracted to him. But it had been so long since she had felt this excitement in a man's presence. She didn't know if it was Devin the man or Devin the star that she was attracted to, and she didn't really care. She felt alive for the first time in years; alive and warm in places no man had touched since well before Jeff's death. She had begun to wonder if she was still a normal woman with normal urges. Now she knew that she was.

The ballad drifted into another, something she hadn't quite expected. She raised her head to smile at Devin, and he smiled back. Then, with a slow, fluid sweep, he lowered his head and touched her lips with his.

"You're so lovely," he whispered. "This has been very special."

It was just a touch, the briefest of kisses, but she knew it for what it was. He had asked her a question. If she answered yes, she could stay. And if she answered no, their time together had ended. It wasn't a threat. He was absolutely right. They had reached the peak of this kind of intimacy, and now they parted or progressed to another. Since the beginning of time men and women had understood this moment and exactly what it meant.

Robin didn't want to leave. Encircled by Devin's arms, she felt as if she was part of something again. She had known she was lonely; she just hadn't known how lonely. She had loved Jeff with all her heart, but his illness had been diagnosed before they'd had time to truly unite. And afterward she had never wanted to burden him with her feelings or problems. He had been given enough to bear.

As if he could read her mind, Devin spoke his question out loud. "Do you want to stay, or shall I have my driver take you back to your hotel?"

"It's been a long time since I've made love to anyone," she said simply.

"Me too."

She read his eyes and decided he was telling the truth. She believed he was an honorable man, despite constant temptation to be otherwise. "Do you think we'll remember what to do?"

"I think it's entirely possible."

She stretched up on her tiptoes and placed her lips against his. His arms tightened around her, and his hands urged her closer.

She was so quickly immersed in desire that there was no time to rethink her decision. She had no hopes that she would ever see Devin again or that this night would lead to something real and permanent between them. This night was a gift from one lonely soul to another, and she gave it generously, without a single doubt that she was doing the right thing.

Chapter Three

"When were you going to tell me? Or were you going to tell me at all?" Devin turned the key in the ignition, and the Cherokee started right up.

Robin heard the slight pause after his first question, a pause where her name should have been. But Devin didn't remember her name. He might not even have recognized her if she hadn't called him Devin.

She closed her eyes and took a deep breath. Then another. The contractions were coming too fast. She was so afraid that the baby had been injured. She had been wearing a seat belt when the car had gone into a spin, but there had been little room between her and the steering wheel. She had braced herself the moment she'd realized there was nothing she could do except slide into the ditch, but she wasn't sure the baby was still all right. She just wasn't sure.

Tears slid down her cheeks. She didn't want to cry. She wanted to be calm for the baby's sake. But she felt as if she was being torn in two, physically and emotionally. She couldn't believe that Devin Fitzgerald was sitting beside her. She wondered if fate was convulsed in hysterical laughter at her expense.

"Where are we going?"

It took her a moment to register his question. Then she realized what he'd asked. "The hospital's…too far away."

"Where is this doctor?"

"Up the road. Turn right. Another mile or two. Maybe…more." The last word ended in a moan as another contraction began.

He shifted gears, and the car began to crawl along the road. He picked up a car phone attached to the dashboard, then slammed it down again. "Damn!"

She tried to breathe the way she'd been taught. But Judy wasn't here to help her. Judy had been her partner in the childbirth classes, and Judy was still in Cincinnati. The baby was making its appearance two weeks early.

"In through your nose and out through your mouth," Devin said.

"What…do you know about…it?"

"I was a labor coach once. For a friend. Just do what I tell you, damn it. In through your nose and out through your mouth. I'll help you count to ten."

"Shut up!" Robin closed her eyes.

"One! Two!"

She slapped her hands over her ears.

He grabbed her hand. "Stop fighting me! I'm trying to help. You've got to calm down!"

"You don't even…remember my name!"

"Look, you only said it once. At a backstage party with sixty people breathing down my neck! And I was embarrassed to ask you again at the hotel. I was going to peek at your driver's license the next morning while you showered. But you left before I even woke up!"

"Just drive!"

He slapped his hand back on the wheel. "One! Two!"

"Stop! Please stop! It's stopped."

"Tell me your name."

"Please! Just drive."

"I'm going to pull over to the side of the frigging road unless you tell me your name!"

She knew he didn't mean it, but his threat of doing something that childish made her realize how childish *she* was being. "Robin."

"Do you have a last name?"

"Lansing."

"And the baby's last name?"

She clamped her lips shut.

"You were going to have my baby, and you weren't going to tell me. What were you going to do? Wait until it was born and sock me with a paternity suit?"

"You bastard!"

"Yeah, you called me that before."

She opened her eyes and saw how white he was, and how angry. "I tried to talk to you. Your manager promised he'd give you my message. That's…all…I owed…you!"

"What's his name?"

She didn't understand. He turned and looked at her.

"My manager. What's his name?"

He didn't believe her. She was filled with such fury that she didn't even consider her next action. She slammed her fist into his arm as hard as she could, then once more. Then she began to cry.

"Damn it! You're probably in transition." Devin

pushed down on the gas pedal. The car began to slide. "We'll talk about this later. Right now we're just going to help this baby get born. Are you with me? Can we do that much right?"

"I'm...not...in transition!" Robin knew exactly what that meant. It was the shortest, most intense—and emotional—part of labor. Right before the baby made its entrance.

"How long have you been in labor?"

She tried to think, but the accident had ruined her grasp of time. "I don't...know."

"Do you know what time it started?" His voice was calm, now. Deadly calm.

She tried to remember. "Seven? Eight?"

"This morning?"

"Tonight."

"Then it's a fast labor."

"The blizzard—" She couldn't finish. She had expected pain, but not pain like this. She wanted to die.

"What are you doing way out here, anyway?"

"I...house-sitting. My managing editor... Florida... I didn't think there'd be a... And the baby's not due for..."

He mumbled something appropriately profane. "Were you going to wait out the storm?"

She nodded.

"Robin, breathe with me. Please. It will help."

She wanted to scream at him again, but she had no breath to do it. She found herself breathing along with him instead.

"Is it helping?" he asked.

"No!" she gasped.

"Then we're going to pant."

She remembered that technique from her childbirth classes. She was supposed to pant like a dog, then blow out all the air, take a deep breath and start all over again. She had been so gripped by panic that she had forgotten everything she had learned. She began to pant with him. Just when she was certain she was going to die, the pain began to subside.

She took a final deep breath. From the corner of her eye she could tell that Devin was looking at his watch. "We're not going to make it to the doctor, Robin. I'm not even sure we could get there in time if the roads were clear and the sun was shining. Your contractions are too close, and they're lasting too long. You're about to deliver."

"No!"

"My house is just up ahead. I can probably get you there. We're going to have to do this ourselves."

She socked his arm again, but weakly. "No!"

"I can get you through this. Damn it, we don't have any choice!"

She was sobbing for real, now. If only she'd left the house at the first sign of snow. But she'd only had a few twinges, nothing more than mild cramps, and she hadn't really believed she was in labor. Then later, when she was fairly certain she was, the snow had been coming down hard. She had expected the labor to last well into the next morning, when the storm would subside and the roads would be clear. She'd thought she could send a neighbor for her doctor if the phones weren't restored. She would have been fine.

She would never have met up with Devin Fitzgerald again.

"Five more minutes," he said. "Just hang on for five more minutes. Then you can have this baby."

She wanted to argue. She wanted Dr. Wright, with his calm voice, capable hands and five hundred babies to his credit. She opened her mouth to tell Devin so, when a new sensation nearly overwhelmed her.

She wanted to push.

She groaned and clamped her lips together again. The baby was coming.

Devin glanced at her, then leaned forward over the steering wheel, gripping it harder. He was whispering something. She thought it was a prayer. She needed prayers, and, God help her, she needed Devin's assistance.

"Pant," he said. "Pant as hard as you can. We're almost there."

She panted, but the desire to push nearly overwhelmed her. An alien force had taken over her body. Her body no longer belonged to her, although she could still feel everything that was happening to it. She squeezed her eyes closed and panted, forcing out air in a gust when she needed to.

"Almost there." The car fishtailed. She could feel it sliding beneath them, but she was beyond concern. The baby was on its way whether this car landed in a ditch or not. She was going to have the baby whether she wanted to or not.

The car stopped, and she heard a door slam. A gust of wind swept over her, and she felt Devin's arms beneath her again. "Hang on. Just hang on another minute."

The contraction ceased, but she knew the respite would be short. Her eyes were still closed, and snow fell against her eyelids. She couldn't find the strength to open them. She knew she was going to need whatever strength she had to bring her son or daughter into the world.

She didn't know how much time passed. Another contraction began, and Devin gripped her harder. She panted, but she was too frightened and too exhausted to control the pain. She made a valiant effort, but the desire to push overwhelmed her. Her body pushed without her help. The baby was tired of waiting.

The snow ceased, and so did the wind. She heard another door slam, and she opened her eyes. They were in a dark hallway; then they were moving up stairs.

"You're going to have that baby in a bed after all," Devin said.

His voice sounded strange. Far away, and sad. She gazed up at his face and saw tears glistening in his eyes.

She had been so angry at him. She was still angry. But mixed with anger was something else, although she didn't care enough to figure out what it was. All her thoughts turned inward. She and the baby were in this together. The baby and her own agony were all she could think about.

She felt something soft beneath her. She opened her eyes again but found she was in darkness.

"The lights are out, Robin. I'm going to have to wash my hands and find a lamp or some candles. Breathe like you've never breathed before."

The last words drifted away, as if he was leaving the room. She wanted to call him back. He had gotten her into this predicament, and he could damn well get her out of it. But she couldn't call him. Another contraction began, and she felt her body bearing down. She had promised herself that she wouldn't scream when she gave birth. She had handled everything life had thrown at her without screaming. But the promise died on a wave of sound that could only have come from her.

The darkness was shattered by the glow of a kerosene lamp. Devin set it on a dresser not far from the bed. "My hands. Then I'll be back."

"Don't go!"

"I have to!"

Her voice caught somewhere between a sob and another scream. Her head tossed from side to side as if it didn't belong to her. Now she could see that she was in a bedroom, but she didn't care one bit. She just wanted the baby to be born. In a snowdrift, under tropical seas, on camelback. She didn't care.

"All right, sweetheart. Let's get this thing done."

She looked up and saw Devin's face. "I can't!"

His smile was brave. "You're going to, whether you want to or not. Your choices are limited."

She felt his hands against her hips, sliding her pants to her knees. She wanted to slap away those hands. She remembered them touching her with this kind of intimacy once before, and then the aftermath.

"Just another couple of inches." He slid off her boots, then the pants and panties beneath them. "Good girl. I'm going to slide a couple of clean towels under you. Now let's prop up your legs. I'm going to have to check your progress."

"No!"

"Robin, sweetheart. Of course I have to check. Unless you want to do it yourself."

She called him something she had never called anyone before. His laughter sounded strained. "You're absolutely right. But I still have to check."

Suddenly whether he checked or not seemed immaterial. She felt the urge to push out their child, and she felt it so strongly that she couldn't do anything except grip the sheets beneath her and bear down.

"Dark hair. Lots of it, I think." His voice sounded strained, too, although he was obviously trying to reassure her. "One more push will take care of the head. Everything's completely normal. No arms or legs in view."

"How…would you…know?"

"You did the damned interview. I was training to be a doctor."

"You quit!"

"Not before I sat through half-a-dozen obstetrics lectures and a trio of movies."

"Movies!"

"Rest. Gather your strength for one last push, okay? Then you can relax and let me take over."

"Never."

She felt a hand against her cheek. "You were there, Robin," he said softly. "I didn't do anything you didn't want that night. And I used protection. You know I did."

"It…didn't…work."

"Let's get this baby born, then we'll talk."

"I'm going to…die."

"No, you're not. I've never lost a patient."

"You never…had one."

He laughed, but it was forced.

She tensed suddenly. Her body seemed to explode. She gripped the sheets again.

"Grab your legs. Like this." He helped her get hold of them. "Okay, pull against them as you push. Push hard. Harder. Let's meet this kid once and for all."

She pushed, despite the pain, despite her exhaustion, despite the indignity of having Devin Fitzgerald between her legs. Suddenly the pain stopped. She felt a relief so total that for a moment she thought she had died. Then she heard a baby's weak cry.

"A boy," Devin said. "Perfect, and breathing on his own already."

She felt something warm against her abdomen. Her legs collapsed to the bed, and she looked down to see her son. "Oh, my God…"

"I've got to find something to tie off the cord and cut it with. Don't move. He needs your warmth."

She heard Devin rummaging around in the dresser, but she felt as if she were floating somewhere far away. Her baby was here. Her son.

"Okay. I've got what I need."

"Is he really…all right?"

"Better than that."

She watched Devin tie off the cord with something that looked like shoelaces, and snip it with what looked like embroidery scissors.

"We're lucky all this stuff is here. My cousin didn't take many of my aunt's things from the house when she moved."

"Your cousin?"

"I bought this house from her. This is the house where I grew up."

She knew exactly where they were, then. The house had been pointed out to her once, before Devin had become the father of her child. She had avoided this road ever since.

Until tonight.

"Okay. I'm going to wrap him up. Then you can hold him. But we're not quite finished with you yet."

She knew she should feel completely humiliated. But all she could think about was the fact that her baby was about to be placed in her arms. Her son was crying. Little tired cries that were growing louder. She wanted to comfort him more than she had ever wanted anything in her life.

Devin nestled the baby in her arms. "If you've got the strength to raise yourself a little, I can tuck another pillow under you to prop you up."

She managed nicely, although she was shaking all over. She cuddled her son as Devin took care of the final details, sliding clean sheets under her at last and covering her with a warm blanket.

"Are you going to nurse him?"

She looked up. Some part of her wanted to tell him it was none of his business, but she couldn't. She had been angry at him for so long. Angry at him for getting her pregnant. Angry at him for ignoring her when she had tried to get in touch with him. But she couldn't dredge up any anger now. Not with her newborn son in her arms; the son he had started on this journey and had just brought into the world.

"Just try and...stop me."

He sat on the bed beside her. "You can start now, if you'd like. It's good for you."

"I'm so weak."

"I'll help."

She started to refuse. But this was her son, and she wanted to comfort him.

Devin unbuttoned her blouse. She looked up at him

as he did. His eyes were on her face. "I have the right to know, Robin."

Robin knew what he meant. Devin believed he had the right to know if this was really his son. She had told him that he was the baby's father, but she had also told him that he wasn't. "Your manager's name is Harry." She felt his hand against her skin and the cloth of her blouse parting. "Harry Bagley."

"He never told me. Not a word."

"I suppose…he hoped I'd just go away."

"And you did."

"I didn't…want anything from you. I…never have. I just thought—"

"I'd want to know?"

She nodded.

He circled her and the baby with his arms, finding the clasp of her bra underneath her and lifting her slightly so that he could undo it. Then he released her and lifted the bra so that she could bring the baby to her breast.

The baby, *their* baby, knew exactly what to do.

"Now, that's a strong instinct," Devin said, watching them.

She began to cry. She didn't know why, exactly; couldn't figure out which of a million reasons had suddenly hit her with enough impact to bring tears.

"Robin." Devin stroked her hair back over her ears. "I'm so sorry I didn't recognize you at first. I can't believe this. Any of this."

She cried harder.

He continued to stroke her hair. He forced a little laugh. "You've got to admit, you looked a little different last spring. Your hair was long. You were thinner."

"Thank you."

"For saying you were thinner?"

"For rescuing me. Us. For helping."

His hand stilled. "I suppose you think I'm the kind of man who wouldn't care enough to help you."

"Exactly."

"I didn't know about the baby, Robin. Harry didn't tell me. Harry's about to be fired."

"No. It's over now. The baby's here. You know…he's yours. That's all I ever wanted."

"And what if that's not enough for me?"

She looked up at him. The baby was still nursing contentedly. She found it hard to be firm with tears running down her cheeks, but she tried. "It will have to be."

"No. This is my son, too. My child."

"We don't need you."

"That's not what this is about. He's my child. I'm his father. *That's* what it's about." He lifted the baby from her arms.

She sat forward, panicked. Then she realized he was only helping her switch the baby to her other breast. She clutched the baby hard when Devin settled him against her again—so hard that he gave a yelping cry of protest before he began to nurse. "You can't have him!"

"Hey, calm down. I'm not going to take him away from you."

"I can support him. I have a decent job here."

"I know you do."

She thought fast. Devin was obviously having an attack of conscience. If he wasn't allowed to do something, the consequences might be disturbing. "Look, start a trust fund…or something." She closed her eyes.

"A college fund in case he wants to go somewhere… more expensive than I could manage."

"Do you think this is about guilt? Do you think that will make me feel I'm off the hook?"

"You're not on the hook. I'm releasing you. Swim away."

Devin was silent. She watched her son nursing. *Her* son. But her emotions were so confusing that she couldn't enjoy it in all the ways that she should have been able to.

"You told Harry I was the baby's father?" he asked.

"I told you I did."

"Then if you try to deny it, I have enough proof to demand a paternity test. Harry will testify."

Her eyes narrowed, and she looked up at him. "Just a while ago you were accusing me…of demanding one."

"Do you have any idea how many women each year claim that I've fathered their babies? Women I've never seen in my life?"

She stared at him.

"I know this is my son." His voice caught. "I'm sorry I doubted you for even a moment. Will you forgive me?"

She didn't nod or shake her head. Her gaze didn't flicker.

"I want to be part of his life."

"No." She had to force herself not to tighten her arms around the baby.

"Yes. He's mine. But I'm not going to take him away from you. I promise that. Just let me visit. Let me be part of his life. Let me watch him grow up. He'll need me, Robin. If you love him, you must know that."

She was trapped, as surely as if she had married this man in a crowded cathedral. They were irrevocably bound together because of the baby nursing at her breast; a son who would need his father.

"You're a stranger." Tears filled her eyes. "It was a one-night stand."

He didn't protest. "We needed each other that night. And now, whether you know it or not, we need each other again. You need my help and support, and I need your cooperation." He touched the baby's head, stroking it as he had stroked her hair. "And he needs us both."

She couldn't respond. The words caught in her throat.

"Do you have a name for him?"

She shook her head.

"He's a North Pole baby. Shall we call him Nicholas? Nicholas Fitzgerald?"

She looked away. She couldn't tell Devin that before the birth she had nearly settled on the name Nicholas for a boy, and that she had only waited until he was in her arms to make the final decision.

It seemed like a sign. She closed her eyes. She could not banish Devin from their lives, despite her urgent need to do so.

He was a stranger, but Devin Fitzgerald was Nicholas's father.

Chapter Four

Devin lifted Nicholas high and watched his son break into an ear-to-ear grin. "Mommy's coming back soon," he promised. "She's always right on time."

Nicholas chortled and drooled simultaneously. At six months he still had his mother's dark hair, but he also had his father's pale blue eyes. His face was shaped like Devin's, too. If Devin had harbored any doubts that this baby was his, they had dissolved the first time he'd gotten to examine Nicholas thoroughly. Devin still had some of his own baby pictures. This child belonged to him.

He lowered Nicholas to his lap, and the baby's chin began to wobble. "You miss your mommy, don't you, Nick? You don't like being away from her for so long. Even if you're with me."

Devin rose and shoved Nicholas under his arm like a football. Nick squealed with delight. Devin began a slow whirl. "And it's a rush to the ten-yard line. Steve Young passes the ball and its a—"

"Touchdown?" Robin slammed the door behind her.

Her arms were filled with groceries. "More boy stuff, huh?" She smiled, but, as always, her eyes were wary.

Devin stopped whirling. "I'm glad you're back. He was starting to miss you."

"Let me put these away, then I'll take him." She kissed the top of Nicholas's head as she passed by, but she was careful not to touch Devin.

Devin followed her into the kitchen, Nicholas still tucked securely under his arm. "I think he's hungry."

"Did you give him his cereal?"

"What little he'd take. He'll want more after you've nursed him."

"I left you a bottle."

"He doesn't want a bottle. He wants his mommy."

"Everybody and their great-aunt Tillie has told me I should wean him."

"Are you going to?"

"Nope." Robin set the grocery bags on the kitchen table. "Not until he wants me to."

"I'm glad."

She looked up at him as if to say that was nice but she didn't really care. He held her gaze, and she smiled at last. "Well, we're in agreement," she said. "That's good, I guess. One decision of about a million we'll have to agree on in the years to come."

"Robin, I've told you before. I'm not in this to control you. I just want to be part of his life."

She didn't answer. Instead she looked away. "Did he get a good nap?"

"No."

"Really? He always sleeps a couple of hours in the afternoon."

"I hovered over him hoping he'd wake up, and he did after half an hour. He's got me figured out by now."

She rummaged through the bags for a half gallon of ice cream and two boxes of frozen vegetables and slipped them in the freezer.

It was Devin's freezer. Two weeks after Nicholas's birth, Devin had convinced Robin to move into his child-hood home. He didn't live here with her, of course. When he was in town visiting Nicholas, Devin stayed nearby at a small bed-and-breakfast with discreet owners who had agreed to keep his presence in the area a secret.

He had wanted to give Robin the house free and clear, but she had refused to accept it. She had refused child support, as well, but he had finally persuaded her that living in his house made sense. She wouldn't have to pay rent for her town house, and she would have more privacy. *They* would have more privacy when he visited, which he did twice a month.

So far they had kept Devin's paternity a secret. Nicholas's birth certificate claimed that someone named "William Fitzgerald" was the baby's father. Since William was actually Devin's first name and Devin his middle name, the certificate didn't lie. There were a host of Fitzgeralds in the area. And since Devin had bought the house under the name "William Fitzgerald," no one seemed to have made the connection to the most famous Fitzgerald of all.

But both Devin and Robin knew it was just a matter of time until the truth was made public. Someone would see Devin at the airport and trace him to the house in Farnham Falls. Someone would see him in town despite the fact that he came and went under cover of darkness.

But Robin and Devin were hoping to keep their secret for as long as possible.

"You must be tired and more than ready to go. I'll take him now." Robin held out her arms.

Devin reluctantly gave her their son. Nicholas wasn't reluctant at all. He began to swat at Robin's breasts with his fists and whimper.

"Just like a man," Devin said.

"I hope you don't mind, but I'd better nurse him now. Can you let yourself out?"

"You know, I wanted to get some pictures of him, and I just plain forgot. You don't mind if I stay until after he's finished?"

She looked up at him. "You were here all afternoon, Devin."

"I was busy. He's a handful."

Devin watched Midwestern manners war with a mother's fears. "I could make dinner while you nurse him," he offered.

"You cook?"

"I'm not completely irrelevant."

"I really think you should go."

"I'd really like to stay."

She closed her eyes. He knew how tired she was. She had managed to work out a way to keep her job and still do a lot of it at home so that she could be with Nicholas at the same time. But the arrangement had taken its toll. She used the days when Devin was visiting Nick to catch up on all her errands. She never seemed to rest.

"Let me cook dinner," he said. "Please?"

"What else do you want?"

"I've always liked the way you come straight to the point."

"I don't like the way you're scurrying around it."

"I want some more time with my son." That was part of the truth, of course, but not all of it. "I don't think that's too much to ask, do you? I'd like to put him to bed tonight."

"I don't know if I have anything in the fridge that you'd know how to make."

"I brought steaks with me, a salad and a bottle of red wine. I can broil. And I can microwave a couple of potatoes."

She opened her eyes. "You planned this?"

"I hoped you'd let me. I still do."

"I don't know if this is such a good idea. We've got things worked out between us now, more or less. I don't like the idea of making changes."

"We're talking about one night, Robin."

She sighed. "All right. I guess it would be nice if you had a chance to tuck Nick in."

He smiled. He supposed, if he was a completely honest man, he would push on and tell her that he would like a chance to tuck her in, too. Right after he'd made excruciatingly sweet love to her. But that was going to have to wait.

He turned away before she could see any trace of that thought in his eyes. "I'll put the rest of the groceries away, then I'll start on dinner. Nick's patience is about all used up."

"Thanks."

He listened to Robin's retreat. He could see it in his mind. The sway of her hips as she walked, the way she pillowed Nick against her soft, soft breasts, the way delicate wisps of hair tickled the back of her neck.

In the past six months, as he had slowly positioned himself in her life, he had memorized every little detail about Robin Lansing.

"You are an insatiable little boy who is always going to get everything he wants, aren't you?" Robin cooed the words as Nicholas nursed contentedly, one hand spread wide against her breast as if to hold her in place.

She rocked him as he nursed. On one of his visits Devin had told her that this rocking chair had rocked generations of Fitzgerald children. She didn't know exactly how that made her feel. She didn't want to be part of the Fitzgerald legacy, but she understood the benefit for Nicholas. She hoped she wouldn't pass on her worst fears to her son—fears that Devin would someday grow tired of this arrangement and sue for custody. Or the opposite; fears that Devin would someday grow tired of this arrangement and abandon the son who had grown to love him.

Devin had given her no reason to be afraid. He had promised repeatedly that he would never take Nicholas from her, and he certainly had shown no signs of tiring of his son. Yet she had experienced so much loss in her life already that she was terrified of losing more. And Nicholas was everything to her now.

Almost everything.

She glanced toward the kitchen. She couldn't see much from this angle, but occasionally she caught a glimpse of Devin striding back and forth. He was large enough to take up a sizable portion of the kitchen, and his long steps took him quickly from one end to the other. In the smallest of rooms he moved with electric energy, just as he did on a concert stage.

She remembered that energy in the most intimate of ways. He made love the way he did everything in his life; with restless intensity and complete concentration.

She remembered.

She shook her head and switched Nicholas to the other breast, trying to put the thought of Devin as a lover out of her mind. He was not here as a lover, but as the father of her son. And despite the arrangement they had worked out one tension-filled step at a time, she was increasingly uneasy.

When Devin had first begun to visit he had been religious about arriving and leaving at the times they had agreed on. Now he seemed to find almost any excuse to stay longer. He adored his son. She knew that was every mother's wish, yet the depth of his love frightened her.

When was he going to realize that he could have more of Nicholas than he was settling for? When was he going to take her to court and demand more?

When was he going to realize that she was so head over heels in love with him that just the sight of him at her front door twice a month made her want to throw herself into his arms and beg him to love her, too?

Robin didn't know when she had fallen in love with Devin Fitzgerald. Perhaps it had been that first and fateful night together. Afterward, despite everything she had told herself at the time, she had foolishly hoped that he would call. She hadn't left Devin a number, but he certainly knew what town she lived in. She would have been easy to locate at the newspaper.

But there had been no phone calls, no flowers or notes. She had continually reminded herself that neither of them had made a commitment. They had indulged in the perfect one-night stand, and it should be a glorious memory.

And it might have been, someday, if she hadn't discovered soon after that she was pregnant.

"How do you like your steak?" Devin came to rest exactly where she had been staring.

"Medium."

"Me too. Another thing we have in common."

"Steaks and one greedy little boy. We're on a roll." She tried to smile.

"I seem to remember more than that. Wasn't there one spectacular April night when we talked till dawn? I thought we'd discovered a lot in common."

Her breath caught, and she looked down at Nicholas. "The thing I remember most clearly about that night was the epilogue."

"Not me."

She looked up again, but he had disappeared. Her cheeks warmed. Their night together—"spectacular," had he called it?—had been off conversational limits until now. Neither of them had mentioned it in all the months since Nicholas's birth. It was almost as if their child had been conceived without sex as well as without love.

Nicholas finished nursing at last, and she laid him against her shoulder to burp him, although he could do it quite well without her help.

Devin appeared in the doorway again. "Would you like me to take him so that you can change?"

"I wasn't planning to."

"Why don't you get into something comfortable? You're home. You should relax."

She would have protested, except that it seemed like a good idea. She was still wearing a dress and panty hose. She held out their son, and Devin came over to take him. He leaned over, and his arm lightly grazed her breast as he lifted Nicholas. Her breath caught. She was acutely sensitive to his touch. She remembered his lips in the same place.

Devin's eyes flicked down, and she realized her dress was still unbuttoned and her bra undone. Her cheeks heated again. She stood and turned away, fastening her bra and buttoning her dress as she crossed to the stairs.

His voice was husky. "Robin, are you getting dressed again so that you'll have more to do when you undress completely in a few seconds?"

"I have some modesty left." She didn't turn around.

"Too bad."

She hazarded a glance over her shoulder, but Devin and Nicholas were already back in the kitchen.

Upstairs, she stripped off everything and decided to take a quick shower. The woman staring back at her from the bathroom mirror couldn't really be in love with a world-famous rock star. She looked much too sensible. Take her haircut, for example. She had cut it short to lessen the demands on her time before Nicholas was born. And earrings. She had given up wearing earrings in her pierced ears because Nicholas liked to pull on them. She wore almost no makeup, and she hadn't gone shopping for anything new to wear since before her pregnancy. She looked a little tired, a little harried.

She looked like every other new mother in the world.

She didn't look like someone who was insane enough to be in love with Devin Fitzgerald.

In the shower she inspected her body with a practiced eye. She was slender again, although her breasts were certainly larger. She had several fine, silvery stretch marks across her abdomen, but it was flat enough to please her. All in all, she had survived the pregnancy well. But not well enough to appeal to a man with his pick of women the world over.

She had planned to dress with that in mind, but she found herself choosing spruce-green leggings and a matching scoop-necked T-shirt that ended mid-thigh. At the last minute she found some simple gold studs that might escape Nick's notice and threaded them through her ears. She added a gold locket just before she started down the stairs.

"Much better," Devin said when she entered the kitchen. "You look…comfortable."

She told herself she wasn't disappointed that "comfortable" was the best he could manage. "Do you need help?"

"No. Sit. Have a glass of wine. The urchin's had mashed banana and rice cereal, so don't let him con you into thinking he needs more."

She looked at Nicholas, who was swatting at toys on the tray of his high chair. He was a beautiful little boy, rosy-cheeked and big-eyed. "He's going to be huge."

"I was a big baby. I'll bring you pictures sometime."

"He doesn't look anything like me."

"No, and I'm hoping he doesn't have your temper, either."

"What's that supposed to mean?"

"Aren't you the same lady who slugged me three times when she was in labor?"

She was beginning to tire of blushing. "I guess I never said I was sorry for that."

"You had a lot on your mind. Besides, it's common knowledge that women in labor like to take it out on their partners."

"You weren't exactly my partner."

"Maybe not, but I got you into this."

"No, you were right about that the night Nicholas was born. We did it together. I remember being there."

"Do you?"

Her voice sounded strangely breathy. "Uh-huh."

"Funny thing. So do I. I remember it well. And I remember thinking how wonderful it felt to go to sleep with you in my arms. Then I woke up the next morning and you were gone. No note. No phone number. Nothing. It seemed like a pretty clear message."

She stared at her wineglass without saying anything in return.

"Why did you leave like that?"

She shook her head. She didn't know how to explain what it had felt like to wake up beside him, to realize what she'd done and with whom. Panic had set in. She was no rock-star groupie, and sex had always meant more to her than pleasure. It had meant commitment and love. It had meant Jeff.

"I picked up the telephone more than once over the next weeks to call your paper and wheedle your name and phone number from them," he said.

"Why didn't you?"

"A lot of reasons, I guess. I was just getting over a

bad marriage and wasn't ready for new entanglements. I was embarrassed that I didn't know your name. And I was afraid I'd make your guilt worse if I called you."

"Guilt?"

"Wasn't that why you left? You felt like you'd been unfaithful to your husband?"

She let out a long breath. "I think you'd better flip the steaks."

"I've done that. They're ready."

She watched him open the oven door and slide the steaks onto a platter. His words were like cannons going off in her head. She didn't want to believe him.

He was seated and they were eating before he spoke again. "Do you have many thoughts about the future, Robin? Do you think you'll stay here to raise Nicholas?"

She shook her head. "No. It's perfect now, and I love Farnham Falls. But I want better schools for him and more opportunities. I think he'll need music lessons, don't you?"

He smiled, and the expression in his eyes was so warm that it seemed to heat the air between them. "Yeah. But they could be arranged anywhere. And when he comes to visit me—"

"He won't be coming to visit you, Devin." She set down her fork. "You can see him here or wherever we are, but I never said that you could take him anywhere without me."

"No?"

She heard the steel in his voice. Her heart began to beat faster. "No. What can you be thinking? He'll go from being Nicholas Fitzgerald to being the illegitimate son of Devin Fitzgerald. What kind of experience would that be?"

"Is that it, or are you afraid I'll forget to bring him back?"

She balled up her napkin and set it on the table as she rose. "I think you've overstayed your welcome."

Devin rose, too. Nicholas, sensing the tension, or perhaps just from exhaustion, began to cry.

Devin stroked Nicholas's hair. "I'm his father, not a kidnapper. I love him. I'll always want what's best for him. And I know that means living with you. But when he's older I'll also want to have him with me sometimes. Surely you can understand that."

She *could* understand it. That was the hard part. She could understand it, but it frightened her so much.

Devin sat down. "Sit down. Please. Finish dinner. I'm not trying to take Nick away from you."

She reached for Nicholas instead, to comfort him or herself, she wasn't sure. She brought him back to her seat.

"How did that get started?" Devin asked. "We're fighting about the future. Who knows where we'll be by then, or what we'll feel?"

"I already know what it feels like to lose the person I loved most in the whole wide world. I couldn't live through it again."

"You won't have to."

"You don't understand."

He didn't smile. "Oh, I think I do. All too well."

She supposed Devin was talking about his ex-wife, although according to everything he'd told her, theirs had never been a fairy-tale marriage. "I'm sorry. I guess you do."

"All these doubts and fears are going to eat away at both of us unless we put an end to them now. And in the long run that's going to be bad for Nicholas."

She nodded, ashamed, but still wary.

Devin reached for her hand and covered it with his. She worked overtime not to touch him, but she couldn't seem to make herself pull away. "We need to give him the gift of our friendship," he said. "Can we work on that?"

"We aren't friends, Devin."

"But we could be. If you'd let us."

She couldn't imagine being Devin's friend. Her feelings were too tumultuous, too intense, for friendship.

"Will you try?" he asked.

She nodded again.

"We'll take it slowly. Then one morning you'll wake up and wonder how you ever existed without my...friendship."

"Think so?" She made herself pull away. She lifted her fork. Nicholas was now playing contentedly with her locket.

"I have to think so," Devin said. "I have all our best interests in mind."

Chapter Five

Robin heard squeals coming from the living room of the house even before she opened the front door. She couldn't fault Devin for playing with his own son, particularly when he only saw him for two days, twice a month. But the squeal foretold a frantic baby by bedtime. On the days that Devin visited, Nicholas was always hard to get to sleep. Already he adored his father, and he seemed to know that if he closed his eyes, when he woke up Devin wouldn't be there.

From the foyer she could see that the two men in her life were playing hide-and-seek. The game was still relatively uncomplicated. At eight months Nicholas had not yet graduated to crouching in closets or basement corners. Devin could hide behind the same sofa time and time again, and it was more than all right with Nicholas.

Robin's head ached; her neck was stiff, and she felt as if she hadn't slept in weeks. She had taken a cut in pay to spend so many hours at home with Nicholas, but there really hadn't been a cut in her workload to go

along with it. Free time was a concept she might resur-
rect when Nicholas graduated from high school, but
until then, she had resigned herself to never reading a
novel, watching a sitcom or going out on a date again.

"You look whupped."

She smiled wanly, too exhausted for once to be wary
of what she was communicating to Devin. He looked
particularly wonderful this afternoon in dark brown
trousers and a woven shirt that was almost exactly the
golden brown of his hair. By the standards of his profes-
sion he was decidedly conservative. No tattoos or body
piercings marred his tanned skin. And she had seen
attorneys and accountants with longer hair.

She supposed that someday she might walk into a room
inhabited by Devin Fitzgerald and not feel this instant tug
at her heart. But she wasn't going to count on it.

"I finished at work," she said. "I thought I'd change
my clothes before I started in on my errands. Is Nick
doing all right?"

"Nick's fine. You're not. No errands."

"Excuse me?" She was almost too tired to be
annoyed, but not quite. Her temper soared.

"I said no errands. You're going to drop in your
tracks, Robin. Please. Take the afternoon off. Spend
some time with us."

If he hadn't said please, she might have thrown a
tantrum right then and there. Realizing how close she
had come to one made her realize something else. He
was exactly right. She was exhausted. She was not
particularly temperamental, yet these days she dissolved into tears at the slightest opportunity. This
morning at work she had snapped at a co-worker for

nothing more than a misplaced comma. She was head-ed for trouble.

She was so lost in her thoughts that she hadn't real-ized how close Devin had drawn to her. She felt his palm against her cheek, and God help her, she leaned into it like a dog aching to be petted.

His arms closed around her. Lightly, as if he wanted to let her know she could step away anytime. "I hate seeing you this way," he said softly. "This is supposed to be a good time in your life, Robin."

"It is." Her protest sounded weak, even to her own ears.

"May Nicholas Fitzgerald and his father have the pleasure of your company at a picnic this afternoon? Just the three of us? Then I'll do whatever I can to help you get everything else finished tonight."

"You? You're the mystery man. You can't even be seen at a grocery store."

"I'll wear a wig and sunglasses."

She gave a dry laugh. There wasn't a wig that had been made that would disguise him. "Even if that worked, you wouldn't know what to do at the laundromat."

"Laundromat? What's wrong with the washer and dryer?"

She cursed silently.

"Robin, you should have told me you were having problems. I'll have them fixed or order new appliances."

"Just the washer."

"Why didn't you tell me?"

She shrugged. She wanted to lean against him and feel his arms tighten around her. But that was exactly the reason why she hadn't told him about the washer. She didn't want to need Devin or anything he could give her. She had to do this on her own, or the consequences might be terrible for them all.

"What else isn't working?" he asked.

"Everything else is just fine."

"Then what else do you have to do?"

"Winter's coming. Nicholas needs a snowsuit and warm pajamas. I have to go to the post office to get stamps and mail a package. I have two sweaters at the cleaners'…." She paused. "This is deadly-dull stuff. Stuff you haven't done in years."

"Let's stop talking about what I haven't done. Will the grocery store and dry cleaner deliver?"

"If you pay them an arm and a leg."

"We'll pay it, then. Do you have catalogs for children's clothes?"

"Yes, but—"

"We'll look through them together tonight and make out an order. Will the rest of this stuff keep until tomorrow?"

"I suppose."

"Then let it go."

Devin was trying to take over her life, but despite her best instincts, she couldn't summon the energy to refuse. "What kind of picnic?"

"The kind I plan and execute perfectly. With whatever you happen to have in the refrigerator."

"There's not much. I could—"

He touched her lips with a finger to silence her. "You could change your clothes and lie down for a few moments of peace and quiet while the kid and I get everything ready."

She was supposed to say no. Enough of her mind was

still working to know that. But the temptation was too great. An afternoon with Devin and Nicholas. The three of them. Almost like a family.

Dangerous dreams.

His arms tightened subtly. She sagged a little closer. "It's going to be winter again before too long," he said. "It's a sin to waste the best days of autumn shopping for groceries and mailing packages."

"I don't know what to say."

"'Yes' will do for a start."

"The last time I said yes to you, Devin, I ended up in a snow-filled drainage ditch having your baby."

"But look how well it turned out."

She felt his lips against her forehead. By the time she was sure he had kissed her, he had released her, and it was too late to object.

"Scoot," he said. "Junior and I have a picnic to put together."

"I don't know…."

"Yes, you do."

And despite everything she had said, and every argument she hadn't articulated, he was right.

Devin plundered cabinets and the refrigerator, dressed Nicholas for a walk in the woods and called the dry cleaners to have them deliver Robin's sweaters and pick up the dirty laundry that afternoon. He ran a test cycle on the washing machine, discovered the problem—as well as the fact that he couldn't fix it—and called the nearest appliance store. They promised him a new machine by the end of the week.

He had made a tentative grocery list and gotten a

promise that they would deliver whatever he ordered in the early evening before he began to worry about Robin. She should have been downstairs by now. He had called up to her once to let her know he and Nicholas were ready. He went to the bottom of the stairs and tried again, but she still didn't appear.

"What do you think, champ? Maybe I ought to go get her?"

Nicholas, who was happily settled in a playpen with a new cloth book Devin had brought for him, just cooed and waved the book in answer. Then he began to gnaw at it.

Devin took the steps two at a time. He hesitated at Robin's door, then knocked softly. There was no answer.

He pushed open the door and stuck his head inside. "Robin?"

She had taken him at his word. She had lain down to rest, and now she was fast asleep.

For a moment he considered leaving her that way. She certainly needed the rest. But he knew she would be mad or embarrassed, or both, if he did. If she had to, she could sleep on a blanket in the meadow where the Fitzgerald men were planning to entertain her.

He crossed the room and sat on the bed beside her. She had changed into jeans, black jeans tight enough to stimulate his imagination—as well as a more visible portion of his anatomy. She had topped them with a royal blue tank top, and she had a buffalo plaid flannel shirt clutched in her hand, apparently to wear over it.

He wondered if Robin had any idea how hard he was finding all of this. He spent four days a month with Nicholas. During those four days he was lucky to spend two hours with Robin. He lived on dreams of her. He remembered the night they had made love. Everything had been so easy, so perfect. They had fit together as if they had been created for that one purpose alone. As passion had built he'd lost whatever objectivity he had started with and made love to her without thought of the future or of keeping a part of himself inviolate.

And the next morning he'd found himself in bed alone.

He had done everything wrong from that point on. He had been reluctant to follow up a perfect night with telephone calls, recriminations and pleas. He had known she must have been upset, to leave without saying goodbye. He had promised himself he would look for her again, when the time was right. But the time hadn't been right soon enough.

He reached out to stroke her hair. He liked her hair short, although he suspected he would like it any way she wore it. The top was still long enough to sift through his fingers when he touched it. He liked the way it swirled like fine black silk when she shook her head. He liked the way it fell into her eyes, the way she pushed it over her ears, the way it adorned her cheeks and the back of her neck.

He was a lovesick fool.

She was sleeping so soundly that his touch didn't wake her. He drew one index finger over her ear and across her cheek to the corner of her lips. He remembered exactly what those lips had felt like as he'd kissed them. She was a generous woman, and for those brief hours they'd had together, she had held back nothing. He wanted to test her lips now, test their softness, their heat, their acceptance of his kiss. He knew better, but he was seized with a longing so fierce that he found he had kissed her before he could talk himself out of it.

Her eyes opened slowly, and, still deep in dreams, he supposed, she smiled at him.

"A kiss for Sleeping Beauty." He sat up slowly. "I couldn't think of any other way to wake you."

"It's time-honored." She smiled sleepily.

"For good reasons." He smiled, too. He was almost afraid to breathe, terrified that something would break the spell.

Something did. A wail started downstairs.

Her eyes widened, and sleep fled. "You left Nicholas alone?"

"It's okay. He's in his playpen. It was just for a minute."

"Oh."

He stood before she could say anything else. "I'll get him. If you're too tired to go on the picnic…?"

"No, I'm coming."

"We're ready when you are." He made it to the door and beyond. She hadn't protested; she hadn't complained. He had kissed her, and she had smiled at him.

He was grinning as he clattered down the stairs to get their son.

"We're going to squash the wildflowers." Robin looked with alarm at the meadow Devin had chosen for their picnic. The afternoon was warm, and bees and butterflies had claimed it as their own. The meadow was only half a mile from the farmhouse through a forest of oak and wild cherry and across a narrow creek with a stepping-stone bridge. She had hiked here once before with Nicholas on her hip, but that day the journey had seemed a hundred miles. Now, with Devin carrying their son, it had only taken minutes.

"What do you suppose happens to wildflowers at the first frost?" Devin held out his hand.

"They burrow underground and wait out the winter?"

"Not exactly. They go squish. Jack Frost steps on them. Think of us as gardeners, spreading seeds for next year's meadow on the soles of our shoes."

She took his hand with some reluctance. This was entirely too cozy to suit the most rational part of her. Her, Devin, Nicholas. A field of nodding wildflowers and a vast, cloudless sky.

He tucked her hand under his arm as if he was afraid she might change her mind. They started down a dirt path. "It would have been a sin not to spend this day outside."

"Did you come here as a boy?"

"When I was a boy this area was fenced for cattle. I suppose I ought to rent it out for pasture. Sarah and her husband did. But I love the idea of it lying here, basking in the sun and producing nothing except chicory and daisy fleabane and black-eyed Susans."

"You know something about everything. You're surprisingly eclectic."

"For a rock musician?"

"I didn't say that."

"No, I did. It's easy, doing what I do, to forget about everything except the day-to-day trappings of fame and fortune."

"I forget sometimes that you have women all over the world sighing as the sound of your voice comes from their stereos."

"You forget sometimes?"

"Not often," she admitted.

Emilie Richards

"I didn't think so. It's always between us. My other life has yet to intrude, but it's always there in your mind."

She wasn't about to confess that she had bought every one of Devin's CDs and that she played them for Nicholas whenever Devin had been away from them for too long. And articles. Lord, the articles she'd read. She regularly stopped by the library to search out the gossip magazines to find out what Devin was doing when he wasn't with her. And now she had a subscription of her own to *Rolling Stone,* although she hid her growing collection when she knew Devin was going to be in town.

"Isn't your fame always in the back of your mind?" she asked. "Don't you always wonder if people react to you as a person or a rock star?"

"People in general, maybe. You? No."

She thought his words were a compliment and she nearly smiled.

"I *know* you're just reacting to me as rock star." He grinned over his shoulder as she narrowed her eyes. "I'm kidding."

"Well, there's some truth to it."

"Is there?"

"Don't you think this whole thing would be easier if you weren't who you are?"

"Sure. I think we'd be married now and starting on our second baby. You would have called me after our night together to tell me you were pregnant. I would have dragged you to the altar. Now I'd get up in the mornings and plow the back forty or deliver babies for a living. You'd stay home, change diapers and feel resentful that you'd been forced to marry a stranger."

"Not exactly a stranger. Close."

"The point is that any scenario can be easy or hard, depending on what we make of it. Musician. Farmer. Doctor. Lover. Friend. Husband." He shrugged.

"You've made this scenario as easy as you can. I'm…surprised."

"What did you expect?"

"Honestly? Bribes I'd have to refuse, for starters. Calls from your manager telling me you were too busy to come this or that month. Expensive guilty gifts for Nicholas because you'd forgotten to show up. Instead, everything seems effortless. You always appear at the front door right when you're supposed to. Alone. Without camera crews or flunkies."

"It's not effortless."

He didn't say anything more, but Robin could imagine the rest. She had seen a little of the way Devin lived. She didn't know how he managed to get in and out of airports without detection. Or how he cleared his schedule without alerting a dozen people where he would be and why.

"Thanks for giving us this time without everything else," she said. "No hoopla. No media circus. Just a father with his son."

"You said 'us.'"

She could feel a stammer coming on. She grabbed a breath of sweet autumn air. "I meant 'us.' It's not easy being a single mom. Being a single mom with reporters camped on her front lawn sounds even worse."

"You could send them out for groceries. Make them do the laundry."

She laughed. "Maybe one of them would baby-sit occasionally."

"I've tried to make things easier on you," he said,

serious again. "As easy as you'll let me. But you know one day things will change, don't you?"

"I don't want to think about that now. Not today."

"Whatever happens, Robin, please don't forget we're in this together. We can solve any problem that arises as long as we don't let it come between us."

She thought about that as they lapsed into a friendly silence. What exactly was there to come between? Surely he had only meant that they were two people devoted to bringing up a happy, healthy child. He hadn't meant to imply more.

But he had kissed her today. Twice. And now he was holding her hand. When she had awakened from her nap, he had been smiling down at her as if he had just discovered the answer to all of life's questions.

She was walking a dangerous path. Not the rambling cow path through a wildflower meadow. But a path destined to bring her to the edge of the great divide that separated her life from Devin Fitzgerald's.

She was lovely in sunshine, lovely in shadow. Right now, sun-dappled shade painted patterns on Robin's cheeks, cheeks that were definitely too pale. Devin was frustrated that she wouldn't take his money or let him do anything to make her life easier. He supposed her integrity was one of the first things he had fallen in love with, so it was unfair to be judgmental. But for months he had watched her trying to carry all her burdens alone, and he had swallowed anger that she wouldn't let him share them.

"He's actually asleep." Robin lifted her hand from Nicholas's fanny, a fanny she had been patting for ten long minutes as the exhausted baby fought a nap.

"Once he's down, it takes an earthquake to wake him." Devin beckoned from the blanket beside the one where Nicholas snoozed in the shade of an oak. "Come over here. He'll be fine."

She seemed reluctant to stretch out beside him, but she fussed with Nicholas's blanket for a moment, then joined Devin on his, sitting cross-legged on the far corner.

"Why don't you take a nap, too?" He crossed his arms behind his head and pretended he hadn't noticed she was still four feet away.

"And what would you do?"

"I'd sit here and watch you sleep."

"I doubt it. You're not a patient man."

"No? You'd be amazed at how patient I can be." He stared up at the sky and held his breath.

He heard movement, but he didn't look at her. He just kept staring at the clouds.

"All right, Devin. Exactly what are you looking at up there?"

He turned his head just far enough to see that she was lying beside him. Not close beside him, but within general touching distance. He turned back to the sky. "It's Mother Nature's version of the Rorschach test."

"Inkblots?"

"Cloud blots. What do you see?"

She was silent for a while. He wondered if she thought he was being silly. "Sea horses and picket fences."

"Picket fences?"

"There."

He supposed she was pointing, but he refused to look. "You're too far away. We're looking at different clouds. Come closer."

"They're the same clouds."

"But from different perspectives."

She edged a little closer. He could hear her sliding along the blanket. "Uh-uh. Same clouds here, too. But the sea horses are gone. Changed into…dolphins."

He edged toward her. "Don't move. I'm going to try to see them your way." He stopped before he got so close that she scooted away again. "Let's see now. Dolphins? Nope. I see…Charlie Chaplin."

"What?"

"There. The Little Tramp. See his cane and hat?"

"Nope."

"Now that surprises me. He's putting on a show for you."

"What else do you see?"

"Bow ties. Circus tents. Madison Square Garden."

"Come on…"

"Actually, that's where I have to be after I leave tomorrow."

"You're doing a concert there soon, aren't you?"

He turned to look at her. "How did you know?"

Her eyes widened innocently. "I guess I saw it somewhere."

"Would you like to come?"

Her head turned, and her eyes met his. "You know I can't. I can't leave Nicholas, and I sure can't bring him with me."

"We don't have to put a sign on his forehead saying he's my love child."

"Love child?"

He turned away from her and back to the clouds. "Do you like the alternatives better?"

"How about son?"

"The night that Nicholas was created, I was more than a little bit in love with his mother. Love child fits."

He heard her draw a sharp breath.

"I wonder," he continued. "Was she a little bit in love with me, too?"

Robin was silent.

"I think she was," he said.

"We shouldn't have discussions like this one, Devin," she said at last. "What's the point? You were right a while ago when you said we ought to give friendship a try, for Nicholas's sake. But anything else will make this even harder."

"Do you think so?"

"We both know there's...feeling between us. We spent the night together once. We delivered a baby together. We're watching him grow up together."

"'Feeling' covers a lot of ground." He rolled onto his side and propped his head on his hand. "What feeling is there between us, exactly?"

She stared at the clouds. "There's more than one, wouldn't you say?"

"What feelings?"

"Anger, for one. Distrust. Fear."

"Uh-huh." He touched her cheek and forced her to turn her head. "But it's not like you to see only one side of something."

"Then maybe it's your turn." Her eyes were so vulnerable that for a moment he wanted to look away. But he didn't.

"I'm not angry with you," he said softly.

"You're angry that I won't let you do more."

"Frustrated. I want to make your life easy. And trust? I'd trust you with my life. You're honest and fair. Intelligent. And you have a down-to-earth wisdom that impresses me every time I'm with you. As for fear…"

"Devin…"

"You're the only one who's afraid. But your fear is between us. You're right about that."

"I don't know who you are. Are you the man who struts around onstage with women screaming and guitars wailing? Or are you the man who comes to visit Nicholas? The man who brings his son floppy-eared stuffed bunnies and tells him hair-raising stories about his own childhood."

He smiled. "Has Nick been passing those on to you? I told him that was guy stuff."

"Who are you?"

"I'm the man who fathered your son, the man you're looking at with those beautiful brown eyes. I'm exactly that man and no one else."

"You're a millionaire who can buy anything and anybody. You have close friends who use drugs and language I don't want Nicholas to hear. You were married to a woman who looks great in videos but has absolutely no soul. You have more women beating down the stage door every night and offering their bodies, and a manager to keep them away from you the next morning. I don't understand your life, and I'm afraid I don't understand you."

His hand still lay against her cheek. "Are you done yet?"

"More than done."

"I hope that means you know you went too far."

Her eyes were still vulnerable. "You wanted to know what I feel."

"You feel confused. I hear that. Let me clear up some of the confusion. I can buy things, probably anything I really want. But I don't buy people. Not ever. And I don't abandon my friends when they need me, whether I like their choices of recreation or language or not. I work on the campaign for a Drug Free America, and that's enough said about that."

"You don't have—"

He ignored her. "I married a woman I thought I loved because I was unbearably lonely. She was a good actress—even better in real life than she is in videos, by the way. I knew three weeks into it that I'd made a serious mistake. I learned everything I needed to know about relationships in the next year, and I never make the same mistake twice. And yes, there are women offering themselves to me at regular intervals and more pretending I've accepted their offers than there are nights in the year. But, Robin, I gave up casual sex a long time ago. There was nothing casual about the night you and I spent together. And I've never given up on love."

"What do you want from me, Devin?"

"I want you to open your eyes. I want you to believe what you see." She didn't answer, and he was glad. Clearly the time had passed when talking was going to do any good. He sighed. He was as afraid of his next move as he had ever been of anything. But he was compelled to make it anyway.

He lowered his lips to hers. "Forget what you hear. Forget what you read. This is who I am."

Her lips were soft and warm beneath his. He could

feel the sun on his back and an ache inside him that was as much emotional as physical. He had kissed her already today, but there was nothing nonchalant in his intent now. He parted her lips and kissed her harder, moving his tongue against hers as his hand slid from her cheek to her shoulder and down her arm.

She made a soft noise—not a protest, but something more elemental and undefined. He felt her hand against his shoulder, then her fingers in his hair. Something more like gratitude than triumph filled him. His hand rested against her side, then slid from her waist upward toward her breast. She was even warmer and softer than he remembered. Welcoming and earthy and lush. His palm rested against her bare skin, and his fingertips slid beneath the top of her bra.

"I've envied my own son," he whispered. Then he kissed her again, slanting his lips over hers with more intimacy.

She moved closer, and both her arms came around him to pull him toward her. He could feel her hands sliding up his back beneath his shirt; soft, smooth hands that were cool against his skin and utterly seductive. His breath was coming in short bursts. He had told her that he was a patient man, but his patience had disappeared with her first sigh of pleasure.

He circled her with his arms and turned onto his side. There was no space between them now. Her legs were taut against his, their hips were joined. He could feel her breasts pressing against his chest, her hands against his skin. His pleasure was so intense that he felt as if he were soaring through the sky, anchored only to her.

He didn't know what would have happened if she

hadn't stopped him. He had lost his head completely by the time she put her hands against his chest and pushed gently. He might have taken her there, on a blanket in the sunshine, if she hadn't stopped him. He had never wanted anything more.

But the moment he felt her resistance, he remembered everything. How much he wanted her, yes. But even more important, how much of her he wanted. All of her. Not just her drugging, ecstatic kisses, her supple, beguiling body. But all of her.

He moved away a little, but he still held her in the circle of his arms. He was content to watch her as he forced his body, his heartbeat and breath into submission. Finally he spoke. "I'm not going to apologize."

"Aren't you?"

"It would be a sacrilege."

"You're intent on making our lives harder, aren't you?"

"That's the last thing I want."

Her eyes were troubled, but her lips curled up in something almost like a smile. "I think I remember exactly what happened to turn me into Nicholas's mother."

"Oh?"

"I've asked myself a hundred times how I could have let that night end the way it did."

"And now you have an answer?"

She didn't speak for a moment. Then she rolled onto her back. Her head was pillowed on his arm. "I'll show you my dolphins and picket fences if you'll show me your circus tents and bow ties."

He settled himself beside her, pulling her a little closer so that her head lay in the hollow of his shoulder. Together they gazed up at the sky.

Chapter Six

"Robin, you're crazy. You know you are." Judy lifted Nicholas skyward and swung him in a circle as his father often did. The baby chortled with delight. "You could have everything you want if you'd just admit some home truths to yourself."

Judy had shown up unexpectedly for the weekend. Robin was delighted to see her, but suspicious about the turn casual conversation had taken so soon after Judy's arrival. In the week since the picnic with Devin she had thought about very little but him. She didn't know how Judy had zeroed in so quickly on her concerns.

Robin waited until the noise had subsided before she answered. "I'm not crazy. My relationship with Devin is an artificial creation. We've been thrown together in a pressure cooker. That's why I… That's why he…"

"You can't even say it, can you?" Judy dropped to a seat at the kitchen table and set Nicholas on the floor with the plastic truck she had brought with her from Cincinnati. "That's why you've what? Fallen in love?"

"That's exactly what I'm not trying to say. I had Devin's baby. He adores Nicholas, and the feeling is mutual. It would be wonderfully convenient for Devin to fall in love with me so that we could be a family. I think maybe he's capable of that."

"You're saying he's a manipulator capable of pretending something like love just to get what he wants?"

"No, I'm not."

Judy leaned back in her chair, her arms folded across her chest. "Then what?"

"I think he's capable of convincing himself that there's more between us than there is, just so he can have more than a few days a month with his son. If he has to put up with me, too, so be it."

"I'm sure you're right. I mean, good grief, what could you possibly have to offer a man like that? You're an ugly brainless twit with no redeeming qualities."

Robin scoured the last pan in the kitchen sink before she answered. "I know I have a lot to offer someone. And someday maybe I'll want another man in my life."

"I see. You don't love Devin. I didn't realize."

Robin was silent.

"Gosh, I'm so glad I understand now," Judy said.

"You really are a monster, you know?" Robin faced her friend, drying her hands on a dish towel as she did so.

"Let me tell you what I see," Judy said. "Okay?"

"You will, regardless."

Judy grinned, but the grin faded. "Robin, I know you loved Jeff. Everybody loved Jeff. He was like a brother to me. You and Jeff were pals for years before you became lovers, two peas in a pod. When you found out he was dying, it was like losing a part of yourself."

"It still hurts."

"Of course it does. It always will. But you've recovered in all the ways that matter. And now there's a man in your life who makes you feel different than you ever felt with Jeff."

"That's not—"

Judy held up her hand to stop Robin's response. "I'm sorry, but I have to say this. You and Jeff would have lived happily ever after if he hadn't died. I believe that. But you and Jeff grew into your love, and it took years. Devin Fitzgerald knocked you over the head on your very first night together."

"We made love because we were both hurting. We needed to comfort each other."

"Baloney!"

Robin was silent.

"You're head over heels, Robin. Have been since that night. That's why you didn't try harder to let Devin know about the pregnancy. You were scared to death. And you're terrified now because what you're feeling is brand-new. And it's uncontrollable."

"*You're* uncontrollable."

"I'm honest. More honest than you've been."

Robin bent to push Nicholas's truck back toward him. When she faced Judy again she nodded. "All right. I'm in love with him. Is that what you wanted me to say?"

"It's a start."

"And Devin is trying to fall in love with me. He wants us to be a family. He hasn't told me as much, but I know that's what he wants."

"How do you know he's not in love with you already? That it didn't take any effort on his part?"

"I don't!"

Judy smiled smugly.

"But I'm afraid," Robin continued. "He wants Nicholas. I've never seen a man so besotted with a baby."

"Don't you think that speaks well for him?"

"Of course it does. Who wouldn't want a man like that? But can't you see? How much of what he feels for me is left over from what he feels for his son? What if we live together, even marry, and it doesn't work out? What if he finds that he doesn't love me at all? Do you know how much chance I'd have of keeping Nicholas in a custody battle?"

"Every chance in the world. He's a rock star. You're a good Midwestern girl."

"At the very least I'd lose Devin, wouldn't I? We couldn't even be friends. And I could lose my son. How can I take a chance like that?"

"Robin, you can't let Jeff's death color every decision you make for the rest of your life. Yes, some day you might lose big time again, because this is the real world. But making sure you have nothing to lose isn't the right way to deal with the future. You're afraid of losing Devin eventually? Well, you don't even have him now. Is that better?"

Robin was silent again.

Judy glanced at her watch. "The man in question is going to be here in about thirty minutes, so you'd better go change."

Robin stared at her friend. "What?"

"You heard me. Devin's going to be here in half an hour."

"How do you know?"

"Because he called me last week and asked if I'd come visit you this weekend and stay with Nicholas tonight."

"That's why you're here?"

"The two of you are going to get away together for the evening. And he knew you wouldn't go unless you had someone completely trustworthy watching Nicholas."

Robin opened her mouth to speak, but nothing came out.

"He's coming to see you. Not Nick. Doesn't that say something to you? And don't be mad. He knew if he asked you, you'd refuse."

"He was right about that."

"Go with him, Robin. Take some time alone with Devin for a change. If the moment's right, tell him what you've told me and listen to his answers." Judy shrugged. "Of course, maybe it won't even come up. Maybe he's not falling in love with you. Maybe you're imagining the whole thing."

But Robin wasn't listening. She was staring out the window, at the yard where Devin had played as a boy, at the old red barn where he and his first rock-and-roll band had rehearsed. She was living in his house. She was the mother of his child. He had obviously stolen the heart of her best friend. In a number of ways she already belonged to Devin Fitzgerald, and she could no longer shut her eyes to what was happening. Slowly, inexorably, he was pulling her into the circle of his life and his arms.

She could have said no. It hadn't been too late. She could have stood at the front door, explained that this was not one of the times they had agreed Devin could see Nicholas and stubbornly sent him on his way.

Instead she was in his Cherokee wearing the new white skirt and sweater that she hadn't been able to resist when she'd gone shopping for Nicholas that week. Perhaps she had known there would be an evening like this one, because no mother with a working brain dressed in white. Nicholas could destroy the outfit with one well-placed burp or a leaking diaper.

But she was wearing it tonight.

"I was prepared for almost anything," Devin said. "Murder. Mayhem. The silent treatment."

"This was disgustingly manipulative."

"I would have preferred asking you for a date, like one grownup to another. But I knew I'd fail."

"When was the last time you failed at anything?"

"When was the last time you went out without Nicholas?"

"What if he misses me? What if he starts to cry and Judy doesn't know what's wrong?"

"You need more faith in your friend and your son. He's only nursing occasionally now, and you took care of that before we left. She can do everything else for him that you could do."

"Are you at least going to tell me where we're going?"

He glanced at her and grinned. Her heart did a back flip. "I don't think so."

She smiled, too. She seemed to be congenitally unable to resist his grins. "I really should be mad."

"But you're finding it hard. Even the best mother needs to get away from her kid occasionally."

"You're right. Anywhere. With anyone who offers."

"With the man in her life."

She didn't know what to say to that. Something had

changed in their relationship, and she didn't remember giving her permission. Yet it seemed too late now to change things back. She felt a glimmer of panic. She needed Devin in her life, but what if this new increased awareness of each other led to a permanent rift between them? What if friendship died, too?

He seemed to read her mind. "You can handle this, sweetheart. We can handle it together."

"I'm afraid we won't."

"I know you are. Let's just take this one step at a time. Okay? And this is the next step. You and me. Without the little guy, for once. But no pressure. One small step. Okay?"

She watched the autumn foliage flash by. Before long their son would be a year old. How long could she continue to fight Devin or her own powerful feelings for him? Did she owe it to Nicholas to reach for the brass ring? To give Devin a real chance in her life? To marry him and give Nicholas the full-time father he deserved?

"One step," she said.

"That's it. That's all I'm asking for." He reached for her hand. "At least for tonight."

Devin watched Robin wander around the suite that he had rented for their evening together. He was perfectly capable of braving fans almost anywhere, but he knew that Robin would feel exposed and anxious the moment he was recognized. So he had found the nicest inn in central Ohio, a small one tucked away in the woods, and he had rented a suite for the night. They could talk, dine in....

He didn't want to think about the rest of it. He had

not brought Robin here to seduce her. Not because he didn't want to. He wanted her with a sexual hunger he hadn't felt since adolescence. But he knew better than to rush her into his bed again. He'd done that once, and he was still trying to work out the consequences.

"We can have dinner whenever you like," he said. "Just let me know."

"You know, when most men invite a woman for a date, it's dinner someplace with crowds of people and a movie theater elbow-to-elbow with strangers."

"We could have done that. But I couldn't guarantee the results."

"Do you ever miss doing things the usual way?"

"Do I miss fighting crowds, talking over the din of a noisy restaurant, sharing you with rows of popcorn-munching strangers…?"

"So I suppose you're saying that there are compensations for the rigors of wealth and privilege." She smiled. "This is so lovely. So peaceful."

"So private."

She looked less pleased about that. "Yes." She turned to look out the window, where birds fluttered and fed at a rustic feeder.

"Would you like to go for a walk? There are trails through the woods."

"Maybe when the stars come out."

"I brought wine and champagne. Which will it be?"

"Champagne sounds like a celebration."

Her back was turned to him, but he heard just the faintest sparkle of distrust in her words. "I thought getting you out of the house was cause for one," he said. "But I hadn't thought any further ahead, if you're worried."

"The last time I was alone in a hotel with you—"

"We conceived a child. I know. Are you sorry we did?"

"Of course not."

"Well, then?"

"That doesn't mean I'm planning to do it again."

"Neither am I. And I'm not planning to take you to bed tonight. So, that said, would you like some champagne anyway?"

"That said, I'd love some. But just out of curiosity…" She turned and met his eyes. "Why aren't you planning to take me to bed?"

He lowered his gaze to her lips. "Let's see. What are the possibilities? I'm not interested in you sexually? That's going to be hard for you to believe since three hours into our relationship I proved that wasn't true. So maybe it's just that I'm not interested in sex tonight?" He smiled a little. "But stand too close and you'll find out that's not true, either. So I guess it's that I care way too much about you to risk scaring you away. Maybe I'm just trying to prove that I can deny myself all the things I really want until you're ready to give them to me."

"All the things you want?"

"It's too early in the evening for this conversation."

"Humor me anyway."

"Robin, you know what I want. You've known for some time. I want you and Nicholas with me permanently. I want you in my bed. I want Nicholas in his bed in the next room. I want us to watch him grow up together, and maybe watch more children, too. I want us to grow old together."

She didn't say anything. She just stood there, breathtakingly lovely in a fuzzy white sweater and a pleated skirt that stopped well above her knees and made her legs look like they were a mile long. He remembered how those legs had felt entwined with his. She had no idea what looking at her did to him or to all his resolve.

"Did you ever jump rope as a kid?" she asked at last.

"No. Not a guy thing."

"There's this rhyme we used to jump to. First comes love, then comes marriage, then comes Robin with a baby carriage. Somehow you and I have gotten everything backward, Devin. We started by having a baby together. Now look where we are."

He stepped a little closer. "Where are we?"

She shook her head.

"I've talked about marriage, but not about love?"

"Don't talk about it. Please."

"You don't want to hear my thoughts on the subject?"

"Not now."

"I'd like to hear yours."

"I believe in it. And the thought of being in love again scares me to death."

He admired her honesty as well as her ability to stay away from the real subject he wanted to discuss. Did she love him? Was she afraid of something that had already happened or just of something that might?

"I'm going to pop the cork on the champagne," he said. "Then we're going to sit over there by the fireplace and talk. Not about Nicholas, for a change. Just about ourselves. Our hopes and dreams. And the little stuff we don't ever have time to talk about. When you're hungry, we'll order dinner. And when you're tired, we'll go home."

She released a long breath, as if she had been holding it and waiting for something. But for what? He didn't know. For a moment he wished he was as self-centered and aggressive as the world assumed all rock musicians were. She was confused, but she was also as attracted to him as he was to her. If he pushed her...

"Make yourself comfortable." He turned away before she could see the temptation in his eyes, and went to get the champagne.

She was amazed how many questions she had stored up to ask Devin. By the second glass of champagne, they were both more relaxed. Conversation flowed along with the bubbly. Robin found herself telling him all sorts of things. About high-school boyfriends, the way that Duke, her childhood cocker spaniel, had kidnapped her Raggedy Ann doll to sleep with every night, the trip to Wyoming she and Nicholas would make at Christmas to visit her parents, who had settled there two years before.

"They want us to come and live with them," she said.

"Have you considered it?"

"They're three hours from an airport. I think it would be harder for you to come and visit Nicholas."

"It might be."

"I don't want that."

He smiled. His fingers dangled just over her shoulder. He dangled them a little lower and made contact with her sweater. "I have a house in the Rockies, near Colorado Springs. Did you know that?"

The casual touch seemed to change everything again. She didn't look at him. "I think I might have heard that somewhere." Actually, she knew all about the house. She had even seen a photograph in an old *Architectural*

Digest. It was breathtakingly contemporary, cedar and glass, with enough square footage to house everyone Devin had ever met. Somehow she hadn't been able to imagine the Devin she knew living there, and that had frightened her.

"I've been staying there when I can."

"Do you think of it as home?"

"No, I think of home as Farnham Falls."

"Oh."

"Do you ever wonder why I bought the farmhouse from Sarah?"

She nodded. She had wondered about that frequently.

"The night Nicholas was born, I was going back there to live for a while. I needed a place where no one would disturb me, a place where I could work on something completely new. I had planned to hole up there for a month or so and see what I could do with my idea."

"Well, things didn't quite work out the way you intended, did they?" She glanced back up at him. He was smiling.

"I think of Nicholas as a new project. A better one than I was planning."

"What were you planning?"

"Well, it's more than a plan at this point. I'm working on a musical. Hopefully for Broadway."

"Really?" She was amazed. She knew he was extraordinarily talented. She just hadn't realized how far that talent extended.

"Really. It's my story, and the songs are mine, but I've teamed up with someone else who's writing the lyrics. It's good, Robin. I don't know if it's good enough, but it's good. There's already interest. Quite a bit of it."

"But that's great. Is that why you've cut back on performing?"

"I want to stop performing eventually, or at least nearly stop. I really love the writing best, and I don't like what performing does to my life."

"But why Farnham Falls? You could have chosen a lot more exotic locales to hole up and work, Devin."

"The show's called 'Heartland.' It's about the way the heartland was before all the family farms began to disappear. For a rock opera, it's disgustingly nostalgic and sentimental." He grinned. "The main musical motif is a lullaby that my mother used to sing to me."

She had often heard him sing an unusual lullaby to Nicholas. She knew the song he must mean.

He had sung it to her when he was carrying her to the car the night he'd rescued her.

Her throat closed, and she swallowed. She was touched that she and Nicholas had somehow shared in this. "So that's why you were coming home."

"Part of the reason. I wanted to reconnect with myself, and Farnham Falls seemed like the right place to do that. I needed to be among people who believed all the things I'd been taught to believe as a boy. I needed to remember…good things. And there was a woman living in Farnham Falls, someone I'd met some months before, who I was hoping to see again. One afternoon I was going to wander into the newspaper office where she worked, look around a little, ask a few questions, find out her name. And if she was there, I was hoping she might just consider getting to know me a little better. Maybe have a conversation like this one."

She supposed her heart was in her eyes. "Please… If that's not true…"

"I wouldn't lie to you. I'm never going to lie to you, Robin. Not about anything."

She didn't think Devin would lie to her. But she did think he might lie to himself. Perhaps he had thought of her. She had certainly thought of him as their baby had grown inside her. But she didn't believe Devin's thoughts had been anything more than memories of a wonderful night when a man and a woman had come together to soothe each other's pain.

Perhaps Devin had planned to look for her. But Robin doubted that he'd had anything in mind except a brief renewal of their acquaintance. In the light of day, she would have proved to be exactly what she was. A Midwestern woman working at a small, inconsequential newspaper. Pretty enough, intelligent enough, but not what a man like Devin was used to. She was proud of herself. She had no desire to be anyone else. But she was also realistic.

She felt his hand settle on her shoulder. "You're homesick, or you were," she said. "Sometimes home looks better than it really is. Don't the rooms in the farmhouse seem smaller than they did to you as a boy? That's how life in Farnham Falls would seem to you if you had to live there day after day."

He nodded, but his eyes questioned her. She could see he didn't understand.

"You were burned out," she said. "Maybe you still are. But that doesn't mean that the things that might help you recover and go on are the things you really want and need for the rest of your life."

He stroked her neck with his fingertips. "Doesn't it?"

"No."

"I don't plan to live in Farnham Falls day after day. That doesn't mean I can't take what's important with me when I go."

She stopped pretending that they were talking in the abstract. "Look at me, Devin. I'm not glamorous or exciting. Farnham Falls might be too small for me, but living your life would overwhelm me. I want stability. Roots. I want the people I love around me, not strangers who come and go. That's what I want for Nicholas, too."

"Am I one of the people you love? One of the people you want around you?"

"It doesn't matter. Because we're not at all the same. We aren't going to be able to fit our lives together."

"You're sure of that?"

She couldn't answer. His hand was cupping her cheek. Her eyes were gazing into the depths of his. Everything she'd said was true. She thought she believed it deep in her heart. But she couldn't answer, because the answer seemed too final.

"You're not sure," he said. "Somewhere inside you there's a voice telling you that with a little compromise, a little discussion, we can work out anything. We aren't so far apart. And there are a thousand places in between where we could be happy together."

It was time to pull away. This was too intimate, exactly what they had to avoid. But Robin couldn't move. She was caught by the look in his eyes, by a deep loneliness that he didn't often let her see, and by something else. Hope? She didn't know. Did it really matter so much to Devin that they find the compromise that would let them live their lives together?

She saw that he was going to kiss her. Loneliness and hope had warred, and the result was this. She saw that she could pull away from him now, that she could stop this before it started again. He had not brought her here to seduce her. At least, not consciously.

She willed herself to move away. This would complicate a relationship already so complex it might never be resolved.

Instead, her hands lifted to his hair, and she sighed. Relief filled her when he kissed her, because now there was no room for doubt or protest. Instead she was suffused with desire. The part of her that still believed all things were possible kindled into flame.

"Just tell me to stop," he whispered against her lips.

"Don't. Don't stop." She was afraid he might. He hesitated, giving them both seconds to reconsider. But she realized she didn't want those seconds. She didn't know what the future held for them. She didn't want to know. She just knew that she needed Devin now. She didn't believe the things he'd said, but she wanted to. She needed to believe, because with his lips on hers, she couldn't bear to let him go. Not ever. Not even if it was best for them all.

"I love you," he said. "Don't ever tell yourself I don't. And don't tell me it's not enough. We can make it enough." He kissed her again. Harder and more intimately. She felt his tongue stroking hers, his hand sliding up her midriff.

Her bra gave way under his capable fingers, and she felt his palm against her breast. Pleasure shot through her, pleasure more intense than anything she'd ever experienced. It had been more than a year and a half since they'd made love the first time, but she remembered every sensation from that night. And this was better.

Because she loved him, too.

Her sweater was snowflake white against the rug at their feet. His blue wool shirt joined it.

She had forgotten how sweet this was, how perfect to have skin against skin, her breasts pressing and molding themselves to the hard contours of his chest. She had forgotten the feel of his lips at her breasts, the erotic enticement of a man suckling where her son still fed. She had forgotten how his muscles rippled under her fingertips, the smooth, cool expanse of his skin, the silky brown hair on his chest.

Her skirt drifted to the floor with her stockings. She helped him slide down his pants until they were gone, as well. She saw how ready he was to take her; that despite his promise of patience, he had none to promise. He held out his hand, and they walked to the bedroom. Twilight filtered through heavy drapes, but it wasn't enough. She stopped beside the bed to turn on the lamp. She wanted to see him as he made love to her, wanted to remember every move, every expression.

He embraced her, his body lean and hard against hers. He was fully aroused, but he didn't hurry her. He stood with his arms around her and kissed her as if they had the rest of their lives to take their pleasure.

She was the one who pulled back the covers, who slid between them and opened her arms to him. She had made love to him only once. He had been a stranger that night. Now, he was not.

"There is nothing that can come between us unless you let it," he said, as he rose over her.

As he sank into her, she wondered if he was right. In that moment there were only the two of them and their pleasure. And nothing seemed impossible.

Chapter Seven

Devin didn't change a diaper exactly the way Robin did, but he got the job done. She watched him fasten the last tab and pull Nicholas's pajamas up to cover it. Devin wasn't in pajamas himself. He was wearing unsnapped jeans and a flannel shirt he hadn't buttoned when he'd sprung out of bed to see why their son was crying.

Robin knew she should have stayed in bed herself. The luxury of having someone else get up with Nicholas was beyond price. But she *had* gotten up. Not because she didn't trust Devin to handle Nicholas, but because she liked to watch him with his son.

They seemed very much like a real family.

"Go warm up the bed again," Devin told her. "I'll be there in a minute."

"Good luck." She blew Nicholas a kiss and followed Devin's suggestion. Back in her bedroom, she stripped off her robe and snuggled deep under the covers, shivering a little at the feel of the cool fabric against her bare skin. Nowadays the bed seemed huge to her when Devin wasn't in it. And there were long periods of time when he wasn't. Since the night they had become lovers again, he visited more often, and he stayed at the house with her when he did. But his commitments still kept him away for long stretches of time. Each time he left, she and Nicholas waited impatiently for his return.

Devin came back and stripped off his makeshift pajamas. He slid in beside her and opened his arms. "He was already falling back to sleep before I closed the door."

"New tooth." Robin nestled against Devin's shoulder and sighed as he wrapped his arms around her.

"It's hard to believe that he's going to be a year old tomorrow."

"I know. I can't believe the first year of his life has already gone by."

"I feel like I missed too much of it."

"Well, you were Johnny-on-the-spot the night he was born."

"No blizzard in sight for tomorrow. High thirties and sunshine."

"I wish my parents could be here for his party."

He paused before answering. "I'd like to meet them."

Robin sighed. "I'd like that, too. But they don't understand about us, Devin."

"Neither do I."

She could feel sleep slipping away from her. Lately Devin had been the soul of patience, rarely mentioning the future. But she knew their part-time relationship weighed heavily on him. It weighed heavily on her, too. She was the only obstacle to giving her son a full-time father.

She loved Devin Fitzgerald. That wasn't in question and hadn't been for a long time. And she believed Devin when he said that he loved her. But she still didn't know if he loved her the way a woman deserved to be loved— for herself alone. He loved his son's mother. He loved the fact that they were a family. But she didn't know if that kind of commitment would hold up under the bright lights of Devin's life.

Right now she and Nicholas were a safe harbor in the stormy sea of rock and roll. But once they were thrown into it, would they keep their heads above water? Or would they sink together?

Would she lose everything again?

"Are you really unhappy with things the way they are?" she asked, when it was clear to her that he wasn't falling asleep, either.

"I love being with you and Nicholas. But I miss you when I'm not."

"Well, we miss you, too. But you've been able to come more often. That's been wonderful."

"It's not easy, Robin. The more frequently I disappear, the more suspicious it looks. And the harder it is on everybody who depends on me."

She had never thought about that. There were probably a lot of people who depended on Devin for their livelihood. He was a big business.

She had never thought about something else, either. Now she wondered how she could have overlooked it. "Is it dangerous for you to come here? I remember you had a bodyguard in Cleveland."

"I take precautions more to avoid detection than for safety reasons."

"I haven't been fair to you, have I? I've been expecting you to keep this up indefinitely."

"I don't want to keep it up. I'm tired. I want you and Nicholas with me, someplace where we can spend all or almost all our nights together. Someplace where I can be sure you're both safe and happy."

"Where? Manhattan? Beverly Hills? Your rustic little estate in Colorado?" Despite herself, her voice was heavy with distaste.

He rubbed the small of her back. "No. Someplace we choose together. I don't own any property that I care about except this house. We could find a community where we feel at home. A good place to raise our family. If you were just willing to look."

"And if we couldn't? What if we found we couldn't make a life together? It would be too late to turn back then, wouldn't it? We couldn't go back to this."

"I know you're afraid. But sometimes people have to move on. Even if it means taking risks."

She remembered that Judy had said nearly the same thing to her. Making sure she had nothing to lose was no way to deal with the future. But she had so much to lose. Devin and even Nicholas.

"Do you know that you were all relaxed against me, and now you're not?" Devin spread his fingers against her back. His thumb began to make slow circles at the base of her spine. "You're stiff with fear. It isn't going to matter how many times I tell you that we can make this work, is it? You're still afraid you're going to lose something precious."

When she didn't answer he turned her onto her back and began to kiss her. There was more than one way to make her relax. She clung to him and kissed him back. They had made love before falling asleep tonight, but now she was ravenous. She wanted Devin inside her, driving out her fears. She knew the time to make a decision was at hand, but she didn't want to make it now. She wanted to forget that things couldn't always stay this way. She wanted to forget that someday he might not be here to make love to her when she needed him.

"Happy Birthday to you..." Devin started the familiar song, and Robin and Judy took it up quickly.

Nicholas beamed at the sudden burst of music from the people he loved most in the world. He clapped his hands, then his eyes widened as Robin walked toward him with his birthday cake. She and Devin had decided on a sparkler instead of a candle. A candle didn't seem nearly special enough for their son's first birthday party.

Nicholas was entranced until the sparkler went out. Then he frowned and pointed. "Da!"

"Sorry, kiddo, I can't bring it back. But I bet you'll like what was under it." Devin took the cake out of Robin's hands after she had removed the spent sparkler and set it on Nicholas's high-chair tray. "Dig in."

"I can't watch." Robin turned away. She'd had the foresight to make two cakes. This one was nothing more than a glorified muffin, but Nicholas didn't know any better.

He slapped his palm into the cake, and it crumbled into a hundred small pieces all over his high-chair tray. Nicholas raised his hand to his mouth and began to sample in earnest as Judy snapped photographs.

"Don't you wish the rest of us could get away with that?" Judy said. "Doesn't that look like fun?"

"Yuck!" Robin went to the counter to get the other cake and slice it. "I'll settle for a fork and a napkin."

"When does he get to open his presents?" Devin asked.

"When we've washed the icing out of his hair. Why, can't you wait?" Robin teased.

"I've drawn up plans. With all the blocks we bought him, we can build a dream city."

"You can build. He can destroy."

"Two sides of the same coin."

"Well, I want to see his face when he opens my present," Judy said.

Robin knew that Judy had bought Nicholas a scooter shaped like an elephant. Nicholas wasn't walking yet, although he was on the verge. But now he could hold on to the scooter and make his way around the house on his feet.

The doorbell rang, and Robin wiped her hands. Visitors weren't common this far out in the country, but some of her friends at work knew that today was Nicholas's birthday. She wouldn't be surprised to find one of them at her front door with a gift.

She wondered if she should invite whoever it was inside to meet Devin. Today of all days the need for secrecy seemed almost obscene. They were celebrating their son's first birthday. They had nothing to hide.

She opened the door, and a middle-aged man with a carefree grin moved back a few paces as the aluminum storm door swung toward him.

"You Robin Lansing?" he asked.

"I am." Another man stepped into view from behind the door. She hadn't noticed him, but he'd obviously planned it that way. Before she could say anything, he snapped her photograph.

"We know everything," the first man said, his grin still in place. "We know you had Devin Fitzgerald's baby. We know he's here. You got any plans for the future with him? Or is he just stringing you along?"

She made it back inside somehow and tried to pull the storm door closed. But the grinning man held the handle. "We hear he's not supporting you. Did you ever think about taking him to court? Or maybe it's not really his kid?"

Robin managed to slam the wooden door and lock it. Then she began to tremble.

"Who was it?" Judy came into the room. She was licking icing off her fingers. "More presents?"

"A reporter." Robin was surprised that she sounded so normal. She was shaking, but her voice was not.

"Somebody from the *Gaz*—" Judy looked up. "Oh." Her eyes narrowed. "So it begins."

"I don't know how they found out!"

Judy frowned. "Oh, come on, Robin. It's a miracle no one in the press found out before this. There's been a conspiracy of silence to protect you. Don't you think your neighbors know? Your co-workers? Everyone's been looking the other way. They love you, and Devin's the local hero."

Robin closed her eyes. There was pounding on the other side of the door, but she ignored it.

"Well, I'm glad," Judy said.

"How can you say that?"

"Because I am. Devin's wearing himself out to keep up this pretense you've insisted on. Now there won't be any more secrets. I wish it hadn't taken a sleazebag reporter to get the show on the road, but I'm glad somebody did."

Robin had expected sympathy. She opened her eyes and stared at her friend.

"What's wrong?" Devin came into the room. "Robin, someone is still at the door."

"'Tis the press," Judy said. "You're going to be in the news, Devin. Not important enough for prime time, probably, but I bet the tabloid shows will pay for this story. And the sleazy supermarket rags." She shrugged.

"Robin?"

Robin turned her gaze to him. "Busted." But she wasn't smiling, and her voice didn't come out as lightly as she'd intended. She felt violated, exposed. But worse—much, much worse—she felt terrified.

"We'll get through this," he promised.

She nodded.

"Do you want me to talk to them?"

"No!"

"Then we have a party to finish. There's a little boy in the kitchen with presents to open. He needs both his parents in there with him."

She heard the words Devin didn't say. Nicholas would always need them both. The time had come for her to face the future. In a matter of hours the world would know everything. They were a family, whether she'd made up her mind to accept it or not.

But she couldn't accept it. She couldn't. Fear was pushing away every other feeling. "I think you'd better plan to leave afterward, Devin. They're going to camp out in the front yard if you don't. And I'm not ready for this."

He didn't say anything for a moment. "What would it take to get you ready for this?" he asked at last. "A signed promise from God that I'm still going to love you when the smoke clears?"

From the corner of her eye Robin saw Judy leave the

room. She and Devin were alone except for the reporter and photographer on the other side of the door. "It's just going to take me some time—"

"You've had time. You've had a year. But when it comes down to it, I don't mean as much to you as your fears. You've never gotten over your husband's death. You would rather lose me than take a chance and try to build a life together."

"That's not true. I—"

"It's true. I'll go say goodbye to Nicholas."

"No, please stay for a while. Let him open—"

"I'm leaving." He turned sharply and disappeared into the kitchen. She wanted to follow him, to tell him that he was wrong and plead with him to hold her.

But she couldn't move. On the other side of the door the reporter continued to pound his fist in rhythm to the agonizing thudding of her heart.

Devin held his squirming son. He didn't care that he would be covered with cake crumbs now, or even, self-ishly, that Nicholas wanted to get down. He just held him as tightly as he could without hurting him.

"I've got to go, partner," he whispered into the baby's dark hair. "I hope you have a happy birthday. Build a city for me, will you?"

He'd heard Robin go upstairs and shut the bedroom door. Judy came to stand in the kitchen doorway, her arms crossed over her chest. Devin had liked her from the first moment he'd met her. She was everything that the small-town Midwest believed about itself. Solid. No-nonsense. Wholesome. Compassionate but never sentimental.

"I couldn't help but overhear," she said.

"It's a small house."

"She's scared to death."

"I know."

"She's afraid you don't love her as much as you love the idea of a family."

"I know."

"There's something you don't know."

"What?"

"She was never sure that Jeff loved her the way she needed to be loved, either."

He didn't answer. For a moment it seemed inconsequential to him what Robin had experienced with her husband. He was so hurt that suddenly everything she felt seemed inconsequential. He had a different bottom line than Robin did. It wasn't that he didn't love her. She hadn't loved *him* enough to try to make this work.

"She's never told me this," Judy said. "But I think Robin believes Jeff married her because he knew, at least on some level, just how ill he was and he wanted her comfort and presence in his life while he fought death. They were good friends, and he didn't want to be alone."

"What do you think?"

"I think it's probably true."

Devin tried to tell himself that this was important. But nothing felt important right now except the chubby-cheeked reality squirming in his arms. "I won't be back."

"You can't mean that."

"I mean it."

"What about Nicholas?"

"That'll be up to Robin." He looked up. He was as close to tears as he had come in his adult life. "I can tell you what the press will do with this story, Judy. They'll eat me alive. I'll be the irresponsible rock star who fathered a son, refused to support him, refused to marry his mother, even refused to fight for visitation rights."

"You could tell the truth."

"I could. But how would she look if I did?"

"Are you going to take her to court? Are you going to seek custody? Joint custody? Because you've certainly proved how much you care about Nicholas. You've nearly killed yourself trying to visit him regularly."

"No."

Judy was silent. Devin kissed the soft, icing-sticky hair of his son and set him on the floor at his feet. "When Robin's panic subsides, she'll realize how much Nicholas needs me. Her attorney can contact mine and work out visitation."

"And if she doesn't?"

There were a thousand voices screaming in Devin's head. He wanted to snatch Nicholas and run. He wanted to stand up to the world and tell them how much he loved this child and his mother—and how in the end it hadn't been enough for her. But one voice was louder than all the rest.

"I love Robin too much to do anything to cause her pain," he said. "Even if she doesn't realize how much Nicholas and I need each other, I'll continue to stay away from him."

"Devin…" She shook her head.

"That's the funny thing about this, you know? I couldn't love her more, and she couldn't believe it less."

"Call me. Any time you need to know what's going on with Nicholas."

He nodded.

"I'm sorry."

He tried to smile his thanks, but he couldn't. He knelt and kissed Nicholas's hair and squeezed him tightly once more. Then he stood and left the house without a backward glance. He couldn't look back, because he didn't know what he would do if he saw that Nicholas was crying, too.

Chapter Eight

If he'd really loved her, he would have stayed to work things out. But in the end he hadn't even loved Nicholas enough for that. For the past two months Devin had disappeared from their lives as surely as if he had never rescued her in the blizzard and delivered his own son.

If he'd really loved her.

She had asked him to leave.

Robin sat at the kitchen table with her head in her hands. She had been trying for hours to put together an entertainment-news column for the *Gazette*. In front of her she had two dozen clips about movies and models and what celebrity had been seen with what other celebrity. All of it seemed so foolish.

All except one clipping.

Devin Fitzgerald was holed up in his estate in Colorado working on a musical that was to debut in San Francisco in two years. His faithful fans would be sorry to hear that he wouldn't be touring or recording for a while, but those in the know said that the musical would be worth the wait.

"He's asleep," Judy said.

Robin lifted her head wearily. "Thanks. For coming to see how we're doing. For playing with Nicholas so I could work. For putting him in for his nap."

"He misses Devin."

Robin didn't answer. She knew it was true.

"I thought we could walk through the woods when he wakes up and look for wildflowers. Take advantage of the warm day. And Nick seems happiest if he's on his feet these days."

"If I can get this finished." Robin didn't want to look for wildflowers. She knew what that would remind her of.

And Nicholas was walking now. Devin didn't even know.

"You're working too hard."

Something snapped inside her. "You're full of criticism today, aren't you?" Robin sighed before Judy could respond. "Oh, Lord, I'm sorry. I really am. It's not true, and if it were, you could have a field day with me."

"You're not at your best," Judy said. "I'll say that much."

"This garbage with the press has really gotten me down."

"Yeah. I'm sure that's all it is."

Robin dropped her pen to the table. "I'm tired of the questions. I'm tired of the odd looks people give me. I'm thinking about quitting my job here and moving somewhere else so I can start over."

"Is there a place like that?"

There probably wasn't. It was only March, but the story about Nicholas had already died down. It hadn't even been that big to start with. Robin had steeled herself to tell reporters that Devin had acted honorably right from the very start, and that the rest of the details were personal and would not be discussed. Devin had refused to comment at all. Eventually more exciting stories had taken the place of theirs.

But Robin was a celebrity of sorts now, the mother of Devin Fitzgerald's son. Someone would always know where she was, who she was. As he grew older, Nicholas would have to field questions.

She thought about the most recent development and decided to share it with Judy. "Devin's attorney has been in touch. He wants the name of mine so that negotiations can begin."

"For custody?"

Robin was puzzled that Judy sounded surprised. "Well, no. He was clear about that. He's not even asking for visitation, Judy. He wants to give us money."

"Oh."

Robin rested her head on her hands. "I don't understand it. Devin adores Nicholas. I'm sure he does. But he hasn't made any attempt to see him since…since he left."

"Did you tell his attorney he could?"

"Of course not! I shouldn't have to. He knows that."

"No, he doesn't."

"Of course, he does. He—"

"Damn it, Robin, don't you see what's going on?" Judy flung her arms out in disgust. "Devin's not going to do anything you'll perceive as a threat. Not ever again. The man's willing to give up his son for your peace of mind. He's not going to ask to visit, and he's sure not going to try to share custody. He knows how scared you are, and he's making the ultimate sacrifice to help you feel secure. If you don't call him and tell him you want him to visit Nicholas, he'll never visit him again. He trusts you to make the right decision, though I don't know why he should."

Robin stared at her friend. When she spoke her voice was barely above a whisper. "How do you know?"

"He told me."

"And you didn't say anything to me?"

"What was there to say? You haven't heard anything that's been said to you for months. The man told you he loved you every which way to Sunday, and you didn't hear that, either."

"He would give up Nicholas?" But even as she asked the question, Robin knew the answer. He would. He had. And deep inside, she had known it for weeks. Devin hadn't stopped visiting his son because the publicity had scared him away.

He had stopped because he loved her.

He loved her that much.

"Call him," Judy said. "Or call his attorney. Make arrangements for visitation. You owe him that much, don't you?"

She owed him more.

She owed Nicholas more.

Most of all, she owed more to herself.

"What if he hates me?" She knew her eyes were pleading for reassurance.

But Judy had none to give. "Maybe he does hate you by now. It's been two months. Maybe he's found another woman. He has more than his share of opportunities."

Robin knew Judy wasn't being purposely cruel,

although it sounded that way. "All right. I hear you. There are no guarantees."

"No guarantees. Exactly. You're the only one who can decide whether loving Devin and going to him are worth what you might lose if it doesn't work out."

The weariness was gone. Suddenly Robin realized how little her exhaustion had had to do with her job and how much it had had to do with Devin. She had been a fool for too long, and being a fool took an extraordinary amount of energy. "I know where Devin is." She held up the clipping for Judy to scan.

"I can stay with Nicholas through the weekend."

But Robin knew she had denied her son a father for too long. "No, I'll take Nick with me. I'm not going to keep him away from his father for another minute. We'll leave as soon as I can get a reservation. I'll walk if I have to."

Judy didn't smile, but this time reassurance gleamed in her eyes. "I'll help you pack. It will be a pleasure."

Snow was falling from a dark sky when Robin emerged from the Colorado Springs airport. She hadn't expected snow, but she had come prepared with warm clothes. Nicholas snuggled against her as she negotiated with a taxi driver to take her to Devin's. Judy, without fuss or explanation, had presented her with Devin's address and telephone number.

"I still don't know," the driver said. He had the kindly face of a grandfather, but their negotiations had been tough going so far. "That's pretty far into the mountains. And the roads are getting slippery."

"Please? I have to get there tonight. There'll be a healthy tip in it for you."

The driver looked at his watch. "All right. Get in. But I'm not going to wait once we're there. I've got to be back in town by ten."

"No problem."

Robin slid into the seat and fastened Nicholas's car seat beside her. She'd come equipped with everything he needed for a short stay except a crib. Devin had never had any reason to buy anything for their son. She had never allowed him to bring Nicholas here. And Devin had loved her enough to accept that, despite his own needs.

She had been such a fool.

Nicholas fussed as the cab negotiated streets, passed the Air Force Academy and started into the mountains. He continued to fuss, despite everything she did to try to calm him.

The ride seemed interminable. Between Nicholas's fussing and the gradual slowing of the cab as the roads thickened with snow, time slogged by. She couldn't even entertain herself by looking out the window. There was a sheer dropoff on her side, and the sight of it made her head reel.

What if Devin wasn't home, after all? What if he didn't want to see her?

The taxi slowed to a near halt. "I don't know if we're going to make it, miss," the driver said. "It looks like they've got the road blocked ahead."

"No!" Robin peered out the windshield and saw what the driver meant. There were wooden barriers equipped with reflectors across the road.

"Happens sometimes when the roads get too slick. Too bad. We're not that far."

"How close are we?"

"Three, four minutes. You could walk it in ten."

The taxi slowed to a stop. The road was wide enough to turn around, although Robin certainly didn't want to watch as the driver got that close to the mountain's edge. She quickly considered her alternatives. She could go back into town and find a hotel. Then tomorrow she could call Devin directly or call his attorney, explain where she was and ask him to have Devin call her. Devin could send someone to get them.

If he still wanted them.

She didn't think she could wait that long to find out. "Is it just along this road?"

"Straight up the road. I been here before. There's an iron gate on the left."

"I can't carry my luggage."

"I'll take it back with me, if that's what you want. I'm going home anyway. I can leave it in the cab. I'll bring it up first thing in the morning if the roads are clear."

Robin trusted him. And she had nothing with her that was valuable, anyway. "Can you wait while I put the baby in his snowsuit?"

"I can wait."

Minutes later she was heading into the snow, Nicholas tucked firmly against her hip. The fussing had stopped the instant they left the taxi. He was exhausted from the trip, but the snow was a new pleasure. She didn't know how long he would be contented, but at least he was snug and warm. The snowsuit was one Devin had sent him from a catalog, and it was filled with down.

She was wearing ankle-high boots with heels that dug into the snow and helped speed her on her way. But when she'd made her decision, she hadn't considered that ten minutes straight up the road meant exactly that. The road was steep, and the air was thin as well as cold. Nicholas was not a small burden. She was tired almost immediately.

For a moment she considered going back. She turned to look for the cab. Through the snow she could still see lights, but they were rear lights. And as she watched, they grew dimmer.

She had nowhere to go but up. Her choice had been made.

"Okay, St. Nick," she murmured. "I'm game if you are. We're on our way to see Daddy."

"Da!"

She smiled in spite of herself. Then she said a short prayer that Devin and Nicholas would someday forgive her for what she had done. She had never been a coward, but Jeff's death had changed her, and not for the better. Afterward she had told herself that life was short and it was important to live it joyfully. But the real lesson she had learned was fear. Fear of pain, fear of taking chances, fear of falling in love again and losing.

She started to hum. She had gone a hundred yards before she realized what she was humming. It was the lullaby that Devin had often sung to Nicholas, the one he was using in "Heartland."

"Remember that?" she asked Nicholas. He held out his mittened hand to catch snowflakes.

She had a long steep road ahead of her. This wasn't going to be an easy hike. But suddenly Robin didn't care. She was glad she had left the warmth and safety of the cab. Glad she was out in the middle of a snowstorm. She was going to be fine. She and Nicholas were going to be fine. They were going to find Devin. She was going to take the biggest chance of her life and win.

"We're going to make it, Nick," she said. "You, me and Daddy. We're going to make it!" She whirled around as Nicholas squealed with delight. Then she continued up the road.

"I know you said you didn't want to be bothered." Mrs. Nelson spoke from a crack in Devin's studio doorway that was just wide enough to reveal her worried face.

"That doesn't seem to have stopped you," Devin said. But he smiled as he did. Mrs. Nelson, the housekeeper, had only been at her job for three months, and he knew that she still expected him to behave with complete disregard for her feelings. He had yet to make inroads into her stereotypes about rock musicians.

"A woman named Judy McAllister's on the telephone. She says she has to speak to you now. I looked on your list, and she's—"

"I'll take it. Thank you."

Five minutes later Devin pulled on the last of his winter gear. His feelings were in such turmoil that he had buried them deep inside him. He didn't have time to feel anything.

"I'm going out for a while," he yelled to Mrs. Nelson, as he started toward the front door. No one else was around, even though there were several members of his band staying at the house, as well as the small staff that worked under Mrs. Nelson's supervision.

Mrs. Nelson appeared from the next room and blocked his path. "Mr. Fitzgerald, it's snowing hard out there. Too hard to be driving down the mountain."

Perhaps she was loosening up after all. Devin spared the housekeeper the ghost of a smile. She was a thin woman, easy to sidestep. "My son and his mother are on the way up from the airport. I've got to be sure they're all right."

"Your son?" She broke into a wide, atypical grin. "Your little boy?"

"That's the one." He looked beyond the door, through the glass that constituted the front of his home. Robin would not like this house. It was like living in a fish-bowl, even though there were no neighbors in sight.

But maybe it didn't matter. Maybe she was just bringing Nicholas to see him. Maybe she was planning to leave again. Judy had been strangely silent about Robin's state of mind or future plans.

The world outside was the winter wonderland that songwriters extolled and small children adored. Devin was less enthusiastic. Judy had seen a weather report, and that was the reason she had called. Robin's flight had arrived in Colorado Springs. Judy knew that from a call to the airline. But Robin hadn't been in touch with her since arrival. Judy was sure that Robin would have called by now if she'd taken a hotel in town for the night. And since Robin wasn't with Devin, Judy was afraid she and Nicholas might be on the way to his house, snowstorm or not.

Devin started toward his car, a Cherokee like the one he parked and drove in Ohio, like the one in which Nicholas had very nearly been born. Surely Robin wouldn't be foolish enough to rent a car and drive unfa-miliar roads during a heavy snowfall. But would she have been able to convince a taxi to bring her here?

He only knew one thing to do. He had to drive down the mountain and look for her, keeping his eyes open all the way. The road was treacherous in a storm, and even the best driver might end up abandoning his car to find help. The snow seemed to fall faster as he settled himself in the driver's seat and jammed his key into the ignition.

Robin was on her way. Nicholas was on his way.

And Devin was on his way to find them.

"Just a little farther," Robin murmured to no one in particular. The only person who might have heard her words was sound asleep against her chest. Nicholas, warm and snug in his down suit, had finally given in to exhaustion.

She had been hiking for more than ten minutes. Twenty minutes, at least, and maybe thirty. She had considered all the possibilities. Either the taxi driver had miscalculated or misrepresented the distance, or she had missed the iron gate.

She wasn't worried, although she was growing tired. She was in no danger of wandering off the road. The snow wasn't thick enough to obscure landmarks, and although the area was remote, she was sure there would be houses up ahead. Even if she didn't find Devin's house, she would find shelter. She and Nicholas were in no danger of freezing to death.

She wasn't worried, but she was sorry the night was turning out this way. She wanted to see Devin right now. She wanted to tell him that she loved him, had loved him from the start. She wanted to tell him that she would brave anything for them to be together. Her days of cowardice were over. She would walk through a fiery furnace for him—for them.

Or a blizzard.

The road made a sharp turn, and she dug in her heels and rounded the corner. She was almost afraid to look up ahead now. She wanted so badly to see Devin's gate that she was afraid she might manufacture one in her mind. She shaded her eyes with her hand and peered into the darkness.

No gate was in view, but a car lay nose down in a ditch just ahead, a Cherokee just like the one that Devin drove.

Nicholas took that moment to cuddle deeper into her arms. She gripped him tighter and started forward. Ten yards from the car, she gave her first shout.

"Is anybody in there?"

Nicholas stirred in her arms again and opened his eyes. He began to whine. "Sorry, partner," she said, "but we've got to find out."

Nicholas began to whimper in earnest, but she pushed on. "Hey, is anybody in there?" she shouted again. The car wasn't badly mired. It looked as if one good yank from a tow truck would set it on the road again. She doubted that anyone inside had suffered more than a bruise or two. She was almost on top of the car when a man's voice sounded from inside.

"You picked a hell of a time for another reunion, Robin."

She gulped in snow and a huge breath of freezing air. "Devin?"

The driver's door scraped against the side of the bank, but it opened far enough for Devin to squeeze through. He shook his head, as if to clear it, then leaned—or fell—back against the Cherokee. "At least I'm not in the throes of labor."

She had never seen a more welcome sight. He was buried in winter wear, layers of wool and leather, but she couldn't have been happier to see him if he had been naked in front of her in a very warm bedroom. She tried a smile but didn't know if she succeeded. "I'm sorry about the timing, but when I make up my mind to do something, I don't fool around."

"Is that so?"

She wished she could see his face clearly, but the snow was falling too fast for that. She didn't know what he was thinking or feeling. She could only go on faith. "Any chance you could come up here so I don't have to shout?"

"Say whatever you've come to say."

Her courage nearly failed her. There was no welcome in his voice. Nothing but caution.

"I've got Nicholas with me."

Devin was silent—an act of great valor, she supposed, under the circumstances.

"I love you," she said. She cleared her throat and said it louder. "I love you, Devin. And I want us to be a family, to make whatever compromises we have to make together. I want you to help me raise Nick. I want to have more children with you." She hesitated. "And I want to get out of the snow. I've had enough of ditches and blizzards. Do you think we could move someplace warm? Like Tahiti?"

He didn't answer. The sound of her words died, and he just stood silently.

"I'm so very sorry," she said.

For a moment she thought she'd lost it all. Then he was scrambling up the bank and gathering her and a wide-awake Nicholas into his arms. "I knew you were coming." His voice was husky with emotion. "Judy called. I just didn't know why."

"I'm here because I've been such a fool. Can you possibly forgive me?"

He kissed her hard as Nicholas swatted at him in welcome and babbled happily.

Despite what she'd said, it felt right to be outside in the snow together. But it would always feel right to be together, no matter where they were. Robin cuddled into Devin's arms and held him tightly with her own. Life came with no guarantees, but she could be sure of two things. She and Devin loved each other, and they loved their son. They were already a family. A very lucky family indeed.

* * * * *

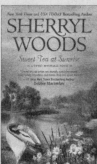
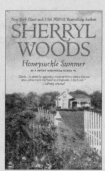

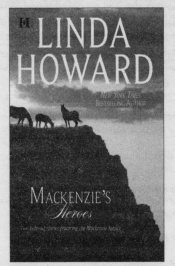

REQUEST YOUR FREE BOOKS!

2 FREE NOVELS
FROM THE ROMANCE COLLECTION
PLUS 2 FREE GIFTS!

YES! Please send me 2 FREE novels from the Romance Collection and my 2 FREE gifts (gifts are worth about $10). After receiving them, if I don't wish to receive any more books, I can return the shipping statement marked "cancel." If I don't cancel, I will receive 4 brand-new novels every month and be billed just $5.74 per book in the U.S. or $6.24 per book in Canada. That's a saving of at least 28% off the cover price. It's quite a bargain! Shipping and handling is just 50¢ per book in the U.S. and 75¢ per book in Canada.* I understand that accepting the 2 free books and gifts places me under no obligation to buy anything. I can always return a shipment and cancel at any time. Even if I never buy another book, the two free books and gifts are mine to keep forever.

194 MDN E4LY   394 MDN E4MC

Name	(PLEASE PRINT)
Address	Apt. #
City	State/Prov.	Zip/Postal Code

Signature (if under 18, a parent or guardian must sign)

Mail to **The Reader Service:**
IN U.S.A.: P.O. Box 1867, Buffalo, NY 14240-1867
IN CANADA: P.O. Box 609, Fort Erie, Ontario L2A 5X3

Not valid for current subscribers to the Romance Collection
or the Romance/Suspense Collection.

Want to try two free books from another line?
Call 1-800-873-8635 or visit www.morefreebooks.com.

* Terms and prices subject to change without notice. Prices do not include applicable taxes. N.Y. residents add applicable sales tax. Canadian residents will be charged applicable provincial taxes and GST. Offer not valid in Quebec. This offer is limited to one order per household. All orders subject to approval. Credit or debit balances in a customer's account(s) may be offset by any other outstanding balance owed by or to the customer. Please allow 4 to 6 weeks for delivery. Offer available while quantities last.

Your Privacy: Harlequin Books is committed to protecting your privacy. Our Privacy Policy is available online at www.eHarlequin.com or upon request from the Reader Service. From time to time we make our lists of customers available to reputable third parties who may have a product or service of interest to you. If you would prefer we not share your name and address, please check here. ☐

Help us get it right—We strive for accurate, respectful and relevant communications. To clarify or modify your communication preferences, visit us at www.ReaderService.com/consumerschoice.

MROM10

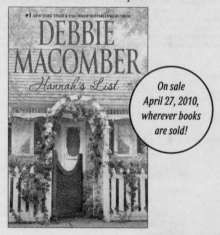